MW01139145

The Highlander

TERRY SPEAR

DEDICATION

Thanks to all my wolf fans who have fallen in love with my medieval Highlanders! There's a little—or a lot—of wolf in all of them! The Highlanders—that is. Well, maybe my fans too.

Also by Terry Spear:

Romantic Suspense: Deadly Fortunes, In the Dead of the Night, Relative Danger, Bound by Danger

The Highlanders Series: Winning the Highlander's Heart, The Accidental Highland Hero, Highland Rake, Taming the Wild Highlander

Other historical romances: Lady Caroline & the Egotistical Earl, A Ghost of a Chance at Love

Heart of the Wolf Series: Heart of the Wolf, Destiny of the Wolf, To Tempt the Wolf, Legend of the White Wolf, Seduced by the Wolf, Wolf Fever, Heart of the Highland Wolf, Dreaming of the Wolf, A SEAL in Wolf's Clothing, A Howl for a Highlander, A Highland Werewolf Wedding, A SEAL Wolf Christmas, Silence of the Wolf, 2014, Hero of a Highland Wolf, 2014, A Highland Wolf Christmas, 2014

SEAL Wolves: To Tempt the Wolf, A SEAL in Wolf's Clothing, A SEAL Wolf Christmas

Silver Bros Wolves: Destiny of the Wolf, Wolf Fever, Dreaming of the Wolf, Silence of the Wolf

Highland Wolves: Heart of the Highland Wolf, A Howl for a Highlander, A Highland Werewolf Wedding, Hero of a Highland Wolf, A Highland Wolf Christmas

Heart of the Jaguar Series: Savage Hunger, Jaguar Fever, Jaguar Hunt, 2014

Vampire romances: Killing the Bloodlust, Deadly Liaisons, Huntress for Hire, Forbidden Love

CHAPTER 1

His side and the back of his head throbbed with pain and the sound of flowing water filled Niall MacNeill's ears. Where in God's wounds was he and what had happened to him? He opened his eyes to low morning light—made grayer by a thick mist. His mind, cloaked in a hazy fuzz, finally cleared enough for him to realize he was on his belly beside a river. He groaned, his head pounding, and he recalled the Murray clansman striking the blow that had knocked him out.

But Niall wondered where in the world he was.

He stared at the river, his thoughts so groggy, he couldn't think straight. The... the Scottish Lowlands. He must have been left for dead.

The back of his head and his side burned.

Gunnolf.

He twisted too quickly to see if his Viking friend, raised as a brother, was nearby. Pain jabbed Niall where he'd been injured—a glancing sword wound in his side, and his head felt like it would split open if he moved again. He moaned a curse.

"Gunnolf," he called out low, trying not to call attention to himself if any of the Murray clansmen were still about.

Gurgling water slipped over the stones near his head, the rushing sound of the river in the deeper part, but he heard no voices. No sounds of human movement. Just the river's flow and birds twittering in a nearby tree.

He prayed Gunnolf was well and not worse off than Niall was. Or worse... dead.

His head throbbed with a perpetual dull ache now. Reaching up, Niall felt the back of his skull. A sticky wetness covered his fingers. Blood. *His blood.* His thoughts jumbled, he could barely remember how he came to be here.

Ambushed! The brigands had struck right after he and Gunnolf had washed in the river, dressed in fresh clothes, and intended to sleep the night. The Clan Murray, he thought coldly, after they'd run into them earlier in the day and asked one of the men if he knew anything about a Frenchwoman living in the region.

Another ragged jab of pain radiated through the wound in his side, and he reached out to scoop up some water in his hands and splashed it on his face, the cold river jarring him from his stupor. Devil take the bastard who'd cut him and struck such a blow to his skull that the man had knocked him out. The man most likely believed him dead.

But where was Gunnolf? Niall had to find him as soon as he was able.

He thought he heard the bleating of sheep off in the distance in the glen and roused himself to a sitting position. Pain in his skull and side stabbed him so sharply, he fought drifting into a cave of blackness again. The groan he heard, he belatedly realized, was his own. Somehow, he managed to conquer the dizziness and focus again on his surroundings.

Woods, green hills, jagged gray stone topping taller mountains in the distance, and the blue river behind him filled his view.

Sheep meant a sheepherder would be nearby, and he could seek his help. As long as the man wasn't one of Cian Murray's men. Though, he didn't think it could be as the Murray Clan had settled farther west, mostly living in the Highlands.

Niall surveyed the brush and trees along the river, his gaze fixing on his sword half hidden in the long grasses and heather. He smiled darkly. He could lose most anything else, but he couldn't live without his sword. Although not having his horse provided more of a challenge also. He needed him back just as much.

Niall attempted to stand, and every move filled him with excruciating pain. He fought an overwhelming lightheadedness and the blackness that threatened to overcome him. After finally standing, listing to the side a little, he retrieved his sword and sheathed it. Then he began the slow walk in the direction of the sheep's calls, remembering the task his cousin, Laird James MacNeill, had put before him. He and Gunnolf were to accompany the Chattan brothers and their kin on the way to see their

3

McEwan cousin and his ward. During the journey, Niall and Gunnolf were to split off from them and continue on their way to the Lowlands, to the area around Banbh. There, they were to locate a French lady whose father had once saved James's life in combat during the Crusades and now needed the MacNeill's protection—without alerting anyone as to their business.

She was here, somewhere in the region, if Niall could discover her location. As soon as he had her in hand, he and Gunnolf would return her to James's safekeeping. But he had to find his friend first. Once they accomplished the task, he and Gunnolf would find some other worthy cause to champion.

For now, Niall concentrated on putting one foot before the other and not collapsing in a bloody heap in the tall green grasses again, worried about Gunnolf, their horses, and another encounter with Cian and his men.

***

An impenetrable mist cloaked the lands in a chilly grayness late that morn, and the area appeared dark and more formidable, Anora thought as she returned home after selling several of her sheep at market in Banbh. A strange red glow in the sky to the north of her stone cottage caught her attention. A campfire? She studied the sight as she latched the gate to the pen.

Her dog suddenly growled a low warning, and she turned to watch him, trying to discern what the matter was. His rusty brown and white fur stood on end, his long flappy brown ears perked up, listening to only sounds he could hear. He sniffed at the air, his white fringed tail stiffening.

Then he sniffed at the ground.

"What is wrong, Charlie?" Anora whispered.

He looked up at her and wagged his tail, then turned his attention to the cottage again.

Not taking any chances, Anora grabbed a pitchfork from the haystack. She had her *sgian dubh* tucked in its sheath at her waist, but she was afraid someone still might get the best of her if she used the shorter knife.

Curses on anyone who might have slipped inside her home to steal from her, *again*. Just because she lived alone, did not mean she was without resources.

Barely breathing, she crept toward the cottage. The tiny stones along the path crunched with every step she took, setting her nerves on edge. With the prongs of the fork, she pushed the door aside. The rusted hinges creaked, and the noise made her stop dead. Her heart thundered so out of control, she could scarcely hear anything else.

The flap of sheepskin over the window on the north side of her house fluttered with the breeze, drawing her attention as Anora peered into the dim light. Not seeing anyone inside, she took a step into the main room. The door to her sleeping room rested slightly ajar, catching her gaze next. Her mind raced as she tried to remember how she'd left it that morning. Closed, she thought. Emitting a low growl, her dog still stood at the front door, and Anora frowned.

"Some guard dog you are," she whispered.

Bringing her pitchfork back to the ready, she steeled herself and angled the weapon up. Holding her breath, she gingerly walked across the stone floor. Charlie ran into the middle of the main room growling more loudly this time, but remaining behind her—her rearguard.

"Shh, you are scaring me more than anyone else, Charlie," Anora whispered, holding her finger to her lips, fearing he would alert whoever might be in her cottage that she had arrived. Not that the creaking door wouldn't have already done so. Though if the intruder was still here, he was being very quiet.

Panting, Charlie settled his rump on the floor and waited for her next command. Her hands clammy as she gripped the pitchfork tightly in her clenched fists, Anora inched forward.

When she reached the simple slat door, she pushed at it with the sharp prongs of her pitchfork, but finding the door resisted her efforts, she paused, trying to figure out what could be blocking it.

Hand on the door, she pushed again and found a chair held it partly jammed in place. She knew she should leave. Someone was still in the room. But it was *her* cottage. Well, she rented it from the local laird, but still, she had nearly always lived here and it felt as though it was hers. She had nowhere else to go and no one else who could take care of this for her. She wasn't going to allow it.

Steeling her back, she again tightened her grip on the pitchfork. If she sucked in her breath, she could slip in through the sliver of the makeshift entrance.

Heart thudding and holding her breath, Anora inched her way through the doorway, careful not to make a sound on the cobblestone floor in here. The windowless room was fairly dark, the scant bit of light filtering in from the main room, allowing her to see the closest objects, the bed and the small table next to it. Everything else faded into the darkness.

Once inside, she saw a large lump of a figure sleeping in her bed, half-buried in sheepskin covers. Her breath escaped in a whoosh. She clasped her hand to her mouth to muffle her gasp. Even though she knew someone had to be in her sleeping chamber, she still couldn't contain her surprise. Not when that *someone* was a large man—half naked!—and sleeping in *her* bed.

Barely breathing, she lifted the chair and set it aside, careful not to make a sound. She opened the door wider to allow more light into the room so that she could see what she was doing better and so that she had an easy escape route, if she needed. Though she fully intended to make the man leave, and not be chased off herself.

She took a deep breath and studied the sleeping figure. His naked back was to her, his broad shoulders muscled and holding her gaze. His hair was dark and curly; his head snuggled against her lumpy wool-stuffed pillow. Still wearing his boots, his big feet hung off the straw mattress, the covers reaching only to his ankles. His arms were well-muscled, way more so than her guardian's had been. Which should have warned her not to trifle with the intruder.

She was still of the opinion that if she threatened him sufficiently, he would leave. It had worked well for her before—on two separate occasions. Not that the men had been so well muscled—or half naked.

Then she frowned. What if under the sheepskin covers, the man was entirely bare? That would put him at more of a disadvantage, she decided.

Courage gathered, she approached the bed.

No naked wanderer was staying in her cottage—in her bed.

When she reached a safe distance from the mattress, she poked at the still figure's back with the point of her prongs. Soliciting no response, she pushed harder with the fork.

The man quickly tossed the cover aside and leapt to his feet on top of the mattress. His dark brows were furrowed. His teeth clenched in a furious expression. His sword was raised to swing at his enemy.

She shrieked.

He towered over her, his dark brown eyes narrowed in hatred. He cursed. His Scottish burr was so thick that she didn't understand his words. Or mayhap he was speaking in Gaelic. A Highland barbarian.

As soon as she truly saw the sword and the intricate carvings on the sloping steel cross-guard, realization dawned and her heart stuttered. He was a Highland warrior, not just some peasant seeking a place to rest.

Anora shrank back, her gaze riveted on his naked chest, a bloody cloth wrapped around his waist, a blue and green belted plaid hung low on his lean hips. She should have been watching the motion of his sword. Instead, she stared at his bronzed, naked skin and the way the plaid hung so very low. She shifted her focus to the dark hair trailing down to his belt and disappearing beneath his plaid.

Until he swung the sword, connecting with the wooden handle of her pitchfork, and then she refocused her attention. He yelled out at the same instant with a robust war-cry. Her heart nearly leapt from her chest.

The sword struck the pitchfork with such force, the jolt sang all the way up through her arm, sending a streak of pain with it. The pitchfork flew across the small room, clattered against the wall, and dropped to the stone floor.

Anora screamed, and then dashed to retrieve the fork, though it was hard to see in the dark. She considered running out of the room, but decided against it and would defend herself in the best way she knew how.

When she grabbed for the farm tool, the man jumped from the bed. He ran only a couple of steps with his giant stride before slamming his boot atop the wooden handle of the pitchfork, cementing it firmly against the floor. He grabbed for Anora's arm with his free hand.

She swung her fist at him, connecting with his jaw. Pain radiated through her knuckles. She groaned and gritted her teeth. His jaw had to be made of granite.

"Charlie! Get him!" She shook her hand as if that would get rid of the pain.

The intruder dropped his sword and grabbed both her wrists, laughing a little as he studied her in the room's dim light. "'Tis a lassie who attacks me in my sleep." He wore a silly smirk on his face, but his husky baritone voice told her that he was not only amused but intrigued. "When 'tis loving that I would seek instead from one as bonny as you. I never fight with a lass."

Charlie circled them, barking, bumping against Anora's *léine*. "Charlie, bite the man!" Anora yelled, hoping that her dog would protect her like he was supposed to, instead of brushing against her gown.

Charlie seemed to believe the knave was playing with her instead, and her dog wanted to join in the game.

When the stranger twisted her in the direction of her bed, she struggled harder to wriggle free, fearing the worse. A half-naked barbaric Highlander wouldn't ask permission to bed her. Not that she had known any personally, but the local laird had warned they were heathens to avoid at all costs.

Unable to loosen herself from the Highlander's firm grip, she kicked his shins with her brown leather shoes, afraid that her struggles were doing nothing more than aggravating him.

"Quit fighting me." His voice was still groggy with sleep and tinged with annoyance as he tossed Anora to the bed as if she was nothing more than a lightweight blanket to be cast aside.

As soon as she was free of him, she bolted from the mattress in panic, trying to get around him. Trying to reach the door.

He was too near, too big, too very muscled and masculine, and standing in her path no matter which way she went. She brushed against him, felt his heat and hard muscles rub against her breasts, the raw power, the tensing of his naked torso, saw the feral glint of something more in his dark eyes.

He grabbed her shoulders and forced her back on the bed.

"Stay," he commanded, like she was a dog.

He sounded like he was used to giving others

commands, and they would obey him. She wasn't *his* to command.

He studied her for a moment, as if calculating her next move, then before she could react, he pulled her *sgian dubh* from her belt and slipped it into his boot! He smugly smiled, as if dismissing her as a threat. She waited, like a caged animal, ready to bolt.

He turned to retrieve his sword. As soon as he leaned over to pick it up from the stone floor, Anora kicked at his hip as hard as she could, unbalancing him. He didn't go down like she'd hoped. He didn't budge but barely an inch.

Her only hope now was to flee. She dashed again for the door. Time to retreat and get help. Though she seriously doubted she'd be successful. So much for doing this on her own.

She fled past him. She only made it to the door's threshold when he grabbed her arm, his grip strong, decisive, overbearing. And then he jerked her toward the bed again and tossed her to the mattress where she landed on her back.

She had to admit she was afraid of him, but also more than exasperated with herself for not having had better foresight. As soon as she'd seen he wasn't a scrawny man, she should have left well enough alone and gone for help.

Not that she thought anyone in the village would help her. Which was why she had made the mistake of confronting him in the first place.

"Stay there. I mean you no harm." He sounded angered and tired, his voice deep and threatening. "Who else lives here, lassie?"

Fear as to what he would do to her if he learned she was alone, mixed with fury that he would take her hostage—washed over her in a cold sweat. She refused to answer him. Breathing hard, she stayed this time, glowering at him, not believing he spoke the truth. If he learned she lived alone, what then? She was strung tight like a new bow, ready to fight him further if he touched her again.

After retrieving and sheathing his sword, and then setting it on the chair, he turned to Anora. She realized then how haggard he looked. Her gaze shifted again to the bloody strip of cloth wrapped around his waist.

He was incredibly handsome, a shadow of a beard covering his square set jaw, a face with character, smiling lines beneath his eyes, and a wrinkle across his forehead. Most women would surely have found him appealing, she imagined. Even she couldn't quash the way her traitorous body responded to him after brushing up against him—the way her breasts ached and felt heavier, the way her stomach quivered with a queer little flutter, the way her heart beat faster as he studied her.

He could pretend he had no interest in her, but she knew the look in his eyes said otherwise. He gave her another long, wicked inspection, raking her with his gaze.

"I must rest a while longer, then I will leave you be," he finally said, sounding resigned. "Where is the man who crofts this land?"

God's teeth, he couldn't stay here. He'd soon learn she lived alone.

"You cannot stay here, whosoever you are." Anora scowled at him as he towered over her, while his darkened eyes studied her as she leaned back on her elbows on the straw mattress. She thought to reason with him even though he was one of those heathens from the Highlands. Surely some were honorable. "What do you want?"

The man's eyes rested on the lay of her gown as the folds dipped between her legs. A glimmer of a smile settled on his lips. He wasn't going to be honorable.

Panic returned. Anora jumped up from the bed again.

His hands flew up to stop her, and he shoved at her shoulders, pushing her to the mattress. "I will stay longer and if you dinna allow me to sleep, I will truss you up first. Will you permit me to rest a wee bit?"

Despite his looking ragged, she couldn't match his strength. Staying here alone with him was not an option, though. Even if he didn't rape her, if anyone should learn she stayed alone with a man through the night, they'd assume the worst of her. Not that she imagined she had much of a reputation anyway because she lived alone. But she liked to think she had.

Anora attempted to stand, and as he empowered her to rise, she waited for a moment, his eyes warily watching her. His whole posture stated he wasn't letting her go. Her meek acquiescence most likely wasn't fooling him.

In a last ditch effort to escape, she dashed for the door.

"Nay!" His singular word filled her with dread, right before he seized her arm and scowled. "I dinna believe this will work."

What did he think? She'd be willing to allow him to dictate to her? Make her his willing hostage?

Never.

TERRY SPEAR

Armed with his sword, he pulled her into the larger room and glanced around at the bare furnishings. "Where is your rope, lass?"

Shaking her hair braided in one long rope down her back, Anora turned her eyes upward to look at him, chin held determinedly, eyes narrowed at him with indignation. "You wish for me to tell you where my rope is so that you may bind me with it in my own home? You must be mad. Who are you anyway?"

He grunted. "You have the right of it, lass. I will tie you up as you willna obey me." He pulled Anora from the cottage and surveyed the byre. "You willna run off to warn anyone that I am here."

She lived too far from the village. Too far from a living soul. If she screamed, no one would hear her. But him. And that would most likely make the Highlander angrier.

Not that she was about to give up fighting him. Just as soon as she had another chance, she was taking it.

.

CHAPTER 2

His head and side hurting something fierce, Niall led the stubborn lass to the byre, not needing this further aggravation. He couldn't believe he'd fought with a pitchfork-armed lassie when he only vaguely remembered entering the cottage in the first place, looking for help.

He hadn't recalled hardly anything, except for seeing the cottage, then barely remembered he'd walked in and found no one. God's knees, she could have run him through with a pitchfork while he was sleeping.

He smiled at the thought, particularly because of just who had been poking him gently with the farm implement. Still, his mistake could have cost him his life if a burly sheepherder had come after him instead.

Then again, if her family arrived soon—he let out his breath with exasperation. He had to get rest.

He glowered, the notion he could be in for further trouble, unsettling him. He glanced down at her unveiled hair. Wisps of chestnut and golden strands mixed together, lightened by the sun, struggling to break loose of their confinement. His scowl softened.

"Are you an unmarried maid?" Mayhap that's why she was so skittish around him. Then again, even if she was married, he was a stranger and had slept in her bed so she had every reason to be wary of him.

He had another thought. "Are you a concubine then?"

He suddenly realized something else, his head clearing a little, not much, but a wee bit. The bed had smelled like her, sweet, womanly, a flowery fragrance, and straw. No man had recently been in the bed.

He glanced down at her then. She lived alone?

The lass glowered at him. "Release me at once, you... you, barbarian!"

Ignoring her demand, he smiled a hint. He couldn't recall any lass calling him such a thing. Most thought he was charming. "If no' a concubine then, does your father manage the croft lands?"

But he now suspected she lived alone. Why else wouldn't she have told him she lived with family?

"Are you always this forceful with the people you first encounter? I imagine you do not win too many new friends this way."

Again, he couldn't help but smile at her audacity. He was a battle-hardened warrior, who had fought numerous times against clansmen who encroached upon the MacNeill lands. Yet, this slip of a woman did something to him he'd never expected. Made him consider hearth and home and a woman to warm his bed in more than a temporary way. He was an honorable man—so he thought—but seeing her lying on the bed, the folds of her *léine* dipping between her legs, and the way she so haughtily considered him, he couldn't help but think of what it would be like to bed such a bonny—and feisty—lass.

Uncomfortable with the way his thoughts were going, he said brusquely, "I dinna seek friendship, lass, only sleep."

"Seek it at the local tavern in the village then. They will offer you room and board for a fair price, or have you no coin or naught to barter with, either?"

He didn't answer her query. He might have thought her perversely obstinate, but he had noted she'd been genuinely concerned about his intentions. He assumed her haughtiness had more to do with covering up her fear than anything else. Not wishing to harm her, he was desperate to get more rest before he ventured out across the glen to search for Gunnolf and continued to look for the French lass.

When they'd been inside the cottage, the lass had been so fearless when she brandished a pitchfork against him, a Highland warrior. If his cousins and Gunnolf, their childhood friend, had seen the way Niall had reacted to the lassie poking at him with the prongs of her pitchfork, they would have laughed their fool heads off.

The fight wasn't out of her yet. He would have to remain on-guard. Because of the wound on his head and his side, he didn't want to battle the lassie any further.

He pulled her into the byre where he was about to search for the rope, but saw a wooden tub used for bathing and still wet from an earlier use. Instantly, he thought of the lass sitting in that tub, wet and naked. He smiled a little at the notion. Mind back on business, he spied the rope hanging looped in several rings on a wooden peg attached to one of the timbers.

She looked utterly annoyed, as if she wished she'd hidden it somewhere else where the likes of him couldn't have found it so easily. He smiled down at her, unable to help himself. He enjoyed how she entertained him, helping to take his mind off how badly he was feeling. She scowled back at him, which made him smile all the more.

He tugged the lass toward the rope as she struggled to loosen his grip on her arm. He could envision her fleeing for the door, attempting another escape, and him running after her to stop her, which would make his head pound even harder, and the wound in his side bleed all the more.

So he held on with fierce determination, while she tried to wriggle free with just as much resolve. She was like a wild cat, only her teeth and claws were still hidden.

Outside the byre, the dog began to bark in an excited tone, greeting someone he must know. Niall's whole body tensed, his blood heating in anticipation of fighting a new battle.

Damnation! What if it was one of the men of the Murray's clan? He looked down at the lass, who had suddenly stilled in his grasp. He could imagine she was thinking her savior had arrived. What if *she* was a Murray? Bloody hell. He hadn't believed so at first as they lived further northwest than this. But what if she *was* kin to them?

Niall jerked the lass toward the narrow window at the

opposite end of the building and carefully peered out.

Wearing a tunic and breeches, a lanky man strolled up the stone path to her cottage, and began whistling some tune.

Niall whispered to the lass, "Were you expecting to see someone? Is it your father, mayhap?"

She didn't answer him.

He reconsidered the man's age and realized he was much too young to be her father.

The sandy-haired man, as tall as Niall, but lean and wiry in build, stopped to pet the dog, peering at the cottage for a moment, then continued toward the door. He had a boot knife, but no sword. He was not a warrior.

As the visitor grew closer to the cottage, Niall shook his head at the lass. "Nay, he is too young to be your father. A lover then, or a brother?"

She mutinously didn't say a word, just glowered at Niall. The last time a bonny lass, such as this one, had given him so much grief, he had kissed her and that had melted the glower away. He didn't believe it would work on the lass though. He could imagine her giving him bloody hell, alerting the man outside, and him coming to her rescue.

"Anora? 'Tis me, Matthew," the man shouted, breaking into Niall's thoughts of kissing *this* lass. "Where is Anora?" Matthew asked Charlie, as the dog stuck close to him. He reached over and petted Charlie's head again, and then continued on his way to the door of the cottage.

Anora. A lovely name for a lovely lass.

"He will know something is amiss when I do not answer him," Anora said, her voice hushed as she jerked her arm in an attempt to free herself, but Niall gripped her tighter so she couldn't break loose.

"Who is he?" Niall whispered into her ear, got a whiff of lavender that scented her hair, and wanted to kiss her in the worst way. What was wrong with him? Mayhap the bump on the back of his head had addled his thoughts more than he had believed.

"A friend, Matthew," she said darkly under her breath, trying to move her face away from Niall's. Her body was so tense, yet she shivered.

Afraid of Niall? Or was the tension more to do with her building anger? He hadn't wanted to frighten the lass.

"And you are alone?" he asked.

The lass shouldn't have been meeting the man when she was unchaperoned. Not when she was an unmarried miss.

Niall shook his head. "He will go away. Be still."

But Niall worried that Matthew might seek her out in the byre next. What would Niall do then? He didn't wish to fight the man unless he had no other choice.

Matthew rapped at the door to the cottage.

Anora struggled to get free from Niall. He was certain she hoped to get Matthew's attention. To ensure she knew she wasn't going to warn the man, Niall pinned her arms close to her body and held her tightly against his chest. "I will kill him if you call out to him," he whispered in her ear.

He didn't believe it would come to that. But if he was in the enemy's territory—and because of his injuries and since he was without his horse and clansmen's protection—he wasn't about to reveal that he was staying here until he'd rested up. In the event those who nearly killed him were still nearby, he couldn't let the word get out that he was here.

Anora was breathing so hard, he was afraid she might swoon from distress. "You are safe with me, lass," he said, hoping to calm her.

She gave him a chilling glower in return, and he grinned. Now, she was like a wild-spirited filly, and he had the greatest urge to keep her for his own, take her back to James's castle, and tame her.

The Highlander's soft breath sent chills sweeping down Anora's spine, and she stared up at the grinning beast. God, he was ruggedly handsome. So much more fascinating than Matthew—the way he touched her, controlled her, and appeared more than slightly intrigued with her. If she didn't get her breathing under control, she was going to faint.

When she never did anything of the sort. The way he was pressing her against his half-naked body was making her lightheaded. She felt his muscles flexing against her as he shifted slightly, trying to get more comfortable, or see out the window, or something. His moving next to her body was making her all the more aware of how hard he was. His mouth hovered over her ear, even brushing it when he spoke to her as if it was a whisper of a kiss, his breath warm, his words hushed, dark with warning.

Anora quieted, listening as Matthew sauntered down the stone path away from her cottage. He disappeared down the road that led to the village, but she hadn't lost hope of escaping. It was just as well that he had not searched further for her, or she suspected the Highlander might have killed him.

Rope in hand, the Highlander pulled Anora back toward her place. Her whole body tensed in preparation for more of a battle. When they entered the cottage, he led her to the sleeping chamber where she renewed her struggle, trying to wriggle free. She wasn't going to be tied up without a fight.

She tried to remove his fingers from their shackling grip on her wrist, but he grabbed her waist, lifted her as if she weighed no more than a sack filled with air, and dumped her on the mattress. When she attempted to get up, he lunged forward, pinning her body to the mattress with his own.

Shocked to the core, she didn't move at first, feeling all that hard muscled body pressed so indecently against her. She hadn't expected him to make such a move, either, completely rattling her composure. She should have been wholly terrified, hating the way he felt lying between her spread legs, the only thing separating them—his wool plaid and her wool *léine*—that barely seemed to exist between them. Not when she could feel his heat pressing against her, his staff taking on a life of its own, growing harder—and she knew exactly what that meant.

At least the shepherdess had informed her greatly of the matter once John had caught Anora swimming half dressed with the butcher's son in the loch. And they thought it past time that she knew about men and women and how dangerous being together like that could be—when she had only been ten summers. Matthew was only two years older than her, so she really didn't understand their concern.

But now, here she was this Highlander's hostage, and why was she feeling so… intrigued, interested, and curious about what lay beneath his wool?

She had to be mad.

"I am too tired for this continued skirmish, lass, though if I were not so exhausted, I believe I would rather enjoy this moment with you." His eyes had darkened to midnight, and his mouth curved up in a sensuous smirk.

He was a barbarian—she reminded herself. So why was she hoping he didn't move off her? So she could feel every bit of him against her for just a while longer?

No man had ever touched her so intimately—and mayhap no man ever would.

Either from the weariness he felt, or the pleasure he seemed to take in lying against her, he made no effort to move from his restful position. Finally coming to her senses, she squirmed in an attempt to unsettle him from his repose.

He cast her a dark smile. "You are making the situation more untenable for yourself, lass, as you are stirring the dragon from his sleep. Take care that you do not wake him too much."

The so-called dragon had stirred from his sleep well before she began to wriggle beneath him. Even so, she grew very still, remembering what her guardian had told her about men when Anora was old enough to understand something about the way men were. Just like a ram that wished to tup a ewe could not hold back his natural urges, neither could a man if the woman encouraged him in any way.

When Anora quieted, the Highlander finally took a deep breath and rolled off her. He pulled her from the bed and sat her in the ladder-backed chair standing next to the bed. He began to tie her to it, and she scowled back at him. All she could hope for now was that she could free herself from the rope while he slept.

After knotting the rope, he considered the way she was bound to the chair, ensuring she was perfectly secure. "That ought to keep you still for a while." Glancing at the mattress, he said, "You could be more comfortable, if you would lie quietly beside me."

Her scowl deepened. What if he woke from his sleep and began to kiss her and touch her and... bed her? What if she went along with it?

He laughed at the look of contempt that must have shown on her face. "I venture not."

Then she scolded herself. She could have pretended she'd stay with the man and then as soon as he fell asleep, escaped.

He walked out of the room. She heard the bolt slide against the main door, but before she could wonder what else he was up to, he returned with another chair. After he shoved it against the door, he sat on the mattress, leaned over, and then pulled off his boots.

"Mayhap I will take you up on your offer," she said sweetly.

He only smiled at her. "Aye, lass. And I would never get any sleep."

She scowled again at him. Why had he said he'd allow her to stay with him if he hadn't meant it?

24

Taking a moment more, he considered the rope that bound Anora and satisfied it would hold her while he slept, he lay back down on the mattress, and pulled the sheepskin over his shoulder. He watched her for some time, his eyelids growing heavy.

She continued to glower at him, just waiting for him to close his eyes, and she'd get free of her rope prison. After he shut his eyes, his breathing grew shallow while his face took on the appearance of a cherub completely at peace with the world.

A cherub. She shook her head. A devil wrapped in his plaid, more like.

The Highlander grew still in sleep, and Anora struggled with the rope as her dog shoved his nose through the sliver of the entrance. Squeezing through, he ran into the room, his toenails clicking in a methodic rhythm on the floor.

"Charlie," Anora whispered as he ran over to her, wagging his shaggy brown tail in an enthusiastic frenzy. "I wish you could go get Matthew."

Charlie plopped his bottom down at her feet. His tongue hung over his teeth while he panted a refrain. Surrounded by a mask of brown and white fur, his deep brown eyes hungered for more of his mistress's praise. At least she was certain he believed that's what her words meant. His reddish brown ears twitched back and forth, his fringed tail sliding over the stone floor like a broom.

Struggling, wiggling, she continued to work on the rope. Charlie curled up in a ball on the tips of her toes, warming them, and promptly fell asleep.

Anora looked down at him. "Oh, Charlie." She glanced

back at the man sleeping soundly in her bed.

She had to get the Highlander out of here before any learned of his presence, and the word spread... and ruined her. Not to mention, she didn't exactly trust herself with him, either.

CHAPTER 3

A candle now glowing in the sleeping chamber, Anora lifted her head and wondered how late it was—only to see the Highlander sitting up on the bed, staring back at her, and her skin warmed uncomfortably. 'Twas bad enough that she was here alone with him, but trussed up and being scrutinized by him made her body heat in a way that both startled and annoyed her.

His dark hair looked mussed and endearing, his masculine lips curved slightly, hinting at amusement. The angular set of his jaw and his cheekbones made him appear sculpted out of the same granite that the cliffs behind her home were made of. Her gaze shifted to his bronzed chest, the bloodied fabric wrapped around his waist, garnering her attention again. How had he been hurt? Had he been fighting someone? Were they searching for him now?

More barbarians like him? She shuddered, thinking how much more trouble she might be in, all because this man took refuge in her cottage.

"It appeared that you needed to sleep as well." He pulled on one, then the other of his leather boots.

"I did not sleep."

Straightening his plaid, the Highlander said, "Oh? It appeared that way to me. I have observed you for some time, lassie." He studied her further as she squirmed against her bindings. "I believe I prefer you this way. I should leave you bound like that so that you willna give me any more grief, but I am hungry and wish for you to prepare something for me to eat."

"You think I will feed you when you have trussed me up thus for so long?" she asked indignantly. Yet she was hungry and had to eat also, and the preparations would take some time if she was to have a meal today.

"Aye," he said curtly, then stood and stretched, but groaned.

Her gaze again latched onto the bloodied cloth around his waist. The wool fabric was his tunic, she now thought, first believing he had traipsed through the glen wearing naught but his plaid, half naked like a true barbarian. He moved to the chair Anora was confined to. Charlie jumped up to greet him.

"Oh, Charlie," Anora said, her voice rife with remonstration, "you are *supposed* to bite him, *not* welcome him."

The Highlander smiled while he untied her wrists. "He is offering Highland hospitality, lass, despite this being the Lowlands. More than that, he knows when a man is friend or foe. So, Anora, where is your father?"

Ignoring his question because she couldn't allow him to know she lived all alone—though she wondered why he had not seemed to worry overmuch that anyone might arrive home and find the cottage door barred, she asked, "Who are you? You carry a fine claymore and your clothes, though soiled, have never been mended. I can see where they could use a stitch or two now."

For a moment, he studied her, as if trying to decide if her knowing his name was a safe thing to reveal. "I am no' from around here."

She narrowed her eyes at him. "Tell me something I do not know. Like your name."

He shook his head. He didn't trust her? He was the one who couldn't be trusted. He'd barged into her cottage, slept on her bed, and used her own rope to tie her up.

She pursed her lips. "I thought you said you were leaving once you had rested." She knew reminding him of his own words would not change the Highlander's mind, but she had to speak them anyway.

"I am hungry now."

He sounded like a man used to getting his way and *that* irritated her all the more.

Anora rubbed her wrists where the ropes had burned, but only because she'd struggled so hard to free herself.

Without him noticing, she slipped the small knife off her kitchen table and sheathed it in the scabbard on her belt. She went outside to the stone well beside her cottage, and was thankful to see the sun had burned off some of the gray mist of earlier in the day, and was still fairly early. He followed close on her heels as if he intended to grab her if she decided to run off. She swore she could feel the heat emanating from him.

"I have chores to do first, before I may eat." Anora hoped he wouldn't force her to bend to his will and have her feed him first, when she needed to pasture her sheep. She'd taken some of her sheep to market at dawn, as everyone opened their stalls at first light. Right afterward, she had planned to start her meal—that would take hours to cook—and pasture the remaining sheep. Until the braw Highlander took her hostage and unsettled her normal routine on market day.

She dipped her bucket into the well. "If you are hungry, you will help me with my chores as you have kept me from my work for a couple of hours and now I am late in pasturing my sheep."

She imagined her dictating to him wouldn't go over well, but she couldn't help it. She had to let him know how she felt. Her guardians had taught her that everyone worked at whatever job they could to put a meal on the table. Not that she had expected her captor to agree.

He quirked a brow at her. Surprised that she would give him an order?

"I will watch you do your chores," he said, a hint of a smile curving his mouth. "If I help you, I could become too thoroughly distracted, and you would attempt to slip away."

Why hadn't *Anora* thought of that? Her main concern had been that he would work for his meal—which only seemed right. Not that it made any difference now.

She'd heard that the Highlanders—though barbarians—did offer a meal to those who visited. But since he hadn't *visited* her and *she* was not a Highlander, she didn't feel the need to abide by *their* rules of hospitality. She doubted if he had bound a *Highland* lass to a chair in her own cottage, she would have felt very hospitable, either.

Then again, maybe a Highland lass would have done anything for the braw warrior. Melted at his touch and offered him much more.

Anora shook her head as she lifted the heavy pail. "You will not help me because you are a man of some… rank and do not work for a living." Although he appeared more like a rugged Highland warrior, not pampered in the least. He still seemed more like a leader of men, rather than someone who was ordered about.

Not taking offense, he laughed. "You are right, lass. I dinna wish to injure myself with doing any hard labor."

"I suspected as much." Anora briskly walked back to the cottage, carrying the heavy bucket of water. Some of it sloshed onto her *léine*.

"I could have carried that for you." He followed her into the room.

"Of course." She poured the water into the kettle "After I had finished with the task."

She really wasn't annoyed with him concerning his not helping her. She did these tasks all on her own all the time, so was used to the work. She lit a fire and watched it for a moment to see it catch hold. The flames grew in height, licking the iron pot with a tender touch. She grabbed a basket off a shelf, and then walked back outside to a small garden.

Imagining she was doing her chores as she would have if she'd had no *visitor*, she ignored Niall this time. Though pretending he was not so near was difficult to do. He remained close by, and she couldn't help but glance at him from time to time to see what he was doing. He was surveying the lands, looking for someone? Listening. His hand rested on the hilt of his sword as if any moment he would be attacked.

And then of its own accord, her gaze wandered over his naked chest again, the muscled smooth planes, the warm, golden color of his skin, his dusky nipples—that she could observe so much better in the misty gray light of day. He caught her studying him and... smiled knowingly, *the rogue*.

The day was cool, but she instantly felt hot.

Reaching down, she pulled up a handful of leeks. Using the small knife, she cut off sprigs of rosemary, thyme, and dill. He frowned a little when he saw that she was armed. As if she could fight him with such a small knife when he was armed with a sword. To her way of thinking, a pitchfork was a much better weapon—well, if the man did not wield a mighty sword.

Returning to the cottage, she chopped the herbs into fine fragments, and then threw them into the pot as the water warmed over the fire.

"At the castle where you live, do you act as a shadow in your servants' presence as well?" she asked.

Dimples appeared on his cheeks before she brushed past him, felt the heat and hardness of him all over again, smelled his spicy masculinity and chided herself for enjoying his closeness, when she should have loathed it. She hated to admit she halfway enjoyed his company, which had her believing she had been living alone for so long she had become daft.

She left the cottage and walked down a short path to a stone building past her byre, dug deep into the ground. The aroma of the earthen walls, like that of a freshly plowed garden, filled the air as Anora climbed down the steps into the cool, damp room, making her shiver. Niall leaned against the doorjamb at the top of the stairs, arms folded, watching her.

She pulled a strip of meat off an iron hook. "We will have pork stew if that should be acceptable to you." Not that she intended to fix anything else. Or that she cared if it was acceptable to him. She was just fortunate enough to have a friend in Matthew. Most renters did not have the luxury of eating much meat during the week like she did.

"Aye, lass, if you are able to prepare it suitably," he said. He sounded serious.

She raised a brow. He cast her an elusive smile. She swore the Highlander was teasing her.

"I will attempt to do my best," she said, only because she always did her best. If he didn't like how she prepared the stew, he could go elsewhere to attempt to secure a free meal.

"Call me Niall—if you please, lass."

Her mouth gaped. He was now trusting her with his name? That did not bode well. What if he thought that because he'd slept in her bed and she was fixing him a meal, it meant he could take other liberties with her? And that's why he gave his name up to her? Unless he was lying and that was not his name at all.

"Those who serve you do not call you Niall, I surmise." Anora headed for the stairs, attempting to learn the truth.

"Two of my cousins are called laird, lass, the eldest having received the title from his da, and the other, through battle. Alas, I am an orphan with naught but the tunic on my back. Not even that at the moment. And, aye, everyone who is friend calls me Niall. You would not wish to hear what my enemies call me."

She closed her gaping mouth. He truly was from a family who ruled others. She glanced at the bloodied bandage around his waist. And he had enemies that could be looking for him.

She let out her breath in frustration. She had to get this man out of here as soon as possible. She would offer to examine his injury and take care of it, if she could. Otherwise, what if it got infected, and he died? It didn't matter the manner in which he had taken over her cottage or ordered her about. She couldn't let the man die here.

She felt a bit of relief that he wasn't a nobleman of title who believed she was of no consequence. Yet, she was a little disappointed as she climbed up the stairs of her cellar while he stood in her path. If nothing else, it would have been a boon to know that a man of some stature had slept in her bed. Not some orphaned cousin of a couple of titled lairds. And that he had no land or way to support himself or a wife and his children, should he have any.

Unless he worked for one of the cousins. "So which laird do you serve?" she asked, trying to ascertain which clan he was with and what his duties truly were.

He only smiled. He had the look of a charming rogue, but he wasn't taking the bait—as he refrained from speaking of his family further.

She attempted to squeeze by him. He leaned close to her and took a deep breath, unsettling her. "You smell of lavender. I wouldna believe a shepherdess would smell so fine."

"I bathed in a tub full of lavender this morning, just for you, so it seems, as I knew you would appreciate the effort."

Niall laughed. "I am glad that you did, Anora."

And then she had a brilliant notion. He smelled clean, as if he'd washed in the nearby river recently, but mayhap he would like to clean off some of the blood around his wound. "Mayhap you would like to use the tub to wash in?"

"Nay, no' at the moment." Again, his eyes sparkled with merriment.

She'd tried. She thought if he was naked in the tub—though she couldn't help wondering just what the rest of him would look like—she could slip away.

"Unless you'd like to join me in it," he said, his voice rough with intrigue.

Her mouth gaped open, then she snapped it shut. Men and women didn't bathe together.

She quickened her pace as she carried the pork into the cottage. How could he suggest such a thing? And now that he had, she couldn't get the forbidden image out of her mind. Not that she was trying very hard—as she envisioned him with his arms wrapped around her body, both of them completely naked in a tub of water in the byre where she bathed. From now on, every time she took a bath, she'd imagine such a thing.

Trying not to think of it further, she laid the meat on a cutting block and began to slice it into cubes. Niall sat down on a chair situated at the table nearby and observed her work.

Not liking that he monitored every move she made, making her feel somewhat self-conscious, Anora frowned at him. "Be sure to make yourself comfortable in my cottage, sir."

"Thank you, lass, I will." Niall rested his elbow on the table with his chin propped on his hand, his eyes half-lidded.

She thought he looked weary, despite his having slept in her cottage for however long it had been. She was about to mention taking a look at his injury, when he asked, "Who was the man who came to visit you earlier?"

Certainly not her rescuer. Though she was glad he hadn't had to fight Niall. She wouldn't have wanted her friend harmed. "Matthew."

"And?" Niall's tone was somewhat condescending, and she didn't like it one bit.

"And *what*?" she asked, irritated.

"What were his intentions?"

She glowered at him. "What do you mean?" She knew what the Highlander was getting at, but she didn't feel a need to defend Matthew's honor. She scooped up the chunks of day-old meat and threw them into the simmering broth.

"I mean, that a young woman, such as yourself, shouldna be seeing a man like that without a proper chaperone."

"'Tis none of your concern." Anora noticed him stiffen a little and the look of disdain on his face. She added, "His intentions are honorable if 'tis any of your business, but what of yours?"

Niall was the one she had to worry about. The Highlander with the hot-blooded gaze and the heated touch. Matthew had never been more than just a friend. If he'd ever looked at her or touched her the way this man had, she might have been married to him already. She shook her head at the very notion.

"If my purpose was other than honorable, you would have known about it long before this." A hint of teasing shown in his eyes as Niall's mouth curved marginally.

Her traitorous heart did a little leap. "You are leaving after supper, are you not?" He could not mean to stay any longer than that.

Niall's eyes sparkled with devilment. Wiping his hand over the smooth tabletop, he said, "I am no' certain. You have been so kind to me, when I truly have needed it, I may wish to stay the eve—at the verra least."

Did he realize she lived alone? Would he not suspect her family would arrive home soon? Before nightfall, at the very least.

Grinding her teeth, Anora stirred the stew. "You cannot tarry here any longer than it takes for you to have your supper. The word will soon reach the village that a man is staying here with me...," Anora said, then hesitated as

Niall's eyes narrowed.

She briefly closed her eyes as she was annoyed with herself for making the slip. She should have said with *us*. Not with *me*.

She looked to her stew again, hoping he wouldn't have noticed. Not that she assumed she'd have much luck with that. He had a warrior's watchfulness.

And she was quite certain she was doomed.

CHAPTER 4

Glad Anora was living alone, Niall was pleased beyond measure at the lass's slip of the tongue. The midnight blue *léine* she wore complimented her blue eyes, so bright and clear, he was reminded of a loch that he and his cousins swam in near Craigly Castle. Her light brown hair was streaked with gold, the braid half undone, the loose strands falling over her breasts, her breath quickened as if she was still afraid of him… or intrigued.

Oh, aye, he believed he fascinated her because of the manner in which she had considered his body when he wasn't looking, until he caught her at it. And made her blush. Niall didn't remember ever having met a maid who could be so charming—in a mulishly determined kind of way.

Was Matthew her only betrothal prospect? Already Niall was thinking the lass deserved better, despite not knowing anything about the man. But if Niall had come to call on her, and knowing she lived alone, he would have searched for her until he found her. Her sheep were in their pen, her dog sticking close to the cottage—so Niall would have assumed the lass was nearby—and he would have located her before he left. Or... he might not have left. He smiled at the notion.

"*Well...,*" Niall said to Anora as she prepared the meal, elongating the word for emphasis, "*that* answers one of my questions. You live all alone. That is even better for me."

He meant only as far as not having to worry about Anora having brothers or cousins or a father who would attempt to slay him for breaking into the cottage and taking the lass hostage. Although, he couldn't help thinking in terms of being with such a lovely—not to mention, high-spirited—lass alone, and the notions *that* led to.

Anora released her ladle, then headed for the door, making him jump from his seat. *And groan.* The lass was way too flighty for his wounded condition.

Before she reached the door, he grabbed her arm—delicately boned in his large hand—and pulled her to a stop, afraid she meant to run off.

"Release me at once!" Anora grasped his hand and tried to peel it from her arm, her cheeks flushed with indignation at being accosted. "Just because I am only a shepherdess and you are a... well, what are you exactly?"

"I am Niall, naught more."

"You are a cousin to two lairds and as such, I assume that is why you are so demanding."

Niall laughed as he released her arm. "Where are you going to now? Are we no' going to eat soon?" He was starving and the aroma of the stew was making him even hungrier. And he was tired. He thought having food in his belly would help chase away the weariness he felt and give him strength.

"I must take my sheep to graze again before the meal is done." Anora strode for the door.

"I will help you." He followed behind her, but the muscle in his side twitched with pain, informing him he would be better off staying behind and resting. He clapped his hand over the wound as if that would prevent it from hurting further. But he couldn't allow her out of his sight.

"Now you will help me?" Anora turned suddenly, catching Niall off-guard.

He barely halted before running into that sweetly-scented body of hers.

Frowning furiously at Niall, she continued, "When you could have carried that heavy bucket of water into the cottage for me?"

"That looked too heavy." Niall folded his arms, head tilted to the side a bit. "I told you it wouldna do for me to injure myself further."

He was loathe to admit he couldn't help the lass with her chores as he would have done so in a heartbeat—not only because he'd slept in her bed, and would now eat her food, but because he was always willing to aid a lass when she needed assistance. No one could ever call him idle. But he knew, too, his physical limitations—with regard to his wounds—prevented him from doing anything too strenuous or he was liable to pass out, and she'd flee and get help.

She glanced at his bloodied binding. "How were you

injured?" She sounded suddenly suspicious and a little worried.

"A skirmish. Thieves attacked me."

She looked up at his face and frowned. "Thieves, yet they did not take your sword?"

"They attacked in the middle of the night. My sword was lost in the tall grasses. They stole my horse and left me for dead."

Her lips parted—soft, pliable, a natural primrose color that begged him to lean down and kiss them.

Then she worried her bottom lip with her teeth and considered his bindings again. "Mayhap I should take a look at it."

He envisioned her warm hands touching his skin in a gentle caress. And he was more than willing to let her do so.

"If you will take off the binding," she said, hesitantly, her cheeks turning rosy, as she glanced from his bare chest to his face. "I will get one of my father's tunics for you. He had two extra ones and either should fit you."

"Aye," Niall said. "Thank you." He couldn't be more pleased that she'd take a look at his wound. Mayhap, she could even help him to heal sooner, and he could search for Gunnolf next.

She returned to the smaller room of the two, rummaged through a chest, and then pulled two tunics out. She rejoined Niall and held the garments up for him to consider. "Which do you prefer?"

"The one that is softest." He didn't know why he said such a thing. Just like with the meal. He would be pleased with anything she offered him. But he couldn't help bantering with her.

Anora laughed. "I did not know a Highland warrior would be so..." She paused as she tried to think of something to say, then shook her head.

"So... what?" He was dying to hear what she had to say to him, considering her mischievous expression.

"Soft." She handed him the linen tunic.

When it came to being around her, wrestling with her, being close to her, he couldn't be accused of being soft. Even now as he took in her scent again, his body reacted.

"Change in the other room if you are shy, while I stir the stew."

"You will try to slip away." She might not attempt such, but he wasn't naïve enough to believe he had naught to worry about concerning the lass. He just hoped she wouldn't faint at the sight of his wound.

Exasperated, she said, "All right then, change in here, and I will wash your garments and mend them before I retire to bed. You can use the water to wipe your wound clean."

Anora poured some of the water onto a clean rag, then looked up as Niall unwrapped the binding, stained with blood. She thought she could manage seeing any injury without showing any kind of reaction.

The red cut streaking across his smooth golden skin while the blood trickled down from the wound made her draw in a bit of breath with surprise. "Oh, my Lord, who has done this to you?" She hadn't thought it would be this severe, particularly as much as he'd been moving about.

She was certain if she had been so wounded, she

would have been flat on her back, unable to move, languishing in pain, wishing she was dead.

"We were ambushed, and when I came to, I found no sign of my horse or the man I rode with. I had to find a safe place to rest. Now you know, but no one else must know I am here until I can regain my strength and search for them."

His dark gaze remained steady on hers, and she had the impression he was pleading with her in a silent way to aid him. She realized then, as much as he was in charge and could wield a mighty sword, he needed her help to see him through. And that made her feel more—in charge of her situation—which she preferred.

"*Who* are you?"

"Niall. I have told you this several times already."

"From which clan, I mean?" She couldn't help but sound exasperated. Because of his staying here, she had to know what she could be involved in. "So I will know them if they come here searching for you."

"Are you from a clan?" he asked her instead.

She shook her head. She had thought the men who waylaid him might have been Normans or Lowland Scots, but maybe they were from another Highland clan. In any event, the situation didn't divine a safe outcome.

"Are you allied with any?" he asked.

"Nay." Anora touched the wet cloth to his skin, and he took a deep shuddering breath. "I am sorry, Niall. Mayhap if you sit down..."

He removed his sword, set it on the table, then sat on the chair.

Anora eyed his sword for a moment. She wasn't used to being around a man who carried one with him everywhere he went. She leaned over and carefully wiped his wound. "'Tis still bleeding. I fear it is too deep and needs to be stitched." She looked up at his face, but found him enjoying the cut of her bodice, and hadn't realized how much it gaped when she leaned over very much. She straightened, casting him an annoyed look.

He smiled when she caught him at it. "Have you stitched a man's wounds before?" he asked.

"Aye, if you can stand the pain. Drink some of this mead, and I will get my thread and needle."

Anora retrieved her sewing materials, and Niall frowned. "Are you sure that you can do this? 'Tis no' the same as sewing on cloth."

She almost laughed. "He who wields a mighty sword is afraid of a needle and thread?"

He smiled.

She had to admit she liked the way he smiled at her teasing. But she didn't wish to let on that she was rather enjoying his being here. Not when he was holding her hostage. Yet, staying here by herself with only her dog Charlie to keep her company was lonely at times. She missed her guardians, whom she had considered her parents—mother and father, even though they were sister and brother—all the more.

"'Tis the same as sewing on cloth, if the man does not scream out in pain too much. Mayhap you should lie down."

"You willna try to leave me, will you?" Niall asked, frowning.

"While you are injured like this? I could not do that to you, nor to anyone else for that matter." Well, she would if he was a real threat to her, but he wasn't. And she thought whoever had nearly killed him might be more dangerous than he was.

Niall retired to Anora's bedchamber, sword in hand, and she was reminded that he could be a dangerous man, too, even if he was wounded. He stretched out on her bed, then she proceeded to sew the deep cut on his side. When he winced, she smiled at a long ago memory. "I am sorry."

"I dinna believe you are." But he didn't sound annoyed with her, only slightly amused.

"Of course, I am. I do not wish anyone this kind of pain."

"Except that I tied you up earlier and held you hostage against your will." His dark, fathomless gaze remained on hers.

"Aye, still I do not wish to see you suffer. This only reminded me of something that occurred some years ago. Do you wish to hear of it?"

"Aye, I wish to hear what amused you so if it wasna about my discomfort."

"'Twas not about your misfortune." Anora took another stitch. "Many years ago, a sheepherder grew tired of eating mutton. So one day, he yearned something powerful for a good cache of fresh fish and determined to try his luck at fishing at the river nearby where trout and salmon are prevalent. After tossing his hook out into the cold waters several times, he grew impatient. He had listened oft to the stories of the villagers and how they had caught this fish or that, and he knew if they could do it, surely he could also.

"As the sun rose high in the sky, so, too, did a stiff breeze. When his line drifted into shore, the sheepherder attempted to toss his hook deeper into the river. A gust of wind carried his hook right before he cast it, snagging it into his back. Having to walk all the way home from the river with a hook in his back was embarrassing enough, as he could not reach the metal barb no matter how hard he tried, but he had nary a fish to show for the ordeal either."

She glanced up from her stitching and saw that Niall was concentrating on her story. "Go on," he said, sounding interested.

She realized then she hadn't shared one of her stories with anyone since her guardians had died.

"When he arrived at the cottage, his sister folded her arms and laughed until the tears flowed freely. The poor sheepherder stormed into the cottage while his sister walked in behind him still snickering. Years passed, and the two often laughed about the situation. But I still remember him wincing so as she pulled the hook from his skin and then wiped it with a cloth soaked with water. His sister smiled, then winked at me, and I stared at the two stitches she had made. She kissed her brother's cheek. 'You should be a sheepherder, as that is what you excel at, my brother,' she said. 'Leave the fishing to other folks.'"

After taking three more stitches to close up Niall's wound, Anora cut the thread with a knife and wrapped a scrap of fabric around Niall's waist, then tied it off. "That should take care of that. You may put on John's tunic while I see to my sheep now."

"Wait," Niall said, and grabbed Anora's wrist. "What about your story?"

She barely heard his words, she was so focused on what his touch did to her—his hand gripping her wrist, not tightly this time, and the heat from his large fingers seeped into her skin. Her whole body warmed with his touch, yet she did not pull away, hating how much she liked the way he affected her.

"What about my story?" she finally managed to answer.

"I thought it odd that you referred to John as such and not as your father."

"That is another story." Anora reluctantly pulled her arm away.

"Will you not tell me about it?"

"I must see to the sheep."

"I thank you for all the generosity you have shown me, lass." Niall captured her hand and to her shock, lifted it to his lips, then kissed her there, and released her.

She openly stared at him, shaken at his behavior— since no one had ever kissed her like that before. She fancied he did so often with the lassies, only she couldn't imagine he would stop there.

"Is that how you show your gratitude to the lasses?" she asked, again feeling way warmer than she should.

"I would show you much more than that if I thought I could get away with it, but I believe that is quite enough for now." He quirked a brow, challenging her.

She thought she couldn't be shocked any further.

"Quite enough for now?" Her voice had elevated a bit. The gall of the Highlander. High-handed, arrogant, and probably loved by all the lasses.

"You think if you shower me with your affections, I will allow you to sleep in my bed with me tonight?" she asked, feeling a wee bit lightheaded.

And she almost wished he would press his lips against hers so she could experience what it would feel like being kissed by such a man as Niall. Only she would not permit herself to entertain the notion any further as he would know just how much he affected her.

He grinned as he rose from the bed and grabbed his sword. "I would think naught of the sort, though if you did suggest it, I would no' object too terribly much."

"I thought not. I will not suggest it." Heavens have mercy and here she was thinking just that—snuggling with the hot blooded Highlander on a cold winter's night. Naked. And his arms wrapped around her while they nestled under the sheepskins.

"I suspected as much. If you would be kind enough to fix a bed of straw for me beside your door, so that I can be sure you dinna slip past me tonight while I sleep..."

"You cannot sleep with me in the same room," she said, so indignantly, she was ready to retrieve her pitchfork and poke him with it again.

"Since your door opens into the sleeping room, I will have to have my bed against the door from the inside. 'Tis the only way I will be sure—"

"You can sleep in the *main* room—by the door!"

"Nay, lass, you could climb out one of the windows in

there while I was asleep. 'Tis the only way we can do this."

"I should not have sewn your wound." Not that she really meant it. She was glad to have done so after seeing how bad it was.

She seized her brat and pulled it around her shoulders and meant to leave the room, but saw Niall pulling John's brown tunic over his head, wincing horribly.

As wounded as he was, he had to be in awful pain, and she felt terrible that he'd had to fight with her to keep her from running away. She wished she could ease his suffering in some way.

But then he said with a smirk, "I have never had a woman see me so undressed before when she is so fully clothed."

Her face heated to hotter than her boiling stew. That quashed any idiotic notion she had about soothing him in his current injured condition.

"I thought you would have dozens of female servants swarming to caress your soft skin with their touch as they bowed to your every whim." Then she stalked out of the room.

When he followed her, she added, "I am glad Matthew is not too proud to work hard for a living. He would have run to aid me without the slightest hesitation."

Anora continued out of doors, and Niall closed the door after her. "Who is he? Is he the young boy who came to see you earlier?"

Niall's calling Matthew a young boy grated on her. As if she was robbing the butcher and his wife of their wee lad. She harrumphed.

"He is not so young. He is two years older than me, and he is the butcher's son." She tried not to appear exasperated at Niall's condescending tone concerning Matthew. She was unsuccessful.

"The butcher wouldna wish his son to marry a shepherdess, would he?"

She gave Niall an annoyed look. Between the two of them, she far outranked the butcher's son. Though that had to remain her secret.

"Who said anything about marriage?" Anora walked over to the sheep's pen.

Niall leaned against the railing as Anora unhooked the gate. "You are really quite lovely. I hadna noticed at first when you poked me with your pitchfork. But since then I have observed, for being a Lowland Scot, that you are really quite attractive."

"What makes you think I am interested in what your thoughts are concerning me?"

Yet she couldn't help but be flattered that Niall would say such a thing. Matthew never complimented her about the way she appeared to him. Sometimes, she felt more like a sister to him than anything else.

Niall gave her another smug smile. "All lassies wish to know what a man thinks of them."

She shook her head, not wishing him to know how much his compliment had pleased her. "I do not associate with men except when I sell my sheep. So it makes no difference how you view me as far as I am concerned," she lied, afraid mayhap he only said so, in the event he might convince her to share her bed with him.

She didn't have much experience when it came to men, and John's sister, whom she thought of as her mother—though it seemed odd at times to think of them that way since they were brother and sister—had constantly warned her how men could say anything to sway a woman to do their bidding.

Charlie corralled her sheep, and Anora walked off to join them. Niall caught up with her and took her arm as they sauntered through the field.

"You do not fear that I will run away now, do you?" Anora asked, surprised at his action, though his touch was gentle now, unlike earlier when she was fighting to free herself.

"Nay, I have too tight a grip on you. You willna get away."

"I would not abandon my sheep. They are my livelihood after all." Anora surveyed the dozen sheep grazing in the field. "You are leaving after supper, and not staying with me in the cottage." She pulled away from him and searched for berries in the grasses.

"How could I live without your kindness? Besides, the view is quite spectacular from here."

Niall considered Anora as she leaned over to pick loganberries, currants, and bilberries scattered in the tall meadow grass, bent slightly in the cool breeze. She stuffed the mixture of berries into a sheepskin satchel at her belt, and then watched her sheep as they grazed in the meadow. Niall observed the hills that surrounded the area and saw no sign of his friend or any others. He had to search for Gunnolf, but he didn't believe he'd get very far with the way he was still hurting.

Turning to face Anora, he pulled a torque from his leather pouch. He had planned to gift the woven metal decorated in knot-work designs to the French lass when they found her to show friendship. But now, he wished to give the necklace to Anora.

"I believe your eyes are as pretty as the gemstone set in this torque." He twisted the chain in his fingers, and saw Anora watching him. "I… would like you to have this in payment for my meal and lodging for the night. It seems only fair that I pay for my way."

But he meant it as more of a goodwill gesture for all her kindness to him and making his stay here so memorable. He would never forget the pitchfork-wielding shepherdess, or the way her warm hands had touched his skin while she sewed up his wound.

"I cannot take your money, or your gifts. You may expect more from me in return. I know how men think."

He stifled the urge to laugh. "Do you now? I meant only to pay for my stay as I would have paid for my lodging in the village had I gone there for the eve."

"Why do you not?"

"'Tis better that I stay here." He slipped the torque back into his sporran.

"Better? Are the men who harmed you still likely to be looking for you?"

Niall said nothing in response. He hoped they were not.

Anora looked up at the smattering of clouds passing overhead as they drifted over the sun, now situated halfway between the earth and the heavens above. "Why me, my

Father? What have I done to deserve this now?" Glancing back at Niall, she said, "And to think early this morn I was praising the Lord that my life was going so well for a change."

"How so, Anora?" His wound began to ache something awful again, and he touched the binding, wishing he could make it stop hurting.

She didn't answer him, her brow furrowed with concern, instead asking, "Are you still in a lot of pain?"

"Some, but I suspect 'twill heal nicely because of your skill with the needle."

"You could still get an infection. That can be deadly, you know." Anora reached over to touch the fabric and frowned to see blood on her fingertips. "'Tis still bleeding. You should not have walked all the way out here with me. One of the local laird's sons was slightly wounded at a skirmish in France, but his cuts became infected, and he died within weeks after high fevers ravaged his body. We were all quite shocked over the whole affair."

"France," Niall said, his voice darkening a bit as he remembered the mission James had sent him on. He thought to ask her if she knew the whereabouts of the Frenchwoman he sought. But then, if she lived way out here, she might not know anything about her. "I thought you said you did no' associate with men."

"I do not. He and his men just stopped here on their way to the village of Banbh to water their horses. When I was at market a month later, I heard what had happened to the poor man." Anora considered Niall's tunic again, and then shook her head. "When we return to the cottage, I will look at your wounds again. You may stay the night, but then you must leave."

"What if I should become feverish..." he said, jesting, loving when she reacted so to his teasing taunts.

"You cannot!" Anora was torn between doing what was right for him—allowing Niall the time he needed to heal before he left—and what was right for her—that he left before he caused her further trouble. "You must leave here after that. Most likely, Matthew will return in the morn, and if he finds you here..."

"You will tell him I am your cousin," Niall said, the teasing light leaving his expression.

She gaped at Niall. Then finding her wits, she said, "He will be surprised to hear that." She didn't believe any of her ancestors would have ever married a Highlander.

"Then a distant cousin."

"You cannot continue to stay here." She doubted Niall would take her seriously though, no matter how vehemently she spoke the words. But more so because she doubted he could safely risk leaving her lands until he had recovered further.

When the sky turned into ribbons of red and yellow silk as the night began to fall, she called and motioned to Charlie to gather the sheep, as she tried to think of some way to get the Highlander to leave.

"Laird Callahan is the local laird and mayhap his physician could see to your wounds. He would want to know that Highland thieves stole your horse and left you for dead. He would not tolerate such criminal behavior here."

Niall only shook his head.

Not that she expected him to do anything else, but it was worth a try.

Charlie chased the sheep toward their pen, nipping at their flanks, moving them quickly as Anora and Niall walked back to the croft. When Charlie had finished corralling the sheep, Anora latched the gate, and then headed for the cottage. She and Niall entered the main room where she lifted her pouch, and then deposited the berries on the table.

"Sit and rest while I get some more mead from my cellar."

"I will come with you," Niall said, looking at her with an expression that said he didn't trust her for a moment.

"You need to rest. I would not leave you to warn someone." Yet, if she had the opportunity, she would be torn to do just that.

Looking distrustful, he wrinkled his brow at her.

She shook her head. "Very well. Follow me if you must." But if he did not rest, he would never heal, and then he would never leave.

Once Niall and she returned to the cottage, she had him remove his borrowed tunic, but he grimaced.

"Here, let me. You are like a child who cannot do anything for himself," she said in a scolding tone.

He smiled at her, probably thinking she didn't believe him to be anything like a child. Not the way her heartbeat accelerated every time she got near him, felt his heat, and smelled his hot-blooded manliness. Why did she never think of Matthew in those terms? Mayhap, because she had never seen him this naked before? Except when he was a scrawny lad. Well, even now Matthew was scrawny, not half as well-muscled as Niall.

She took care to remove his binding and seeing that the wound was only leaking a small amount of blood, most likely from the walking they had done with the sheep, she sighed with relief. "You have not broken the stitching." She rebound the wound and was about to help him pull the tunic over his head when she noted blood along the neckline in back. "What is this? Turn around and let me see your back."

She felt the blood on the back of his head. "You have been wounded here also."

"Aye. 'Tis a hard head I have, though the brigand thumped it hard enough to knock me out. 'Tis probably what saved me, as otherwise, I would have continued to battle him. And there were more waiting in line to fight me."

"Oh, Niall. All right. I must tend to this also." She grabbed a cloth and moistened it, then began to wash the back of his head.

"Ow," Niall said, when she touched the wound.

"I am so sorry. Just a little more. Good thing 'tis no longer bleeding. And now at least 'tis cleaned up. You should have told me you were injured there," she scolded. "Does it pain you very much?"

"Some, lass. 'Twas why I wished you to settle down with me and let me rest."

"I am sorry. Had I known..."

"I doubt you would have seen me as anything but your enemy still," Niall said, giving her a small smile. "Thank you,

Anora." He stood, took her hand, and again he kissed it. He was looking down at her, his eyes smoky with desire, and she was fairly certain he wanted to kiss more of her than just her hand.

And she wanted him to. Yet, what if he wanted more than that? Despite his condition, she suspected he could still ravish her, if she offered him the chance.

She snatched her hand away and hurried off to poke at the stew meat—a much safer task. "'Tis almost done."

She stirred the stew for a moment, then turned her attention to the berries she'd gathered in the grasses. After throwing them into a small pan, she placed it over the fire and added honey to sweeten the softened fruit. Afterward, she covered the mixture with finely ground hazelnuts and brown breadcrumbs, set the pan back into the embers, covering it with a cauldron overturned on top of it to form a lid.

Anora finally ladled stew into clay bowls.

Niall leaned over to enjoy the aroma of the highly spiced, thick-gravy stew. "You would make a nice addition to my cousin's staff."

"Because I can cook?" She snorted. "I work for none but myself. I have my cottage and my sheep. Slave away in a kitchen to serve meals to you and your cousin, the laird?" Not to mention they were Highland barbarians. "Once you leave here—tomorrow, early—you will forget all about the likes of me and my cooking."

"I willna forget you all that easily, lass, with the crystal blue eyes, and lips like that of the pink primrose that grows wild in the meadow."

She was waiting to hear more. She'd never heard a man describe her in such a beautiful way and she truly loved it—even if he wasn't being completely honest with her.

Niall frowned, considering something else about this man who had come to see her earlier. He didn't know why, but he truly didn't care for this man who sought audience with her when she was all alone. "Has this Matthew of yours kissed those lovely lips…"

Her eyes narrowed. "Matthew is not mine and…"

Charlie suddenly rose from the floor and gave a little woof.

Niall's body tensed with a warrior's wariness. The only good thing was that if anyone had come for him, he doubted the person would have knocked. He glanced at Anora. She had lost all the color in her face. They both turned to face the door.

A knocking on it made Niall jump from his chair, curse harshly under his breath when his head and side hurt like the devil, and he unsheathed his sword to face his foe. He hesitated to consider his next move. He didn't want Anora in harm's way should there be a fight. He glanced at the one small window on the backside of the cottage, thinking she could make her escape that way.

Anora stood and stared at the door as frozen as he was with indecision.

All he could think of was that some of the Murray clansmen had discovered Niall's body had disappeared and were now searching cottages in the area—to make sure they killed him right this time. But then again, why would one of the men knock so politely on the door?

CHAPTER 5

Charlie wiggled back and forth before the door, wagging his tail in anticipation at seeing the person or persons outside the cottage, when a man from beyond the door called out, "Anora?"

"'Tis only Matthew," Anora said, feeling greatly relieved that the visitor wasn't a man who wished to kill Niall.

Though she didn't know how she would explain Niall's presence here and her whole body warmed with embarrassment. She was certain Matthew would not like this business at all. She glanced at Niall, a tightly wound warrior ready to kill, and at once she felt a sense of panic. How could she explain her "cousin's" plaid garment indicating he was a Highland barbarian?

"If you are supposed to pretend you are a relation, you should not be wearing thus," she whispered frantically, motioning to his plaid. "And you must put your sword away at once."

"I am your Highland relation. Go then," Niall said, as he walked with her to the door, then sheathed his sword. "Remember, I am your distant relation, Niall, who has come here to stay awhile."

"Awhile?" she asked, her heart still in her throat as she looked up at his determined expression.

"I must heal from my wounds," he said.

"They are not all that great," she countered, frowning at him. Yet she knew he was right. He should rest for a few more days at the very least. His wound could cause him further difficulty if it became infected.

"Anora!" Matthew called out.

"Answer the door," Niall said softly with a barely concealed threat.

She ground her teeth. Charlie bounced around at the door, waiting eagerly.

Heart pounding, Anora pulled it open.

Matthew looked in and glared at the man who stood behind her, wearing her guardian's tunic, the plaid reaching his knees, and the sword sheathed at his waist. Charlie jumped against Matthew's legs, trying to get his attention.

"Who is he?" Matthew said, his blue eyes glowering at Niall, and then Anora.

"He is a distant cousin on my mother's side, Matthew. He just learned my father had died and came by to see how I was doing," she quickly said, anxious that she sounded... anxious.

"Why is he wearing his tunic?"

She'd never thought Matthew would recognize the

tunic, and she had to come up with a quick plausible explanation. "A branch tore his own and the garment was soiled from his journey here. I was going to wash and mend it after we finish our meal. Would you like to share some pork stew with us?"

Niall gave her a growly look for asking Matthew to join them, but what if Matthew had become suspicious if she had not?

Matthew again considered Niall's appearance, who was looking very warrior-like as if he wanted to throw her friend right out the door. Then Matthew turned his attention to Anora, not answering her question. "Where were you earlier today? I looked everywhere for you."

"I sold some of my sheep for quite a price to Laird Callahan today at market. He said I had the best looking sheep he had seen in a long time." Truth be told he always said that to her and always bought more than anyone else did.

"Is he still trying to convince you to join his staff at Braybrooke Castle?"

Niall watched her, waiting for her answer as he retook his seat.

"I will not give up my croft to work for him at his keep," she said. She loved her way of life here.

"Your work there would be easier than maintaining this place of yours and if that old profligate king of ours keeps raising our taxes, forcing Laird Callahan to do the same, you will lose everything you own anyway."

Anora's face felt hot. Niall's expression showed he was highly amused. What if he was close to the king? Mayhap he was loyal to him, just as much as he was to his Highland laird. She had no idea.

"I do not believe we should say anything about the king in front of my guest, Matthew."

"Why ever not?" Matthew asked as he glowered at Niall. "Do not tell me this relative of yours favors the king? Besides we have always had this discussion, and we both feel the same way." Matthew gripped Anora's shoulders and pulled her close, his blue eyes appearing as lust-filled as Niall's had earlier. Which shocked her. She'd never seen him look at her in that way. "Why will you not just say aye, and marry me? You would no longer have to pay rent and you could move in with my family and me."

Anora frowned at Matthew's familiarity with her and pulled free.

"We have company, Matthew." She returned to her stew and poked at it some more, unnerved by all the unwelcome attention, when in the past, she had always wondered why he hadn't shown her more affection.

Especially since he had talked of marriage numerous times before. But it bothered her that he would do so in front of Niall, as if attempting to prove to her distant relation that Anora was Matthew's. And it further disturbed her that Niall would see it. Men and women did not shower each other with affections freely in front of others. What would Niall make of it? That she and Matthew behaved even more intimately when no one was about? Aye, that's exactly what he would think.

"You didna tell me, my cousin," Niall said, as he sat taller in his chair, eyeing her with disapproval, "that the lad had proposed to you."

She swore Niall said lad in a derogatory way that meant he was too young to think of marrying anyone. Niall's words were sure to irritate Matthew, even though he had enough of a scruffy blond beard that proved he was not some young lad.

"So Anora has told you about me," Matthew said, his face brightening, Niall's comment not having the effect on Matthew that she suspected Niall was trying for. "That is a good sign. I do believe I will have some of that stew of yours, Anora."

Niall furrowed his brow at her friend, looking disgruntled that he'd join them. She felt likewise, not wishing to keep up this ruse any longer. Though she truly thought Matthew would have been suspicious if she hadn't invited him to join them at the meal. Tension filled the air between Niall and Matthew, and she was definitely caught betwixt the two.

Matthew sat at the table, leaned back in the chair, and said to Anora, "I brought you a slab of beef as well, but left it packed on my horse in case you were still not here. I was worried sick about you earlier today."

She felt badly about that. She knew he hadn't lied and it would be the only reason he had returned this eve to check on her.

"I am sorry you were troubled about me." And if he'd known what had happened to her when he'd come by the first time, he would have had every right to be concerned for her welfare. But he could have been—and still could be—in danger, if Niall believed Matthew to be hazardous to his own welfare.

Anora poured stew into a bowl for Matthew, while Niall took another scoop of his and said, "She makes the best pork stew I believe I have ever eaten."

She smiled a little at Niall. She was pleased he thought so.

When she set the bowl before Matthew, he took hold of her wrist and raised her hand to his lips, then kissed it, his blond mustache tickling her skin. "I missed you, Anora."

Her mouth gaped and she quickly clamped it shut. He had *never* kissed her. Not once in all the years they had known each other. How could he do so in front of Niall? Her body burned with mortification.

"Oh bother, Matthew, I only saw you last eve." She pulled her hand free, then walked back over to the fire. Why was he acting so smitten with her all of a sudden?

"Last night?" Niall said, sounding like he was her brother and ready to take them both to task.

"Aye, I had supper with Matthew and his family," she explained, not liking that she felt she had to, or that Niall was acting like he really *was* her relation.

"Oh," Niall said, then poked his spoon into his stew and scooped up a generous portion of thickened broth, herbs, and pork.

Properly chaperoned, she wanted to tell the Highlander, and it was none of his business.

"How long will you be here?" Matthew asked Niall, studying him.

"Not long," Anora said, ensuring she set the rules as she stirred her stew again. She couldn't sit with the men, fearing Matthew would read her expression or body language and know nothing was as it seemed. She felt she was better off keeping busy.

"I have some business in the area. I dinna know how long that will take," Niall said, countering her, then took another bite of his stew. "Come join us, Anora."

"Mayhap after the meal I could step outside with you, Anora, and watch you while you wash your cousin's tunic. I thought I might have a word with you... alone," Matthew said.

She saw Niall narrow his eyes at her and shake his head subtly, telling her to say no.

"Nay, Matthew," Anora said, letting out her breath. "I believe Niall is afraid to be left alone while he is here." She didn't know why she said it that way, because in truth it was much like poking the lion with her pitchfork. Mayhap in a devious way, she *wanted* to see his reaction.

Niall smiled, the look pure evil like he intended to get her back for saying as much. "Rather, I have had this discussion earlier with my cousin that now that her guardian has died, she should be chaperoned when she is with a man."

"What about when she is with *you*?" Matthew said, then sipped his mead as he studied Niall, looking perturbed.

Anora hadn't expected this turn of events. She hadn't believed Matthew would be a little envious. No one had ever really acted interested in her, and even Matthew had been more of a friend than anything else.

"I am her relation," Niall said evenly.

"A distant cousin, she has said. Distant relations are

known to have wed, and beyond that... well, suffice it to say, your being her relation does not stop you from taking advantage of her while she is here alone with you. Should you not stay at the inn in Banbh for the time-being?" Matthew asked, his question sounding more like a command.

"My cousin insisted that I stay here with her as I have run out of funds for now," Niall said, then offered him a smug smile.

Anora could have told Matthew he *wouldn't* change the Highlander's mind. Even if he'd had the funds.

"I would be willing to loan you the coin as I do not mind aiding a relative of Anora's in circumstances such as these."

Anora stared at Matthew in disbelief. He was extremely careful with his money, and he would never hand it out to anyone, particularly a stranger. She was always surprised when he brought her cuts of meat—when he could have sold them for a profit.

"I thank you, but I would miss her delightful cooking too much and certainly her company." Niall winked at Anora, making her heart skip a little and her face warm a lot. He looked down at his empty bowl and said to her, "I do believe I am still hungry."

She glowered at him, took his bowl, filled it to the brim, and set it in front of him, none too gently. Did he think she was a serving wench in a tavern, only he had no intention of paying for his meal?

Niall grinned at her. "Thank you, Anora."

Matthew said, "I would like more, too, Anora, if you

could fetch me some more."

Anora shook her head as she took Matthew's bowl, then refilled it. She swore the two of them were competing with each other to prove how much they appreciated her cooking. Before, Matthew constantly compared her meals to his mother's, and they had never stood up to the scrutiny. After that, she'd quit inviting him to eat with her. John had loved her cooking, but she had thought mayhap he hadn't known any better since she'd learned how to cook from his sister, and so he'd been used to her meals.

She couldn't help but be pleased Niall seemed to truly enjoy her cooking. She suspected if Matthew had said anything disparaging about the food, Niall would have told him what a fool he was. Actually, she almost wished Matthew would, so Niall could set him straight, and mayhap in the future, Matthew would watch what he said about her meals.

After placing the bowl on the table before Matthew, she grabbed Niall's torn tunic, careful not to allow Matthew to see the blood on it, but when she walked toward the door, Niall said darkly, "You must stay and visit with us until we are through, Anora. You have not even touched your own bowl of stew."

"But I was just going to soak these—"

"Nay, we will suffer without your company," Niall said sternly.

Annoyed to high heaven, Anora set the garment aside, scowled at Niall, then returned to her chair.

"I will have to learn to be more forthright with you, Anora. You usually are so headstrong," Matthew said, chuckling.

Niall offered a small, devious smile. "I can imagine so. It must be my commanding personality."

"Demanding, meddling, domineering, I can think of many names to call you, Niall," Anora said, as she squirmed in her seat, not liking that the men were working together against her. As much as she *wasn't* hungry now, she began to eat her stew.

Matthew studied Niall. "You do not look too much like someone who is related to Anora. You are much darker than she."

Niall took a deep breath and nodded. "Many of our relations have dark hair. Is that not so, Anora? She takes after the Danish side of the family."

Anora stood, making Niall touch the hilt of his sword. She masked the alarm that filled her heart. "I was just going to get the dessert."

"You are too nervous, my cousin. Sit, keep us company, and finish your stew."

Gnashing her teeth, she sat back in her chair.

Matthew considered Anora next as she took another bite of her stew. "You say Niall is related to your mother, but I have heard it said that your mother was from France."

CHAPTER 6

Learning of Anora's possible French connection, Niall stared at her in disbelief. She *couldn't* be the lass that James had sent him and Gunnolf to fetch and return home. Could she be? Her accent wasn't in the least bit French sounding. Her voice was a mixture of English and Lowland Scot's.

"Well," Anora said, as she ran her hand over the wooden slats of the simply-fashioned table, "I have heard it said my mother was French as well. Strange how rumors will surface that are completely unfounded." Anora said no more concerning the matter.

Matthew resumed eating his stew as if that was the end of the discussion.

But Niall studied her posture—the way she fidgeted and the way she avoided looking at either of them. He had to learn more about her. James had no idea what the French lass looked like. And he certainly hadn't known exactly where she lived—just in this general area—so she might be a shepherdess—*the* shepherdess right under his nose. *Mayhap.*

He wished Matthew would leave so he could question her further. *Now.*

And then what? He hadn't thought that far into the future, unsure as to what they would find. A lass married or an unmarried maid living with a family. He hadn't thought he'd find her living alone, managing her own cottage and sheep. He knew she wouldn't want to leave it all behind, if she was the one he was sent to find.

James had been adamant that her life would soon be in danger. And as soon as they found her they needed to move her at once to Craigly Castle. James had been afraid to send any more men than Gunnolf and Niall, concerned that if there were too many of them, and the wrong people learned they were searching for her, she and they would be at further risk. Which happened anyway when Cian and his men attacked them.

When Anora finished her meal, Niall said, "Why do we no' have the dessert, then Matthew can leave before 'tis too late." He knew he couldn't tell Matthew to decline eating the sweet berry mixture and leave at once without both Matthew and Anora becoming suspicious, as much as Niall wanted to order him to do so.

"Nay, I will help Anora wash the dishes from supper," Matthew said, smiling at Anora, acting as though Niall had no say in anything.

Niall cast him a caustic glare that if he'd seen it, the man would surely have taken heed. Anora did see Niall's reaction, knew he was angered beyond reason, and quickly reused the bowls to fetch the berry dessert for them before Niall said something further.

"You have no need to stay," Niall said again. "I will help Anora wash up after the final course."

"Nay, I am happy to help Anora clean up. Hmm," Matthew said, as he inhaled the intoxicating aroma of the berry-honey mixture. "I do not believe I have ever been offered such a delightful dish as this before, Anora. Having a relation visit improves the menu."

Now *she* gave Matthew a highly irritated look.

Before Matthew could ask for a second helping of the dessert, Niall finished the last of his in a rush and rose from his chair. Matthew didn't have time to react before Niall took hold of his bowl—one last uneaten bite of the tasty confection sitting in the middle of it—and stacked them together.

Anora's lips parted in surprise.

"Now that we are done, we can wash up and retire for the night. Anora and I have a long day ahead of us—as do you—and we need to get our rest before 'tis too much later. Anora?" Niall said, waiting for her to agree, his look as stern as he ever used when he wanted someone to do his bidding, and he knew the person would be reluctant to submit.

She gave Niall a scowly look, then grabbed his bloodied, torn tunic, hiding the blood stains from Matthew's view. "Niall's right," she finally said, though it looked like it was killing her to say so. "He is leaving early in the morn and needs to get his rest."

Touché, little one, Niall thought, giving her a small

smile, but he wasn't about to do as she wished.

Matthew grabbed the bucket of water heating over the fire and carried it outside. "Mayhap tomorrow I can return after my work is done," he said to Anora, as she and Niall headed outside with him.

"Anora was mistaken in saying I was leaving so soon. We havena seen each other in so long, we need some time together, *alone*, visiting, for old time's sake," Niall said, quickly washing the bowls in the heated bucket of water. "You will be able to see her any time after I leave." Unless, she was his French miss and then it would be another story.

His brow furrowed disagreeably, Matthew eyed the two of them standing so close together as she took the washed bowls and dried them, and he seemed to draw other conclusions.

"All… right," Matthew said to Anora as she finished drying the bowls, "Let me have them and I will take those inside for you."

Had he wanted to prove he could help with the bowls also? Niall nearly smiled. Matthew gave him a glower and headed inside.

Anora washed out Niall's bloodied tunic, scrubbing, beating it, acting as though she would have liked to have beaten the wearer of the tunic instead.

"Why did you no' tell me your mother was from France? You were trying to give me away," Niall said, glaring at Anora. Though the matter of her being French was what interested him the most. He would discuss it with her once Matthew had left the area, and they were settled down for the night.

"I told you that the notion that you were my distant relation would be hard for any to believe. Besides, like I said, there is no proof my mother *was* from France."

"Why did you no' say that I was related to your father instead?"

"He was from France as well—so the tale goes. Another *unfounded* rumor."

"The sheepherder?" Niall was truly suspicious of her birth place.

Anora smiled. "I told you that was another story. Mayhap I can tell you that tale another time, however."

The English were not on the best of terms with the Franks and if they'd learned she was living here, would they think to take her hostage if she was nobility?

Matthew's boots tromped across the stone floor toward the door, catching their attention.

Niall asked her, "Do you love him?"

If she did, that would further complicate issues. Niall would have to convince the butcher's son to go with them.

"Shh, he is coming," she said.

Niall shook his head. "Then you dinna love him."

He was glad to hear it. If she was the woman he sought, he was taking her to Craigly Castle no matter what objections she might raise. The problem was he had to find Gunnolf, and ensure she *was* the right woman. He couldn't afford to take her to Craigly and then learn that the woman James sent him for was still here in the vicinity—and in possible danger. Not to mention, he had another slight difficulty with having lost his horse. And, God's knees, his wounds precluded a rigorous journey for at least another day or more.

Anora lifted the bucket to obtain water from the well. Niall stepped forward to do the task, but Anora shook her head. "You could pull your stitches loose."

Matthew exited the cottage and saw Anora lifting the heavy bucket from the well. He gave Niall a blistering look and then hurried to help her, which annoyed the hell out of Niall. He would have done the task if he hadn't been worried he'd never heal in time to leave here soon.

"You should have waited for me to get the water for you, Anora," Matthew said.

"You know I must do this several times a day without your assistance, and poor Niall has hurt his back or he would have helped me with the water."

"Oh," Matthew said, looking askance at Niall, and he didn't appear to believe Anora. "I did not know."

"That is quite all right, Matthew," Niall said, as he rubbed his lower spine with the back of his hand, damned irritated. He sounded like a weakling, rather than a badly wounded Highland warrior.

Matthew stored the beef in her cellar and returned. Finished with cleaning Niall's tunic, she wrung it out and said to Matthew, "I thank you for the beef. You are as kind as always."

Matthew rested his hands on her shoulders. "Can we take a short walk...," he asked, looking into her eyes like a besotted fool, "*alone*?"

Niall opened his mouth to tell him in no uncertain terms that he couldn't.

"Not tonight, Matthew." Anora smiled and quickly

pulled free. "I am sorry, but I am very tired. You know how wearing 'tis for me to go to market and now with company..."

"Very well, I will be gone for the next three days on a shopping expedition. There has been such an uproar at Banbury as the word reached us this eve that rumors abound that a French spy has been murdered there. Now, I will have to go to Coventry instead."

"A spy?" she asked, sounding alarmed.

Niall frowned at the news. If Anora was French, would the king of Scotland, or even Henry, his brother-in-law, king of England, suspect her of being a spy? Mayhap that was why James had sought to have her brought under their protection.

"Aye, and they are searching for any others, believing he had been with at least another man. Anyone who is not local in Banbury is suspect."

"I have not heard this," she said, looking pale.

If she had nothing to do with the matter, why was she looking so worried? She couldn't be a French spy, could she? But what would she have knowledge of, living in the countryside beyond the village of Banbh?

"Of that I have no doubt with living out here as you do." Matthew sighed.

"Did they say who he was? What his business there was?" Anora asked, appearing as though she was attempting to be casual about it, but Niall noted she was wringing her long braided belt with her hands.

"'Tis difficult to say how much truth he spoke." Matthew shrugged. "But what they did get out of him was that it seems he was looking for someone named Asceline. Does not that mean little noble one... in the English version of the name? Or the French's?"

Niall studied Anora as she slowly shook her head. "I would not know."

"Aye, well, Anora, I did not think you would have company like this. You never do. Had I known, I would have spent more time with you earlier in the week."

Anora cast him an easy smile, as if this topic was less difficult to deal with. "We were both busy with other matters this week, Matthew. You know we do not always have the time to be so carefree."

Matthew pulled Anora close—and her eyes widened. She quickly placed her hands against his chest, appearing to be an unwilling participant in Matthew's sudden action—and then he kissed her cheeks. "I will think of naught else while I am away from you, Anora."

"You will only be away for three days," she said, her posture stiff, the color in her cheeks high.

"Aye, and it will seem like an eternity." Matthew pressed his lips hard against her mouth.

She didn't kiss him back and her hands curled into fists at his chest before he released her and smiled to see her cheeks full of color.

Niall was ready to unsheathe his sword and threaten the man with bodily harm. He didn't believe Anora liked Matthew's kiss—the way her face was now pinched with annoyance.

She quickly turned to see what Niall thought—and witnessed his scowling face—before she blushed anew.

"Well, I will see you as soon as I am able, Anora." Turning to Niall, Matthew said, "And should you be done with your business here before my return, 'twas a pleasure having met Anora's distant relation. She did not tell me she had any. I assumed she was all alone in this part of the world."

Niall nodded stiffly. He stepped closer to Anora as Matthew mounted his horse and rode back into town. Anora gathered up her bucket and the wet tunic, and headed toward the cottage. Niall rushed after her.

"Has he kissed you like that before?" Niall didn't know why he blurted out the words, but there was no taking them back now.

He didn't like to see a man force a kiss on a woman, no matter the reason. Then again, they might kiss all the time, and she was just embarrassed that Matthew did so in front of Niall. Still, Niall didn't like it because Matthew was not tender, but showing possession—letting him know that Anora was Matthew's lass.

Anora ignored Niall, pushed the door open, then walked inside, and set her bucket on a shelf. She laid his garment on a rack above the cooling embers. The wet cloth dripped into the fire. The water droplets sizzled, sending ribbons of smoke curling heavenward.

She turned suddenly, then headed back toward the door while Niall grabbed her arm. "You havena answered me."

"I believe he was showing off to my distant relation," she said, annoyed, gazing up at him with her beautiful blue eyes that he found he could lose himself completely in.

"You mean he was envious of me? He shouldna have kissed you the way that he did," Niall growled.

"He wishes to marry me." Anora sounded as though that was a good enough reason for Matthew taking advantage of her—when it was not.

"But you dinna wish to marry him."

Anora pulled her arm free from Niall and headed back out of doors.

"Where are you going now?" He felt he couldn't take another step, his head and side were paining him so.

"You wished for me to make a bed for you to sleep on tonight. Remember? I am tired so I will gather the necessary straw and make a bed for you as you have demanded, and then retire."

"You are truly the kindest woman I have ever known," he said, gritting his teeth against another sharp pain in his side. He desperately needed to lie down.

She frowned a little at him as she headed for the haystack in the byre. "You only say so because you have lost your horse, have no money to go elsewhere, and are not sure who else may come to your aid in your time of need."

"True, but still I have never had someone do so much for me without having to pay for their services."

"Then if that is so," Anora said, stopping in her footsteps, and then turned to face Niall, "I would not trade my life for the sort of existence you must suffer. And here I always thought your kind would have been so content."

"The problem with having money and power is that there is always someone who wishes to take it from you."

"Even if you have very little, there is someone who is

bigger than you who wishes to take it away from you."

"You mean the tax collectors?"

"Aye." Anora picked up an armload of straw.

Thinking only to help and finish this task as soon as possible, Niall reached down to gather some of the straw. Instantly, he felt a sharp stab of pain in his side and his head, and groaned. God's wounds, he hated feeling this badly.

Dropping the armful she'd gathered, Anora ran to his side and touched his arm. "You have not done yourself further injury, have you?" She sounded so worried, her concern touched him.

"It hurts when I bend over," he hated to reveal.

"I will check to see if it is bleeding when we get inside. Why do you not go back to the cottage and take off your tunic while I gather the straw for your bed?"

Still not trusting the lass, Niall shook his head.

"Oh, stewed boar. You do not believe I am going to run away with you injured here like this?"

He gave her a small smile. That's exactly what he believed.

Anora took a deep breath and let it out. "Very well, but do not do anything more to injure yourself or you will never leave here if you do."

He was amused at the way she dictated to him.

"It grieves me to think you dinna wish for me to stay longer," Niall said, with a teasing tone of voice, as she gathered the straw. Then he grew serious. "I am sorry I cannot assist you in your efforts as Matthew would have done."

And sorrier still that he might have to take her from here against her will, as he suspected she wouldn't leave her home unless he forced her. She seemed happy here, but if it meant her safety, she was going with him. If she was the lass he sought.

Anora shook her head as she carried an armload of straw into the cottage. "Matthew would be furious if he were to learn you slept in the same room with me this eve."

"I willna tell him, if you dinna." Niall smiled a little at the notion, thinking of just how much he'd like to tell the man that. Not to cause Anora any grief, but because Niall hadn't liked the way Matthew had kissed her so... against her will.

Setting the straw aside on the floor, Anora considered Niall, then the straw. "I will have to make at least two more trips to the byre to fashion a proper bed of straw for you. Remove your tunic first. I will check your wounds before I gather the rest of the straw."

Meaning to make light of a situation that bothered him more than he wished Anora to see—he hated that anyone would have to fuss over him about an injury—Niall pulled the tunic over his head and said, "I believe you rather like to see me undress."

Her cheeks grew flushed, but her gaze didn't waver as she stared back at him.

He loved it, particularly since as soon as the words were out, he'd hoped she wouldn't take offense and realize he was only jesting with her, trying to get her attention off the fact he was so injured.

"I have seen men's chests before. Yours is no different

than the rest," she said haughtily.

"Have you now? Whose? Matthew's?" He couldn't help sounding so aggravated. The man had forced his kiss upon her and not in a loving way at all. More of possessiveness, telling Niall he'd claimed her. He didn't want to think she'd been with him in a more intimate way.

"Heavens no."

Niall was somewhat relieved to hear it. "Whose then?"

Anora unwrapped his binding. "My… father's."

"And?"

Anora looked up to see Niall studying her. "No one else."

"I suspected as much." Then he frowned as he considered her words. "You have done it again. You mentioned the sheepherder, your… father? Was he French?"

"He was a Scot," she said. "Born and raised here." Anora pulled the bandage free from Niall's chest and some of the dried blood pulled at his skin. He winced, biting back the pain.

She frowned. "I am sorry. I will wipe it clean again. The stitches have held, but you really must lie down."

"You know I canna let you out of my sight, even for a moment."

"I am hurt to think you regard me as having so little character, but I will clean your wounds, replace your bandages, and finish making your bed. I am afraid I will have to fetch some more water."

"You wear me out with all of this walking back and forth."

"Then you may stay here..."

"Nay. I will carry some of the straw as long as I dinna have to bend over."

Anora smiled. "I do believe before long I really will wear you out."

He didn't like the vixen-like smile she gave him, as if she thought to sneak out when he was too tired to notice.

After lighting candles in the main room and the bedroom, they obtained the mead and another two armloads of straw, then retired to the cottage. He realized then, her dog had been absent all this time.

After stacking the straw with the rest, Anora grabbed the used bandage and wetting it with water, touched Niall's chest with a tender sweep of the cloth. He shivered at the feel of the cold liquid against his skin. She reached up to feel his forehead.

"I worried mayhap you were becoming feverish. You are not, thank the Lord." She wrapped a new bandage around his chest, then Niall pulled his tunic back over his head.

He couldn't have been more relieved that he was not feverish. He had to get on his way soon. He was about to inquire about the dog, when Anora walked into the main room and blew out the candle, then called for Charlie. After some length, he bounded through the front door.

"Have you been chasing rabbits again, Charlie?" She closed the door to the cottage with a creak and a clunk, then bolted it. "Come on, Charlie." She motioned for him to go to her sleeping room.

After Niall closed the door behind them, Anora pulled

the straw in place beside the door. "Where is he going to sleep?" he asked, suddenly wary.

Charlie sat in the middle of the floor, wagging his tail as he looked from one to the other for attention.

"I do not know. Sometimes he sleeps at the foot of my bed, sometimes next to the door."

Niall frowned.

Anora laughed. "Have you never had a dog to sleep with?"

"The dogs are used for hunting, naught more. They are kept in the kennels. The people live in the castle."

"Which castle?"

"None that I will speak the name of, lass." Not until they were well on their way, if she was the French lass he was meant to protect.

"Still afraid to reveal too much about yourself?"

"I could say the same for you, lass."

Anora's expression turned to concern, then she quickly rummaged through a trunk, found two more blankets, and pulled them out. "My father used these. They are longer than my blankets. They should work well for you."

She walked over to the door and laid the blankets out lengthwise over the straw and added her father's pillow. She blew out the candles, then moved toward her bed in the pitch black room, except her dog suddenly yelped, and Niall suspected he'd gotten underfoot.

"Oh Charlie. I am so sorry, pup," she said, mere inches from Niall, who was about to take her hand and lead her to her bed when her warm fingers touched his bare chest, the contact sizzling.

And she gasped.

CHAPTER 7

"Come now, I am no' such a frightening prospect as all that," Niall said to Anora, who was standing in front of him in the dark.

He took her hand and kissed it. She didn't object, and he reached up to explore her face with his fingertips and found her lips. He touched them with tenderness, then lifted her chin. When she took a deep breath, he smiled, then kissed her lips with a sweet and rather unassuming kiss, by his standards.

He was glad when she didn't step away from him or push him back.

"I wondered what it would be like to kiss the woman who poked me with a pitchfork earlier this day." He loosened her hair from the ribbon that barely confined it and gently pulled her closer. "You intrigue me more than any other woman I have ever known."

"Mayhap, then," Anora said, as she tried to wriggle

free from him with a subdued air this time, unlike the energy she'd expended in the effort earlier in the day, "you will have to arm your ladies with pitchforks when you return to your castle."

"They would not know how to use them as well as you do, lass. I would be afraid they would do me bodily harm."

She chuckled softly. "Had you not knocked the fork from my hand with your sword, I may have done you harm also."

"Nay, lass. Though you pretend to be harsh, you are as gentle as the lambs that you tend to." Niall reached up and ran his hands through her soft, silky hair, then kissed her lips again, pressing his mouth more firmly against hers. He was tender though, not forceful—like Matthew—willing her to partake in the kiss, but ready to part company if she was unwilling.

Anora could feel Niall's heartbeat quicken as his chest touched her breasts. She closed her eyes as she felt his hand slip down her back, pressuring her to feel his desire for her as he leaned close to her. By the heavens, he felt so... so... masculine. She should be pushing him away, but she couldn't. She'd never felt a man up close like this, pressing indecently against her, wanting her, and despite knowing how mad it was to think such a thing—she wanted him right back. What was the matter with her? She was his hostage for the moment—naught more.

"Oh, Anora," he whispered, "you should discourage me."

He was so different from Matthew—so in charge and commanding. And yet, he had his tender moments like now.

His lips begged for more, and she loved the way he pressed his against her mouth—warm and appealing—not like Matthew's as he had mashed his lips hard against hers. She'd wanted to shove Matthew away—and would have if it hadn't been for Niall watching, and she had been afraid he might draw his sword if Matthew became angry.

But with Niall, she wanted desperately to lean into his kiss.

And she did, ignoring the warnings her guardians had given her about kissing men and what that could lead to.

She cupped his face, angled hers, and kissed him on the mouth, as gently as he had her. She loved hearing the hitch in his breath, the way his arms wrapped around her, and pulled her even tighter. But then he groaned, and she was certain it *wasn't* a groan of lustful need.

He was hurting.

She pulled quickly away from him. "I am so sorry."

"Ah, lass," he said, his voice dark with desire, "'tis naught to be sorry for."

"You are hurting," she said.

"Aye," he ground out, sounding frustrated. "Though to be sure, for a moment, I forgot all about the pain. To bed with you, lass." He took her hand and led her to her bed.

She shook her head. "We cannot..."

He let out his breath. "I only wished to lead you to your bed so that you wouldna trip over your dog anymore, or me either, for that matter." He sat her down on her bed. "Again, I wish to thank you for your generosity, Anora. I fear I wouldna have found a more helpful soul in this shire."

"I wish... I wish you had not been injured here, but I..."

What? That she had changed her mind about his being here? If they'd kissed any further, and he hadn't been injured, she could imagine where that would have led. And she was afraid she would have encouraged it. But she couldn't say she welcomed his presence because they'd soon part company, and she was certain now she'd miss him. "I am glad I could help," she finally said.

He kissed the top of her head, and she sighed deeply.

"Night, lass." Niall left her and settled onto his mattress of straw.

Anora realized just how honorable the Highlander was and couldn't help but admire him for it. She removed her outer *léine*, and laid it upon the chair, then climbed into bed and pulled her sheepskin covers over her shoulder.

Niall chuckled.

She smiled, envisioning Charlie curling up with him. "Have you a guest?"

"Aye, it seems Charlie thinks I have joined him on the floor."

Anora laughed. "Good, 'tis too warm for him to sleep with me. I am glad he has decided to sleep with you." After some silence, Anora worried about Niall. "He is not hurting your injury, is he?"

"Nay, wrong side." The straw moved some more and then everything was quiet. "Who were your parents, Anora?"

A prolonged silence ensued as Anora thought of what to say that would keep her secrets as her guardians had warned her to do. "Did I not tell you? I am a princess who has lost her kingdom. A kind sheepherder and his sister took me in."

The room was quiet for some time, except for Charlie's whimpering as he dreamt his dog dreams.

Then Niall broke the silence again, jarring Anora fully awake as she was just drifting off to sleep. "So you truly do come from France?"

"How would I know that for certain? I was very little when I came here. If I spoke another language, I have forgotten it in its entirety." It was true she never had spoken it since she was little. Jane made sure of that.

Niall turned to face Anora, then said, "*Comment vous appellez-vous*?"

Surprised to hear him speak French to her, Anora responded with some hesitation, realizing she'd remembered quite a bit. "*Je m'appelle* Anora."

"How do you know French if you did not come from France?" he asked.

"Some of the villagers are French."

"Oh? I would suspect they would keep this to themselves," Niall said, sounding suspicious. "So if your father died last year, when did your mother die?"

"The queen? Well I do not know if she has even died yet."

Niall chuckled and she liked the sound of it. She loved to tell stories and was glad Niall didn't mind. "The shepherdess who was your mother," he said.

"I never knew John's wife. She died before John's sister, Jane, brought me here."

Niall had to know the truth about the lass and the more she spoke of her family, the more he was concerned that they *had* come from France. Whether she was the woman he sought was another story. Was she truly Asceline? The French count's niece, a countess in her own right?

Niall placed his hands behind his head as he stared at the shadowy form of the dark timbers crossed high on the ceiling above. "You are a fine story-teller, lass."

"Thank you. My father always told me stories before I retired to bed for the evening."

"Your guardian, the sheepherder."

"Of course. I am sure my father, the king, would not have had time to tell his children any stories at night."

"I will be sure to tell my children stories before they retire in the evening," he said, thinking of how no one had done that with him or his cousins growing up and how much his own children someday would most likely enjoy such a thing.

After some silence, Anora said, "I did not know you were wed. Is she a fine lady from a fine background?"

He smiled. "I am no' married, Anora. I only meant when I have wee bairns one day..."

"Oh."

"Have you no sisters or brothers?" he asked.

"I imagine my father, the king, would have had many to ensure he had an heir for the throne. Such a thing is very important for the continuation of the kingdom, you know."

"Aye, I know." He only just managed not to shake his head even though she could not see him in the dark.

"As for John, he had a son and two daughters, but his wife and children all died before I arrived, his sister told me."

"Why did he take you in instead of one of the other villagers? Or if you were the king of the Franks' daughter, why not the local laird?"

"John's sister brought me to him."

"Aye, but why would the laird of the local area no' have taken you in since you were a French princess?" Niall imagined she would have made a good bargaining tool for someone. Not that she was truly a princess, but that she was one of the French nobility.

"How would I know that? I was only six at the time. But John and his sister were very kind to me."

"How do you know you were a princess and not just a little girl?" Had she been so young at the time that she truly didn't remember who she was?

"My father always called me his little princess."

Niall chuckled. "I see. Which father, Anora?"

"Both to be sure."

"But... you said John was not your father."

"Aye. I was never to call him that, but I still fondly think of him in that way."

"Are you certain that your mother was not John's wife?"

"Do you not think I would remember my own mother?" Without waiting for a response, Anora added, "I do not really remember my real mother, but I know the lady who lived with John was his sister. They fought often, just like sisters and brothers always fight. Just like the English king and our Scottish one and their brothers fought while they were growing up together, I imagine."

"Aye," Niall said. "My cousins and my friend Gunnolf, who are like my brothers, were like that. Silly squabbles about naught. Who fought better, which of us was a faster runner, who was the best swimmer among us. Unlike King Henry who continues to fight with his brother over the rule of England."

"Among you and your cousins and Gunnolf, who fought the best? Ran the fastest? Was the best swimmer?" she asked, curious as to what Niall would say.

"Me."

Anora laughed. "Aye, because your cousins are not here to dispute your claim."

He chuckled.

She grew quiet then. She was tired, but... she had to admit, she hadn't had anyone to talk to like this in well over a year, and she knew she needed to sleep. She couldn't help wanting to speak with him further.

"You really will not stay very much longer, will you?" she asked, not truly wishing he'd leave, but she couldn't say that—knowing he'd be gone, and she was afraid she'd feel a terrible loneliness. For a time. Like she did when Jane had died. And then John. But she reminded herself it wasn't the same because they'd been like family to her. Once Niall was gone, she'd be back to her usual life—such as it was.

"I will remain here as long as is necessary," Niall said. The straw scratched the floor when he rolled onto his side.

She frowned, wondering why he would want to stay any longer than necessary when she was certain he had business to conduct. Then she realized he hadn't meant that he *wished* to stay, but his injuries most likely made it necessary. And he had no horse.

If things had been different between them, she'd love to have more of his kisses when he was no longer hurting from his injuries. She enjoyed his companionship and wished he would stay longer. Though she knew that was not a good idea. Not when men could be after him and wish to kill him. And not when it could hurt her reputation as an unmarried miss. Just as Matthew had said, distant cousins married, and even closely related ones did. So that would not keep tongues from wagging.

But then the news about Asceline and the French spy began to nag at her again.

Anora said, "You know, you must not tell anyone that I am a princess. John and his sister always told me to tell no one."

"Then why have you told me?" he asked, sounding as if he didn't believe a word she told him, which was the way she hoped it would be.

"I believe you are in a similar predicament in that you cannot tell anyone who you are for fear that those who attempted to kill you will try again." After some silence, Anora said, "I must graze the sheep in the pasture in the morning, but afterward we could search for your friend."

That had bothered her also. She wasn't certain Niall was strong enough for the task though. She thought she could look for his friend, and prayed he would not be dead somewhere near where Niall had been struck down.

"It would be too dangerous until I have healed some," Niall said.

"I could look for him," she said, not to be dissuaded if

he thought she could help his friend.

"Nay. 'Twould be too dangerous for you as well, lass. But I appreciate your offer of help. Anora, you seemed worried about the French spy who was murdered. Did you... know him?"

She chewed on her bottom lip. How would she know the man? Matthew had said nothing about what he was called. "I thought you were tired and wished to sleep."

Niall let out his breath and sounded exasperated. "Answer the question, Anora."

Her heartbeat sped up a bit. She'd only believed Niall had been a traveler in the area and thieves had attacked him to steal his horse. But what if he was not? What if *he* was trying to discover her identity and wanted her dead?

She bit her lip and frowned. Now what was she to do? Or say without giving herself away? Who was he really? Who did he work for? The French? The English?

Oh, aye, he was a Highlander to be sure. His brogue and clothes and commanding attitude were more than enough to prove just where he came from. But the French or the English might very well have hired a braw Highlander to learn where the French lady was living and bring her to them.

She never suspected she would have to worry that Niall was someone like that.

She closed her eyes, irritated with herself for the further predicament she was in. God's teeth, what if he realized who she was and she had to kill him? And then dig a hole large enough for him in her garden, and somehow drag the Highland warrior out to the hole and bury him?

Oh, aye, that would be an easy task. Well, and the killing also. Not that she wanted to even think of such a thing. Or that she could do such a deed.

Niall chuckled, breaking into her dark thoughts. "I believe your dog is chasing something in his dreams."

She smiled. No matter what she worried he might be, the Highlander was endearing—to an extent. "Sheep probably."

"If you were a princess..."

Anora laughed—the sound fake even to her ears. "I should not have mentioned it."

"Do you have any proof?"

"I need no proof." She only jested. No one ever believed her. She was a teller of tales. Always had been.

"Anora," Niall said very seriously, "I am cousin to James of the MacNeill Clan, laird of Craigly Castle."

She barely breathed, waiting for him to say something further. Why was he telling her who he was now? When she didn't say anything, he continued. "Do you know of us?"

"Why... why would I know of you? I know no Highlanders. Not until you came upon my cottage." Which was true.

"My cousin, James, and his brothers all fought in the Crusades. A man called Jacques Ponsot, Count of Carcassonne, saved James's life during a battle with the Saracens. He begged James to take care of a wee lassie living in this region should he return to France and learn she was in harm's way. Do you know him?"

Chill bumps raced up her arms. Aye, she knew him. The uncle who had shared with her many a tale after her mother had died before Anora had been sent away. She said nothing. What was she to say that would not give her away?

"He said if he ever sent a missive to James, it meant the lass's life was in grave danger. He said he wouldna be able to state such in the missive, but that James was to assume as much. He knew if he sent it, it could very well be intercepted by those who could do her harm. He intended to meet us at Craigly Castle as soon as he could."

"Oh?" she said, very softly.

"He asked that James send someone who he regarded as the most honorable and capable of men to fetch her and return her to Craigly Castle for safekeeping until the count could come for her."

"And you are the most honorable and capable of men," she said, a smile curving her mouth. She couldn't help it. The poor Highlander had lost his horse, his companion, and was sorely wounded.

"Aye," Niall said, as if he was ready to take her on the rough journey right this very moment, that would no doubt kill him in his current condition.

She didn't say anything, still thinking about his injuries and how he couldn't manage the trip when he said, "Anora?"

"I have no cousins," she said softly, repeating her dying guardians' words—*you have no family. They are all dead. Trust no one.*

"He would be your uncle. You have no relations nearby, so Matthew said," Niall countered. "Did this uncle never mention us to you? That if you were ever in danger, we could take you away to safety?"

Again, she said nothing.

"Lass?"

"I have never heard of you or your kin or of an uncle who fought in the Crusades alongside your cousins. You—if you think I am the lady—are mistaken." She hadn't known her uncle fought in the Crusades, or anything about the MacNeills, so she was being truthful. And certainly, she had never received any word from him in all the years she'd lived here.

"Mayhap he wasna able to send word to you, afraid someone else might intercept the missive," Niall continued, his voice gentle, coaxing, as if he was attempting to cajole the truth from her. "And as of a certainty, he still didna know your exact whereabouts."

The room grew quiet, except for the brushing of Charlie's foot against the floor as he chased something in his dreams.

Niall shifted on his bed of straw again, and she worried he might be hurting and unable to sleep. "If you were six when you came here, and you are now...," he said, and paused as if waiting for her to fill in her age.

She sighed as she thought the matter over.

"Are you still awake, Anora?"

"I was counting."

After much silence, Niall said, "Dinna you know how to count?"

"Of course I know how to count. How would I be able to keep track of my sheep if I did not know how to count? How would I know if I had received the correct payment for my sheep when I have sold them in the village or know..."

"I am sorry, Anora. So how old are you?" Niall sounded slightly amused—to her further annoyance.

"I just count more slowly when 'tis this late at night when I have to rouse so early in the morn."

"Just answer this for me and you can sleep."

"I am one and twenty." Anora rolled onto her side, then closed her eyes.

Niall sat up on his makeshift mattress. "If you are one and twenty now, and you came here when you were six, that was five and ten years ago."

"Aye."

"If that is so, the English were having trouble with the French at the time."

"From what I understand, they are always having difficulty with the French of one kind or another."

"'Tis true." Niall lay back down and stared at Anora's bed.

"I am a shepherdess."

"No' a princess?"

"If you will let me sleep tonight, I will be a shepherdess again or a princess or anything you desire, as long as you allow me to rest."

"Anything I desire?" he said, a teasing tone to his voice.

She shook her head. But she assumed Niall was awake because he was in pain and wanting to learn if she truly was the one he sought.

The question kept running through her mind—was he truly a friend of the count, her storytelling uncle, and intended to take her to safety, or was Niall good at telling stories also and was truly working for her enemies?

CHAPTER 8

At daybreak, Niall left Anora's cottage in search of Gunnolf. Feeling relatively sure she wouldn't have any trouble at the moment, he wanted to see if he could locate his friend, and together, mayhap they could determine if the lass was the one they sought. He was fairly certain she was.

His side ached with every move he made, and he hoped that once he walked a bit, the stiffness in his muscles would lessen, but the pain wouldn't subside. He had walked too much as he'd followed Anora about to ensure she didn't run off the day before, not that his concern could have been helped. But he was sorely paying for the effort this morn.

For a while, Charlie chased after him, though Niall repeatedly told him to return to Anora. She needed Charlie's protection, and Niall didn't want anyone to be suspicious if he saw him with her dog.

But Charlie continued to chase along the burn and

return to his side as if Niall was taking him for a jaunt in the woods. Niall was anxious to return to Anora as soon as he could, but he had to learn what had become of Gunnolf if possible.

He would never forgive himself if he found Gunnolf nearly dead, and he had not come to his aid.

No matter how hard he looked, he could not find any sign of the man. Had he gone in a different direction? Found refuge with a farmer?

Niall stopped to breathe through the pain again, gritted his teeth, and forged on.

***

Early that morn, Anora rubbed her eyes, then reached over to her table to light a candle. "Charlie," she whispered, not wanting to disturb Niall if he finally was able to sleep. Her dog did not greet her like he normally did.

A shiver of dread crept up her spine. He should have been poking at her with his wet, cold nose long before this, eager to go outside.

She fumbled with the candle. After lighting it, she stared to see the straw bed had been shoved away from the door. Niall and Charlie were gone.

No matter how much she told herself Niall must have needed to leave the cottage for personal business, she couldn't help worrying he was trouble. Yet, the cottage seemed so empty without his domineering presence. She should be glad he was up and about and not languishing from a fever.

Anora quickly climbed out of bed, then reached for her *léine*. She lifted it off the chair in a hurry and something fell to the floor with a clunk. Looking down, she found the lovely torque Niall had offered her in payment for his stay, sitting in a coil on the floor. She leaned over and picked it up, then ran her hand over the smoky quartz. No one had ever given her a gift such as that. It was precious and she would cherish it always.

After pulling the chain over her head, she slipped into her gown, and carried the candle with her as she opened her door to the main part of the cottage. She stared at the room left unchanged from the night before. She peered out the window facing the sheep's pen. Still seeing nothing amiss, nor any sign of Niall or her dog, she set her candle on the table, and blew it out.

Anora walked outside and saw Charlie running through the meadow, his tongue hanging out, his brown ears flying. The sky was awash in a soft yellow and pink sunlight.

She whistled for him. He barked and ran for her. Relieved to see him, she patted his furry head. She wondered if Niall had gone in search of his friend.

"Where did Niall go?" she asked, as Charlie pounced on her, wagging his tail in a vigorous fashion, whipping a whirlwind of air in its path. "Well, come on, we must take the sheep out this morning. I feel as though I slept not at all last night."

Yet, she couldn't push aside the anxiousness churning in the pit of her stomach. She had wanted Niall to leave, aye. But he was too badly injured to travel far. And she didn't even want to think about what might happen if he attempted it.

Had he decided she was not the woman he sought and

went in search of the right woman?

Thinking of the way he kissed her with tenderness and caring, Anora wondered how he'd view her if he knew who she truly was. He would probably wish he hadn't touched her—concerned that her noble family, if they learned of it, would want his head on a pike—and that saddened her.

She opened the gate to the pen, then motioned for Charlie to take the sheep out. He nipped at their withers and headed them out to the nearby hills.

She was unable, or mayhap unwilling, to refrain from thinking about Niall and how he'd made her feel—like a woman, desirable, even interesting. She was so wrapped up in her thoughts that she nearly missed seeing movement on the horizon. Men on horseback crested one of the hills, their swords glittering in the early morning sunlight. Her heartbeat quickened. Who were they?

The men were dressed in plaids much as Niall had been, not breeches like the locals wore. Were they Niall's men, searching for him? Or the men who had tried to murder him?

Panicked, Anora ran for the cottage. She dashed inside and stared at the hearth where she'd hung Niall's tunic to dry, meaning to hide the torn garment.

Finding it had vanished, she realized he must have left her behind. She prayed he would be safe from these men, if they were the brigands who had wounded him so. And that he would not fall ill from his wounds. Or that they would catch up to him again.

Grabbing her staff, she ran back outside to see Charlie waiting for her in the meadow. Trying to appear as though she had nothing to hide, she walked out to join him. She frowned when one of the men motioned to some of the others to go to Anora's cottage. Five of the men split off from the main group, then headed in her direction, as the rest continued toward the village. Anora stood her ground and waited with her sheep, her heart skipping beats. She tightened her hold on her staff. The men galloped toward her, sending muddy earth flying in their wake, alarming her sheep. They scattered in all directions.

She ground her teeth, trying to control her anger while Charlie hurried to corral the sheep some distance from the men.

One of the men took the lead and pulled his reins in sharply, galloping within inches of her. She fought jumping back, her heart beating against her ribs, her breathing unsteady. She would not let these brigands see that she was frightened of them or their actions. The others joined him, standing a ways off. Dirty, red-bearded, middle aged, the man regarded her with cold gray eyes—the leader of the group, she assumed. He looked like he would enjoy killing just for the sake of doing so, and she worried he might harm her sheep or her dog. Or her.

"We are looking for some men who have escaped us who we believe may have come this way." His accent sounded very much like Niall's—the same heavy Highland burr.

"What men are these?" she asked, frowning up at him, not about to be intimidated, even though he and his men *were* intimidating. But she believed showing weakness would only get her into worse trouble.

"Two Highlanders who have stolen from us."

Furious with these men when they had stolen from Niall and nearly killed him, she narrowed her eyes. "I have no knowledge of these men." And she didn't. Niall didn't steal anything from anyone.

Glancing at Anora's cottage, the Highlander said, "Who resides there?"

"My father and brothers and me."

"Where are they now?"

"In the village."

"Banbh?"

"Aye."

"You are here alone?" the man asked, brows raised, not believing her, she thought.

"Nay," she said, very sincerely.

He frowned at her. "I believe you are by yourself, lassie."

That didn't bode well and a shiver shook her. "The field is full of sheep and my dog is here with me. And, too, here, you, and your four men are. How might you think I am alone?"

The man cast her a tight smile. "You have quite a wit about you. You will come with me. I wish to inspect this cottage of yours."

"May I place my sheep back in their pen first?"

"'Twill take too long."

"I will have my dog take them back. It will not take him long." She would not leave her sheep out without her being with them to watch over them.

Anora motioned for Charlie to return the sheep to their

pen. She strode toward home, but the Highlander reached down to grab her arm, making her step away from his grasp.

"Come, ride with me," he said, his voice a command, sounding irritated that she would avoid his grasp.

"I am afraid of horses. I do not wish to ride. I shall walk."

"You have naught to fear from my horse. He is extremely gentle. And it will take us too long for you to walk." He leaned over and grabbed for Anora's arm again.

Instinctively, she reached up with her crook, hooking it over his arm, and yanked as hard as she could, nearly unseating him from his horse.

She had done it without thinking of the consequences as she would have reacted to any man who had attempted to accost her. One of his men rode up beside her and jerked her staff from her hands.

Instantly, her skin chilled with concern now that she was mostly defenseless. Not that being armed with a staff had made her that invincible against Highland warriors. Her knife would not protect her, either.

"'Tis a lassie with spirit," the leader said, and yanked her into his saddle.

Anora screamed out in surprise.

Ignoring her, he kicked his horse to a gallop.

Terrified of the horse and the man holding her, she took in deep breaths to calm her racing heart, shutting her eyes so she couldn't see the way the earth moved so quickly beneath them.

When they reached her cottage, he lowered her to the ground—his sudden gentleness worrying her more than when he acted the barbarian. He dismounted.

Feeling unsteady and shaken, and worried about what would happen next, she waited for Charlie to corral the last of the sheep in her pen, then hurried to lock the gate.

Two of the men searched her home.

When they exited the cottage, the scrawniest one said, "They are not here."

They. Niall and his friend? As much as she'd hoped the men didn't mean them, she feared they did.

"Search the other buildings," the leader said, motioning to the byre and cellar. When the men moved toward the other buildings, he led Anora into the cottage and looked about the main room for a moment. "Light a candle."

She did, and he made her walk in front of him into her sleeping quarters.

God's teeth, how was she to get out of this? She feared what he wished to do to her.

"Set the candle on the table."

She thought to unsheathe her knife. She was afraid he'd kill her before she could escape. She set the candle on the table.

He immediately grabbed for her knife, quickly disarming her. She scowled at him. He smiled a little and considered the straw mattress on the floor, then the bed. "Where do you sleep?"

"On the floor," she said firmly, hoping she hid the way she was trembling.

"And your father?"

"In the bed."

"And your brothers?"

"In the main room, but they have removed their mats for the day. I rose late to do my chores and neglected to put my bed away," she said quickly.

"Which do you prefer?"

Not understanding his question, she frowned at the hulking brute, just as muscled as Niall, just as tall. "What do you mean?"

"The floor or the bed?" He shut the door behind him with a clunk.

Goose bumps trailed down her arms and with her blood rushing in her ears, Anora glared at him. "My father and brothers will kill you if you touch me."

She knew her words wouldn't deter the barbarian. But she didn't know what else to do or say. She spied the pitchfork on the floor, half-buried by Neill's makeshift straw bed.

"We will be long gone before they return," the man said, his gaze raking over her in a predatory way. He unfastened his belt and set his scabbard on the chair.

Anora swallowed hard. "I thought you were in a hurry to search for these men who have stolen from you."

"I am. Only it willna hurt to take a respite from the task at hand to enjoy the company of an attractive lassie such as yourself before I move on."

"What about your men?"

He removed his plaid. "What about them? Do you desire their company as well?" He shook his head. "We dinna have time for everyone to enjoy you as I shall."

That's *not* what she meant.

Still wearing his tunic, he stepped forward to touch Anora's face with his meaty, dirty hand, and she moved back. "The baron who manages this shire will not be happy that you have trifled with his subjects so."

"He will never know."

Anora dove for the pitchfork, grabbing a handful of straw along with it in her haste. She brought the weapon up to defend herself. The man seized his sword, unsheathing it from its scabbard in a swift movement. He struck at Anora's pitchfork with a mighty swing. Determined as she was and more prepared this time, Anora hung onto her pitchfork. She swung it back at the villain, hitting him squarely in the shoulder. The strike knocked him off balance—just a little. Only enough to make his face redden and his mouth turn into a scowl.

He said something in Gaelic, cursing she suspected.

"You will pay with your life for this, woman," he growled.

She would have anyway even if she hadn't fought him, she was certain.

He hit her pitchfork with his sword again, knocking it out of the way. He grabbed it and pulled it from Anora's hands. In anger, he threw it aside. No longer armed, she ran for the door. After pulling it open, she dashed into the main room, and headed for the front door. She hoped to heaven she could get away from him when she hadn't been able to escape Niall yesterday.

She knew though, as soon as she ran outside and the other men saw her, they'd catch her if this one didn't. She didn't stand a chance against so many.

She snatched at the door handle, but he caught her arm, and jerked her aside. "I have never heard of a sheepherder keeping a pitchfork in his sleeping chamber. I will have my way with you as I intended. And if you make it worth my while, I might even allow you to live."

When he pulled Anora toward the small room, she hit him in the eye with her fist. She wouldn't make it easy on him.

He twisted her arm behind her back hard. She screamed out in pain and tried to jerk free.

The front door creaked open. Before she could see who it was, her attacker turned to look. His face lost all its color.

Niall. Quickly, she stomped on the man's foot. He lost his hold on her, and she ran into the other room. After slamming the door behind her, she grabbed the pitchfork again, and waited a moment. The two men slashed at each other with their swords in the main room. The clanging of metal filled the air.

Her heart thumped hard. What of the other men? She couldn't let Niall fend for himself against all of them. And he was sorely wounded already.

"Oh, Niall," Anora said, swinging the door open.

With her pitchfork readied as Niall forced the man back toward her bedroom—right where she was standing with her pitchfork ready. But she was unsure as to how she could help. Niall thrust at the man again. Taking a couple of steps back to avoiding being stabbed, he suddenly stopped when he felt the prongs of her pitchfork pricking his back. Without a place for him to maneuver, he couldn't react fast enough to fight Niall who surged forward, his sword poised to kill the man.

Niall made one final thrust, the sword sinking into the man's chest. The villain sank to the floor.

Her breath catching in her throat and her hands shaky—just as her legs were, Anora stared at the man lying on her floor. She looked up at Niall, her skin suddenly chilled. "What of the others? They are in the byre and the cellar."

"No longer." He pulled her against his body with his free arm and hugged her soundly.

"You did not kill them, too, did you?" How could he have managed? One man against that many?

"They would have killed me had I no' done the deed to them first."

"How were you able to kill all of them?"

"I am about the best swordsman there is, lass. I was lucky to kill the two who were drinking of your mead in your cellar, then took care of the two in the byre who had curled up to take a nap in the hay while the other was busy with you."

Her whole body chilled with the disagreeable notion. "Oh, Niall. I thought you had gone for good."

"I was looking for Gunnolf, to see if I could learn where he had gone. I found no sign of him. I hadna thought these men would search here since they hadna before now. I believed they'd left the area completely. You are all right, lass?"

"Oh, aye, but if it had not been for you…" She took a shuddering breath and fought the tears welling in her eyes.

"They will kill us both now."

He shook his head, and then slipped her *sgian dubh* out of his boot. "Keep this with you. I will take the bodies south and stage a battle of epic proportions, leaving their horses to graze in the heather."

Unable to stand any longer, Anora pulled away from Niall and sat down hard on her chair. A million thoughts were rushing through her mind. A million *what-ifs* as she tried to sort out ways in which they could get caught up in this.

Niall walked into the other room and reached down to take coins from the brigand's sporran still tied to his belt lying on the floor. She frowned. "You cannot steal his silver."

"He willna be able to spend it where he is going. Besides, 'tis blood money paid by whoever wants to locate the French lass. The silver is yours to do with as you wish."

"He would have killed me," Anora said, as she stared at the man. "Wait, he is looking for her also?"

"Aye," Niall said, studying her closely. "He learned Gunnolf and I were making inquiries as to the lass's whereabouts. We hadna thought a fellow Highlander would be working for the French count. Her uncle believes this count wishes her hand in marriage and once he has claimed her title, her lands, and an heir, he willna need the lass any longer. Once the count learned you lived, he sent negotiators to your... I mean, her uncle to work out an agreement, but her uncle said no. The man will stop at naught to have you returned to France before your uncle can see to your safety."

But what if Niall and his family worked for this man instead?

"Come, help me move him. We must get rid of him quickly before anyone comes back to investigate," Niall said, reminding her of the more current problem they had at the moment.

"The rest of his men went to Banbh. What if they return?" she asked, terrified the others would discover she had any part in this. But then she realized she could not leave her sheep or her cottage.

"All they will find is a shepherdess here still tending her sheep."

"Oh, Niall, I am afraid."

He cupped her cheek and looked down into her face with concern and pride. "Is there anywhere else you could go with your sheep? A pasture where the men would not find you?"

"Nay, I will stay here. If I were to go to Matthew's home in Banbh, I could run into the rest of their men. There is no pasture land that would hide me from these men. You are right. The only way to handle this is for me to pretend naught has happened. I am used to telling stories."

Still, he didn't budge from where he stood. "Lass..."

She shook her head. "'Tis the only way, Niall. As long as they are not found dead here, well, even if they were, they would know I had not killed all these men. But then they might stay to see if you returned. You must go."

"I will be gone only for a while." Wincing, Niall pulled the man from the room.

Anora jumped up to help him. "Are you still hurting?"

Niall nodded. "I need for you take a look at my bandages, but later. I must move these bodies at once."

"What of their horses?"

"They will graze happily in a pasture, part of the mock battle I will arrange. Of course, I will keep two of them—for one is mine and the other is Gunnolf's."

Her lips parted in surprise, she glanced up from the dead man to see the strained look in Niall's dark eyes. She knew from Niall's account, these men had attempted to murder him and stole his horse. But knowing that one of the riders Niall had killed today had ridden his own horse made it so much more real. She'd hoped his friend had gotten away. Her stomach tightened with the horrible notion that he had not.

Was Gunnolf dead? She prayed it was not so.

***

After they pulled the dead man into the garden, Anora ran back into the cottage to retrieve her pitchfork so no one would think she'd used it on the man who had tried to rape her. She grimaced at the sight of the blood left streaked across her stone floor as they'd dragged the man's body outside. She'd have to clean it as soon as she could. She returned the pitchfork to the byre, then saw the boot of one of the men poking out from a pile of hay.

She gasped. "Oh, Father in heaven, this Highlander will be the death of me." She pulled aside the hay when Niall led two of the horses into the byre.

"Help me to get the men on their horses, and I will take them far away."

"All right." Anora helped Niall with the first of the men.

Though he was trying to use only his strength to lift the brigand, she could see the strain on Niall's face, the sweat on his brow, and the pinched expression as he groaned a little with the effort. He was hurting badly, and she did her best to lift as much of the man's weight as she could.

After settling the two men on two of the horses, Niall said, "If you will bring two of the horses to the cellar, I will haul them up from there and you can help me again."

"I am deathly afraid of horses. You get the horses and I will retrieve this villain's tunic and belt that he removed in my room." She should have gotten them when she retrieved her pitchfork, but her thoughts were so scattered with concern, she wasn't thinking clearly.

Niall nodded and strode to the place where the villain's horses munched on her garden. She scowled at the sight and hurried into the cottage.

The brigand's effects in hand, she hastened to help Niall heft one of the men who had been in her cellar across the horse's back.

"I am glad you came into the cottage when you did. Thank you," she told Niall.

Her muscles already straining from helping to lift these men, she was certain she would be aching from all the effort later today. But she couldn't help worrying these men's friends would soon return.

"I only wish I could have come to your rescue sooner. One of the men in the byre had the gall to fight me." They heaved the brigand who she had fought in her cottage onto a horse behind another man. "I knew the man who attacked you. He is known for his attentions toward the ladies."

"Was," she said dryly.

"Aye, lass."

When all of the men lay across their saddles, save one who Niall stacked with another, he mounted his own horse. "Are you certain you will be able to manage, lass?"

"Aye." She wasn't sure he could do this alone, and she'd much rather be with him than alone if the others returned to look for their men. But she knew it would be dangerous if she went with him and the rest of their kin found them together. She worried, too, for Niall. What if they caught him? What if he was in so much pain from his own wounds, he could not return? Or if he did, what if the men were here at the same time and caught him upon his return?

He hesitated to leave her behind.

"The others may suspect something is wrong if I am gone, too. What if they were to stay until I returned? As dangerous as the situation is, I believe it would be better to do it this way. If anyone asks, they came, looked for you, found naught to concern them, and left. They will never suspect I had anything to do with making their men disappear. I will tidy things up," she said, the blood left in a trail on her main room floor instantly coming to mind, sickening her. "Then I will tend to my sheep as though naught is wrong."

With her stomach twisting in knots, Anora waited for him to agree.

Niall gave her a small smile. "You, bonny lass, would make any Highland warrior proud."

And then he turned and headed away from her home

with his silent party.

Tears filled her eyes. She couldn't help worrying that he might never return. And she couldn't help how much his words affected her. She couldn't remember anyone saying he was proud of her.

As soon as Niall disappeared beyond the hill, she dashed back inside the cottage to clean up the blood. After scrubbing away all of it, she pulled the straw for Niall's bed under her own. Then she hurried into the byre and looked at the blood that spotted the hay. Her heart thundered in her ears as she feared the men would return at any time and she was still not done.

Quickly, she used her hoe to move some of the dirt about to absorb the blood. Then with her pitchfork, she pulled the straw over the area, and raked out the hay to make it appear as though it had lain there for some time. If anyone found her so out of breath, most likely flushed as hot as she felt, and her hair in disarray, what would they think? Mayhap that the brigand had had his way with her and not that she had just helped hide evidence that all their men were dead.

Trying to slow her breathing and act as though nothing was amiss, she returned to her cottage for her bucket, and after filling it with water, started a fire to cook her dinner like she would do any other day. Only this time her hands shook as she prepared the meal. And her heart was still beating way too fast.

All she could think of was the dead man who had lain on her floor, and she glanced in that direction, again looking for blood, as if it would suddenly reappear. She would see it in her mind's eye forever.

Then she worried about Niall again—how dangerous it was for him and in his weakened condition also. What if he took a tumble from his horse—and that brought fresh chills to her overheated skin—remembering the one that had injured her so as a young girl. What if he was too weak to climb back into the saddle once he took care of the men? Or he passed out from the exertion?

And then what if the brigands found him?

She had to quit thinking like that. He would be fine. She couldn't think of it any other way.

She gathered herbs and tossed them into the pot. Afterward, she took the beef that Matthew had hung in the cellar the night before, then returned to the cottage and skewered the meat with a long metal rod. When she hung the meat over the fire, the juices dripped into the flame, making a sputtering sound.

The clip-clop of horses cantering toward her cottage had her heart pounding all over again. Running to the window, she peered out to see several men enter her yard on horseback. Two dismounted and headed for her cellar, and she gasped.

"Oh, I did not check the cellar for blood," she said under her breath, her skin prickling with fresh tension.

CHAPTER 9

About eleven Highlanders dismounted and while some entered Anora's byre, another threw the door to her cottage aside, making her jump back as the door slammed against the wall.

She told herself not to wring her belt between her hands, to look the blackguard in the eye, and to quit shaking!

The black-bearded Highlander stood before Anora, his blue eyes hard, and said, "Where is Camden?"

"Who?" She thought she sounded firm, unafraid.

His eyes studied her, watching her every reaction, and she was trying her hardest not to react as though anything was wrong.

He tilted his head to the side, considering her appearance. Trying to learn if his man had had his way with her? If she'd been willing? Or if he hadn't had time to do the deed and left in a hurry? Because she wasn't screaming and wailing, this man had to know Camden had not raped her.

As much as it was killing her not to blurt out which way the men had taken off so she could be rid of *these* men—she waited for him to answer her, still not lowering her gaze. And she knew it was a challenge, but she couldn't act meek and mild. 'Twas too late for that.

"The man who came here with four of our men to search the place," he finally said.

She attempted to steady her breathing before she spoke. "He came and then he left." She tried to sound sure of herself when she felt anything but.

"Oh?" He looked suspicious. "We havena seen him. Which way did he go?"

"In that direction," she said, motioning in the opposite way that Niall had gone and was afraid her hand shook, so quickly dropped it to her side. "He found naught here to interest him."

The Highlander's eyes narrowed again. "That is hard to believe once he spied you in the pasture."

She'd made an awful mistake. Why had she not told them what she had planned to? That they had thought they spied Niall heading in that direction? She made up stories all the time—but never under duress like this.

"He was quite forceful, that is true, but when one of his men shouted that he had seen one of the men they were looking for or some such thing, I could not hear all that well because the other men were outside and well... Camden was here with me. But he took off with his men. Now that they are gone, I can prepare dinner for my family for when they return, and take my sheep back out to pasture as they need to be fed as well."

She hadn't meant to explain all her plans for the day, but once she got to talking, she couldn't quit. Did he see how nervous she was? If so, mayhap he would believe his presence frightened her after what Camden had tried to pull, and she thought he intended to do the same.

Two men walked into her sleeping quarters to search there and not finding anything, walked back into the main room and shook their heads.

"Nothing there, either," one of the men said as he returned from the byre.

She wanted to sigh with relief, but her stomach was still twisted into knots.

"Find anything?" she heard a man say to another as the men left the cellar.

"Blood from the meat the woman hangs in the cellar is all that I found."

The mention of blood had her heart skipping beats. She barely breathed.

Without another word to her, the man in charge of this group turned and walked out the door with his men. Anora finally took a shaky breath. The men mounted their horses, then took off again.

For a moment, she stood frozen, relief—that they believed her, and apprehension—that they would soon discover no sign of their men, filling her with mixed emotions.

She again prayed that Niall would be safe from harm as she ran back outside to pasture her sheep. "Charlie!" she called. He bounded in from the field, making her frown.

"Where have you been when I could have used your help? Some guard dog you are."

She couldn't settle the way her heart was pounding, and the worry the men might return when they never found their comrades in the direction she had sent them.

Anora motioned for the dog to take her sheep out and fairly out of breath, she hurried out to the field and found her staff where the man had thrown it. Nearly the entire time she was with her sheep, she watched the horizon for Niall's return. And in the opposite direction—for the brigands as well.

***

Travelling west in a stream while towing the horses that carried the dead brigands, Niall was certain he couldn't be dying. He was in too much pain for it. His thoughts focused again on Anora, fearing for her, despite believing the choices they'd made were the only ones they could have. He'd hated having to ask Anora to help him heave the Murray bodies onto the backs of the horses because of his damnable weakened condition. And he hadn't wanted to leave her behind to face the rest of the men who had come with these Highlanders. The lass should never have had to deal with any of this.

Wanting to get back to her as soon as possible, he needed to take these men far enough away, covering his tracks as much as possible, so that no one would find them soon. While he walked the horses, he also searched for any sign of Gunnolf. Earlier, when he'd looked for him, Niall had been on foot and had not been able to cover that much distance. He'd been in as much pain then as he was now though.

His side hurting him something fierce, he crossed two streams and then proceeded to walk along another for several miles, ever vigilant in the event anyone caught him hauling the dead men. He'd come up with what he believed was a plausible enough explanation just in case—they were his brethren, and he was the only survivor. He at least had the wound to show for it. Though how he could explain the stitching...

If it came to that, he hoped no one would ask to see his wound. If he ran across the Murray clansmen, he knew he wouldn't live through another battle.

The area was isolated—scattered trees, the sound of a breeze ruffling their leaves, the water trickling over the rocks in the stream, and the horses splashing as he led his party toward their temporary resting place. The sky was filled with clouds, but thankfully it didn't look like it would rain anytime soon.

When he finally found a secluded area surrounded on two sides by hills, a river on the third, and trees on the fourth, he thought it the perfect place—an idyllic spot for the horses to graze. Though the area would soon offer a macabre setting once he arranged all the bodies where it would appear as though the men had fought well.

He really didn't want to set them up in such a manner—as they had *not* fought well—too busy drinking of the lass's mead, or taking a nap in her byre. He would rather the leader of these men knew the truth. But to Niall's way of thinking, it would be better to simulate a great battle had occurred so that the rest of their men would not believe the fight had taken place at Anora's croft.

Feeling as though he could pass out at any moment the way he was aching, Niall set about the task of preparing a small battlefield. At least he would not have to lift any more bodies onto the backs of horses.

Even pulling the bodies off the horses hurt his side though, and he cursed a couple of times, worried Anora's stitches might have pulled loose. He gritted his teeth as he leaned down to move another body. The pain shrieking through his side was the worst he had ever suffered. He wanted desperately to sit down and try to breathe through the pain, but he feared if he sat, he would never get back up.

Struggling to finish his work so he could leave and return to Anora, he unsheathed the men's swords, and rested them beside their fatally wounded warriors. He positioned the men to rest on their sides or backs in very nearly the same position as when they had fallen after he killed them before they were able to retaliate to much of an extent. He would never have managed to survive the ordeal—wounded as he was, and with so many to fight—if he hadn't taken advantage of the situation.

He studied the last man for a moment longer, wondering what to do with him. He no longer wore his plaid or his belt and no one would probably believe the man had rushed off to hunt him and Gunnolf without first redressing. Hating the odious task, Niall dressed the man in his plaid and belt, then situated him on the ground face down—in disgrace—for what he had been about to do to Anora.

Niall stood back and observed the men in their final

moments of glory—as much as none of it was true—and satisfied it looked as realistic as possible, he took hold of Gunnolf's horse's reins. Niall mounted his horse, and again used the stream to hide his trail.

He went in a different direction this time, still looking for any sign of Gunnolf, and prayed that he would find him and return to Anora and see that she was safe.

* * *

Guardedly relieved that the Highlanders had not returned, Anora stayed out in the meadow the rest of the morning. Several times, she'd been tempted to walk in the direction of her cottage, though she needed to let her sheep graze longer. But she was dying to see if Niall had made it back to her home.

When the sun grew high in the sky, she returned with her sheep, trying not to run, praying he was in her bed sound asleep. She hurried to pen up her sheep, then rushed into the cottage, no sign he was here, then raced into the sleeping room.

"Niall?" she said, crossing the floor to the bed in the dark and ran her hands over the sheepskin covers. Tears filled her eyes. He had not returned and she feared the worst. Either he had run into trouble with someone, or he had collapsed from his injuries. Or both.

She was torn with trying to locate him, though on foot, she was afraid she'd never find him. Wiping away tears, she vowed to check on the meal, in the hopes that he would still return and he'd need sustenance right away.

After checking on her soup, she stared out the window. Not seeing any sign of Niall, she threw chunks of bread into the kettle, and stirred until the bread dissolved, thickening the soup to perfection.

"Go to the door and listen for Niall," Anora said to Charlie, hoping her dog would pick up sounds of Niall's return, if she could not hear him. If Niall did not find his way back to her cottage, she was searching for him, despite being certain he wouldn't wish it. And the greater uncertainty that she wouldn't be able to locate him.

Charlie sat at her feet. She frowned at him. "You are a good sheepdog, but not good for much else."

Charlie wagged his tail. Anora chuckled, tears suddenly trickling down her cheeks with worry for Niall.

"What is so funny?" Niall asked, as he pushed the creaking door aside, then entered the room.

She wheeled around, her heart giving a little start. Then relief at seeing him alive and well washed over her. She released her ladle and ran to him and threw her arms around him, hugging him to her breast.

He grunted a little, and she worried about his wound, but she could not let go. "Oh, Niall, they returned. There were eleven or twelve of them. I told him his men had headed northwest, but I could not be sure."

Niall brushed a curl of hair off her cheek and gave her a light embrace in return. "Good, lass. Did you miss me?"

She couldn't help the tears in her eyes that were running again down her cheeks.

"Nay, lass. 'Tis all right just yet."

She felt so needy, wanting more of his touch, a tighter embrace, but he seemed distracted.

"The soup is ready, but I should check your bandages

first before we eat." But she didn't let go of him.

He kissed the top of her head. "Aye. Let me remove my belt. I hoped you would take a look at them when I returned." He pulled away and unbuckled his belt.

Anora stared at Niall's tunic, surprised he still wore John's tunic when she had not seen his own drying over the fire.

"What is wrong, Anora?" he asked, as he put his sword on the table.

"You are wearing John's tunic. Where is your own?"

"I hid it in the byre this morn. It would not have been a good idea to leave it lying about. Besides, you have not mended it for me yet." He gave her a small smile.

Loving the way his mouth curved up in a teasing light, the way his dark brown eyes met her gaze and held it, the way he touched her with a tender caress—she realized just how much she had missed him.

Anora took a deep breath, glad he was all right. "Aye, 'twas much too wet last night. I will mend it today. My stitches may not be as fancy as what you are used to though."

"You dinna have to worry about such things, Anora. I am sure they will be much grander than what I would do with the garment."

Anora smiled. Niall groaned as he lifted his arms to pull off his tunic, and she quickly reached over to assist him. "You must lie down. You will never heal if you do not rest."

She laid the tunic aside and unwrapped the bandage with a gentle touch. When she pulled the last layer from his chest and saw fresh blood, she frowned. "You are bleeding again. You must quit doing such strenuous tasks."

"I will ask Cian Murray and his clansmen to leave me alone until I heal properly should I encounter them in your byre again." He smiled tenderly down at her.

"Did... did you have any trouble?" She was afraid he might have had to fight more men, and hoped he had not. She carefully wiped the blood from around his injury.

"Nay, lass." He caressed her hair, and she looked up at him.

Her eyes were still teary. "Did you see any sign of your friend?" She had been afraid to ask, fearing his friend was dead.

He let out his breath. "Nay."

Anora swallowed hard, worried he had not survived.

"It doesna mean he is dead. Just like I wasna. The Viking is even harder to kill than me."

Anora took a deep breath, certain Niall said so more for her benefit than anything. He looked more than anxious about his friend, no matter the face he tried to put on for her. "I will have to get some more mead to drink with our meal. Why do you not sit for a moment and rest? I will help to wash you as well."

This time, Niall did as Anora suggested, no longer worried that she would tell anyone about his presence here. How could she? She'd helped him get rid of a bunch of dead men, and the ones still living would most likely want her dead now, too. If they learned of it.

Anora retrieved the mead, but before she could return to the cottage with the refilled flask, a man called out to her.

"Oh, Master Basil," Anora said, whipping about, her hand to her breast. "You frightened me."

Matthew's father looked similarly to Matthew, lanky like him, only a little taller and a lot grayer. He had a shiny spot on the top of his head, too, where the hair had fallen out. He was a kindly gentleman, with warm green eyes, and she oft wished his wife treated him with kindness like he treated others.

"I am concerned that a group of Murray have been searching for a couple of thieves. With you being out here all alone...," he said.

"Aye, well, my distant cousin is here with me, and we are just fine," she quickly said.

"My son told me about him. Niall, Matthew said his name was. How do you know this man is your relation? Is he French?" Master Basil glanced back at the cottage, his brow furrowed.

She was afraid he wanted to see Niall and question him or confront him or something.

"'Tis truly terrible about these men—stealing and the like. I hope Matthew has taken a proper escort," she said, not wishing to answer the question one way or another.

"Is this... relation of yours still here?"

"Uh, aye, but he had a bad night last eve and is sleeping this afternoon. He had injured his back and 'twas bothering him something fierce." She tried not to wring her belt through her fingers, a bad habit she had when she was nervous.

"Aye, Matthew said that, too. Are you sure that you are all right? Matthew said that the man would not let you out of his sight." Matthew's father looked back at the cottage, while Anora took a step in that direction. She was glad Niall didn't come out to see Mr. Basil, when after all Niall had been through, he needed to rest.

"We are just fine. Well, I must see to my meal. Would you care for some? I thank you so for the beef you sent me. That is what I am cooking this afternoon." She offered, to be polite, but she knew he would not sit down with them to eat. His wife would have a fit if he ate with Anora and hadn't had her approval first.

"Nay, my dear. If you are all right then, I will check on you later since Matthew is not around to do the task. We do not like it that you live out here so far from the village the way that you do. 'Tis not safe for a woman alone. Good day."

Anora watched as Master Basil walked back down the path to Banbh. Upon reaching the road, he glanced back at her, wherein she smiled and waved at him, glad he was leaving. He waved back, but didn't smile, then continued on his way.

Once he had disappeared from sight, Anora ran into the cottage with the mead. "I am so sorry, Niall," she said, glancing at the chair where Niall had been sitting. Not seeing him there, she looked around the room. "Niall?" she asked, then rushed into the smaller room. She found him lying in her bed with the covers pulled over his head. She lit a candle.

"Are you all right?" He'd worried her to death.

He pulled the covers aside, and she touched her fingers to his temple. He took her hand and kissed it. "I am fine.

You told the man I was resting, and I came right in here in case he wished to investigate your story further."

"Matthew's father would not have done that." At least she didn't think so.

"I dinna believe he thinks I am your relation."

Anora smiled and moistened a cloth, then washed Niall's chest. "How could he have? I have no relations that live here, after all."

Niall frowned. "You are no' a princess."

"Nay, I am not a princess. Where would you have gotten such a notion?" Anora said, chuckling, and finished cleaning his chest and his arms. "You must sit up, so that I may bandage you again."

Niall sat up with Anora's help, and she wrapped a clean bandage around his chest.

"You dinna mind if I stay longer?" he asked. "I willna for verra much longer. Mayhap just this eve.

She looked away, then, not wanting him to go. But she knew it wasn't safe for him here. She met his gaze again. "You saved me from a fate worse than anything I have ever feared, even riding a horse."

Studying her, Niall nodded. "Then mayhap I can show you that a horse is naught to fear."

"Nay. I need not have anything further to do with animals bigger than my sheep," Anora said firmly, and headed back into the main room.

Niall followed her and took his seat at the table, while Anora ladled soup into bowls. Returning to the fire, she pulled the roast from the spit and laid it onto a wooden platter, then brought the meat to the table. Niall eyed the beef with a smile.

"You may cut it, if you like, and aren't hurting too terribly much." She was afraid he would do it whether he was hurting or not, just too prove he could. She should have just carved it herself.

After slicing a piece off, and without taking his eyes from his duty as he slid the sharpened knife through the meat, he asked, "What ship were you on?"

Surprised he'd bring it up, she wondered how long he'd been considering the matter. She had thought he hadn't believed her.

Anora took a spoonful of her soup. "When?"

He frowned at her. "When you were six, of course."

"I... do not remember that much when I was six. Do you recall anything when you were that old?"

Niall nodded. "Aye, many things. I remember riding on the hunts, fighting in mock skirmishes, swimming in the cold loch. Some of the ladies of my clan tried to teach me how to dance, even. We laughed hard as I recall. They were a patient lot."

"When you were six?" she asked, incredulously.

"Thereabouts," he said, smiling.

"And now?"

"I believe I can dance fairly well. But as to this other matter... you said you had lost your kingdom."

"Aye, was that not a good story?"

Niall studied Anora for a moment, and she swore he saw right through her. She struggled to come up with another subject to talk about when he asked another question.

"If I were to question the inhabitants of Banbh, what would they tell me of you?" He skewered a slice of beef and set it on her plate. He lifted another slice for his own.

"I do not know. I know very few of them." Anora took another sip of her soup, again, trying to come up with something else to talk about, but other than his friend or worrying that the Highland brigands might return, she could think of nothing else to mention.

Niall noticed Anora running her hands over her tasseled belt and wondered if the lass was like a bard who made up tales to entertain. Some of what she said was mayhap true and mixed in with more of a made-up tale. He wondered.

"You are no' a princess." Not a princess, Niall thought, but a countess. *The* countess he was looking for.

Anora laughed. "What difference does it make? If I were a princess, no one would believe me anyway. And the king, my father, has long since given up on me, if he is even king any longer. If I had a princely brother, he would not want a shepherdess sister... so I am a shepherdess, naught more."

"Philippe, the Amorous? King of the Franks is your father?" he suddenly asked, worried that mayhap she was a princess, not the countess he was seeking, or the count had lied to James.

She frowned at Niall. "I know that is what the English call him, but..., 'tis all an unfounded rumor, I am sure. But aye. That king. Or mayhap, my father was the king's younger brother."

"Hugh... he was in the Crusades. Philippe had been

excommunicated and couldn't serve due to falling in love with the Countess of Anjou and abducting her."

"He was in love with her, so I have heard."

"But he already had a wife."

"Aye. Or mayhap, my father was a..." She worried her lower lip and shrugged. "A fisherman who fished me out of the sea."

Niall studied her for some time, trying to decipher her words, which of it was true—if any of it. "But if you were a princess," he said, humoring her, "you could live in a castle, have servants carry out your every wish, marry a prince, a duke or a king..."

"Until someone wishes to take over my castle and then I would be hiding with a sheepherder in some meadow nearby some town like Banbh."

Niall frowned at her. "The count said your ship was overtaken by the English and for many years the family thought you were lost, along with everyone else aboard the ship."

"I have never been at sea. I told you it was just a story. Have I told you the one about the page who stayed beyond the castle walls after the gates were shut, and every night, the gate guard would have to open the portcullis to allow him inside?"

"Let me guess," he said. "'Twas a French castle."

"Mayhap. This happened for several nights in a row. The page wailed and carried on outside the gates, until the gatekeeper would let him in. On the last night, the king decided that the boy, who was seven at the time..."

"And you were?"

"About six, I guess," Anora said, as she swirled her mead in her cup, "anyway the king said the boy would have to stay out for the night all that eve. The page wailed and lamented, begged, and screamed. 'Twas something awful to hear, but finally he fell asleep, and when the gates were opened in the morn, the boy was cured of his late-night wanderings."

She *had* lived in a castle. With the king of the Franks. Devil take her. Was she telling the truth? Or reliving some childhood fantasy? He had to know if she was the right woman.

Anora smiled again. "I told you it was a story."

"And the boy's name?"

"Pierre."

"A French boy?"

"I would assume. The name does sound French after all."

"'Tis no' a true story."

"Nay, 'tis not. You are right."

He didn't believe her. Niall sipped the remainder of his broth from his bowl, making her smile. "Would you like some more?"

"If you dinna mind. I thought you were angry with me for asking for more of your pork stew last eve."

"Nay, I did not like that the two of you seemed to be competing over me, however."

"Competing? Me?"

"Of course, not you. Where would I have ever gotten such a notion?" Anora returned to the table with the bowl full of soup for Niall, refilled his cup with mead, then sat back down at the table.

"You could be French," he said slowly, watching her reaction.

"I am not French," Anora said, looking like she stubbornly resisted the idea. "I am a Scot."

Niall nodded, but he was certain she was not. "If you were sailing from our coast..."

"What makes you think I was on a ship? Did I tell you the story of the fish that got away?"

Niall laughed. No matter how much he had to learn the truth from her, he couldn't deny she amused him with her tales. "I dinna know what to think of you, lass."

"Good, that is how it should be. If you thought I were a princess, you might insist I go back to live with the king..."

She paused, arched a brow, and he smiled. "Or mayhap he would wish to marry you off to someone of nobility."

Anora refilled her cup of mead. "I like my life as a shepherdess. I would never wish for it to be any other way."

"But if you were a princess..."

Anora stood abruptly. "I must clean out the sheep's pen. Please rest awhile, and I will see how you are in a bit."

"You willna stay with me while I finish the delightful roast you have made for us?"

Anora sighed, then retook her seat. "I believe you are the most handsome man I have ever encountered."

Niall raised his brows at hearing the news. "Whatever made you think to say that, Anora?"

"Poor Matthew, he has a weak chin and an unmanly nose. Now you, your jaw is strong and persuasive."

"I thought you said I was demanding."

"Commanding, you said. And you have the loveliest dark brown eyes, like a stormy dark sea."

"That you have never been on."

"Aye." Anora frowned as she stared at her empty cup.

"Why do you not marry Matthew?"

"Did you not hear him? He wishes for me to move in with his mother and father. His father is like Matthew, kind and helpful, but his mother, ah, what a nightmare that would be, only I would have to live it all day long."

"What is wrong with Matthew's mother?" Niall finished his beef, then stood to carve another slice. As he sat back down, he looked up to see Anora watching him, and he smiled. "I believe I should take you with me when I return, as James's cooks could learn a thing or two from you." But that was not the real reason he wished to take her to Craigly. He feared she was the countess, and not only that, but he didn't wish to leave her behind in any event.

"I like where I live just fine. As to your question, Matthew's mother is the most critical woman I know. She bosses Master Basil before the sun rises in the morning until way past the time when the sun has set. She is so argumentative. If you say the sky has clouds, she will say it is mostly filled with the sun. She says my cottage is too frilly for her taste..." She motioned to the baskets hanging on one wall, "...while to me, hers is cold and austere."

And Anora did not love Matthew. Why could she not admit that?

Anora grabbed the empty bowls. "I must wash these now and you must get your rest." Anora headed for the door, and Niall joined her, sword in hand. "Where are you going to now?" she asked.

"I will help you."

"What if Cian's men return? You should lie down."

"I enjoy being with you, but more importantly, if anyone should return, you may need my protection again."

Anora shook her head and continued out the door. "You should rest."

After washing her dishes, she set them on a board to dry, then heard a horse whinny inside her byre. She turned to Niall and frowned at him. "Do not tell me you brought all of the horses back with you. And housed them in my byre?"

CHAPTER 10

"Nay, no' all the horses are in the byre. Only Gunnolf's and mine," Niall told Anora, seeing how concerned she was as she stared at the building as if it suddenly had spawned *mnathan nighe*, the fairies carrying omens of death.

He'd rethought the matter and knew leaving his and Gunnolf's horses in the woods nearby would not be a good idea. He'd had enough trouble already with getting them back. Trying to reach Craigly Castle on foot would not be a viable option.

The notion of riding anything at the moment, though, was making him ill.

He believed if he did not lie down soon, he would collapse at any moment, his head and side aching, his body overheated from exertion, his vision blurring with pain, it was so intense.

"I need to find the lass—the French countess." Niall sounded as weary as he felt, instead of determined as he needed to be. But he wanted her to know how important this was.

Truth be told, he didn't believe he could ride any further, but he had to quickly move the horses from Anora's byre in the event any of Cian's men returned and discovered them there.

Anora furrowed her brows as she studied Niall. "You... cannot go anywhere." Her lips parted as she suddenly appeared shocked, or concerned. "You... your face." She reached up to touch his forehead. "'Tis flushed."

She placed her cold hand on his hot skin, and he shivered. God's teeth, he was burning up.

"Oh... oh, Niall, you are feverish. You must go inside and lie down."

Her concern for him touched him. But he had this business to take care of.

"I must find the lass," he insisted. "And Gunnolf."

"Nay, you cannot go anywhere. I..." She took a deep breath. "I can... search for Gunnolf."

He noted that she did not offer to find the French lass. "'Twould no' be a good idea for you to go alone," he said, dismissing the notion.

"I could inquire in the village. I know these people, Niall. I am safe there."

He snorted. If she was truly the one he sought, she was not safe in the least. "Mayhap we could go together." If she rode with him, mayhap if they located Gunnolf, his friend could coax the truth from her and they'd continue on their way to Craigly.

"Nay," she said, taking Niall's arm firmly and forcing

him to retire to her bed, shocking him that she was so determined and concerned. "Lie down. I will do this. You cannot go anywhere. What if you fell off your horse on the way? Just... passed out on the road or in the woods? Then what would I do with you? I would have to leave you and continue on to the village by myself and make inquiries there. Mayhap someone has taken Gunnolf in."

Niall shook his head at the image that his falling off his horse brought to mind. Though the way his head was pounding again, he could imagine doing just that. Yet, he didn't believe she'd leave him behind to suffer. Then he considered that if he did collapse, what if Cian's men came across him? He would be a dead man.

"I wouldna fall off my horse," he said. "I was born to the saddle."

She shook her head. "Nay. You cannot go."

He began to rise, but felt so dizzy, he slumped against the mattress. She seized his arm and scowled at him. *Him*, a Highland warrior, who had fought many battles.

"You must stay. I will not have you die on me after I worked so hard to stitch you up." She chewed on her bottom lip. "Then again, mayhap, we can wait for Matthew to return—" Before she could say anything further, Niall cut her off.

"That willna be for two more days. 'Tis dangerous to keep the animals in your byre."

"But you said you would leave them far from here."

"The Murray horses, aye. Not mine and Gunnolf's. Think you I would allow Cian's men to steal them again? I will leave in the morn," Niall said, taking her hand and squeezing it.

"Oh, Niall, you are so hot. Let me get you something to drink to cool you down." She quickly got him a tin of water. "I… I would go with you if I could."

He drank the water, then studied her expression. She looked serious.

"To look for Gunnolf," she said quickly, as if afraid Niall was thinking she might be the countess. "But I am afraid of horses. You see, once there was a squire who was thrown from his destrier during a joust. He died from head injuries suffered from the fall, the healer said."

In disbelief, Niall stared at Anora. "How do you know of this squire? The French castle?"

She licked her lips as if in nervousness—as if she was afraid he believed her to be the French lass he needed to find. "'Twas a story, but just the same I am afraid of horses."

Was she just making up another story? He didn't believe so.

He was thinking he should take her with him back to Craigly Castle as well—even if she was not the lass James wished him to locate. What if the locals believed she was a French spy since she seemed to have French roots?

"Sleep." She frowned at him. "And, Niall?"

"Aye, lass," he said, wiping his brow with the wet cloth, feeling as though his skin was roasting on a spit, while inside he was shivery and cold.

"Do *not* die on me while I… take care of some chores."

He cast her a small smile.

***

Armed with a *sgian dubh* sheathed at her waist hidden

beneath her wool brat, Anora stalked toward Banbh, intent on learning if Gunnolf had managed to reach the village and found shelter. If she could find him and he had not been sorely wounded, she would take him back to her cottage, and then he and Niall needed to leave as soon as was possible. *Without her.*

They could not house their horses in her byre for very long. If Cian and his men returned, 'twould be too dangerous for Niall. And mayhap even for her, since she had misdirected them when they were attempting to hunt Niall down.

Once she reached the village, she hurried through the main road through Banbh, passing the first of the two butchers' stalls that was already closed. When she approached the second butcher's stall, she tried not to draw attention to herself.

Master Basil's back was to her as he nodded to his wife, who waved her finger at him and pointed at the meat he was about to carve. That was another reason why Anora didn't want to live with them. The woman nagged him before sunup to well after sundown. Anora had no plans to ever move in with the butcher and his wife.

She stalked past a mercer's table dealing in wool, the merchant hurriedly packing his goods away before nightfall. Quickening her pace, she practically ran past the hogs' market, wrinkling her nose at the stench.

Making her way to the tavern on the other side of the village, she noticed a tall man wearing a gray hooded cloak, speaking to a merchant. When the merchant took notice of her, he pointed at her, making the other man turn to look.

Her skin crawled with warning.

As they watched her, Anora said, "Good day to you, Master Burland." She considered the stranger further. His nearly black eyes and black curly hair looked familiar somehow. "Do I know you?" Anora asked the stranger. She should have left well enough alone, but if he hadn't looked so much like someone she had known...

"You would do well to move along, take care of whatever business you have in Banbh, and return to your sheep at once," the merchant said, his blue eyes narrowed. Master Burland grumbled something inaudible, then turned on his heels and then continued to put away his iron works.

"You seem familiar. Are you from around here?" she asked the stranger again. He shook his head. She couldn't place his shadowed face, but she was certain she had seen it somewhere before. "Good day to you then, sir," Anora said, and hurried the rest of the way to the tavern.

She had never been concerned about visiting the village before. But ever since Niall had warned her she might be in danger, she worried—what if he spoke the truth?

Glancing back to look at the stranger, she noticed a tell-tale sword swinging at his hip under his cloak as he cut down through an alleyway nearby. A whisper of dread crept through her. The man was not dressed as one of Cian's clansmen. But he appeared to be armed like them.

She opened the door to the tavern, her eyes adjusting to the lower light inside. A smoky peat fire blazed at the hearth. Several men were seated at long wooden tables, drinking ale. Conversation filled the room until some of the men turned to see who the newcomer was, and then everyone stopped talking. She wanted to tell them to continue with their conversations, not wanting the attention.

"What do you want here?" a gruff voice said, startling Anora.

"Oh!" she said, her heart beating furiously, and turned to face Michael, the tavern keeper. His red shaggy hair and beard were in disarray as usual. "I did not hear you approach. I am looking for a man."

One red eyebrow shot up.

Her blood heated with embarrassment.

A grizzled old man with yellow teeth and a graying beard patted his lap. "Come, sit your arse down here, lassie, and you need look no further."

Several other men, young and old, laughed. "You dinna want the auld mon. Come, sit here," a younger man said, who looked like he wasn't even growing any whiskers yet.

"The man," she said, her voice lowered as she spoke to the tavern owner, "is a... well, a Viking."

This time both of Michael's brows rose. "Indeed." He folded his arms, looking stern, yet she swore a hit of amusement flickered in his dark eyes.

"Aye." She began to wring her tasseled belt between her fingers. "He... I found something of his."

"You do not say."

"Aye. I do."

"The mon's name?"

She swallowed hard. She wasn't sure if the tavern keeper would have heard the story of how Gunnolf supposedly stole Cian's horses or not. But if Gunnolf was here, he had to come with her and see to Niall. And the two had to get on their way.

She licked her suddenly very dry lips. "Gunnolf," she said very quietly.

From the tavern keeper's neutral expression, she couldn't tell if he knew him or not. But he finally tugged at his beard and said, "A pack of bloodthirsty Highlanders descended on the village, questioning everyone as to who you were and where you reside."

She barely breathed. The men who had injured Niall. But... but the tavern keeper had not told them who she was? And the villagers had not, either? Shocked, she hesitated to say anything.

And then she said, "I thank you and the others."

He grunted.

"Do you know anything of the stranger cloaked in gray wool?"

"Another foreigner, a Frenchman, inquiring about you. There are five of them, I have heard tell."

Five Frenchman?

"About me? Whatever for?" A chill ran up her spine.

"Seems everyone is interested in the wee French lassie these days," Michael said. "Mayhap even this Viking you seek?"

"You have seen the man? Where is he? Is he all right? Uninjured?" Hope sprang anew that Niall's friend was well.

Michael shrugged. "I have heard tell of him as well. I have no idea where the mon is now. I have also heard you have a visitor."

Her whole body warmed.

"'Tis said he is a distant relation. But you have no relations in these parts."

If Cian learned of it…

"Uh, aye, but…" What could she say? Don't tell Cian or his men, should they come back to inquire further? She released the stranglehold she had on her tasseled belt and folded her arms. "He… he has hurt his back and so is staying with me until… until… well, I imagine by the time I return, he will even be gone."

The tavern keeper smiled marginally.

"He will be." She thought if she said so and the word was to get out, everyone would presume Niall had already left. She had to return to tell him Gunnolf was alive. But she wished to find the Viking herself and take him home with her. "You… you have no idea where his friend… I mean, the Viking is?"

This time Michael smiled broadly.

She could not believe how rattled she was becoming.

"Nay. I would hie yourself on home now. I have heard rumors the Highlanders might be willing to pay to learn the whereabouts of this Frenchwoman. Mayhap she should find somewhere else to stay. I have business to tend to. Off with you, lass."

Anora felt a mixture of hope and despair. She could not leave her cottage, her sheep, her livelihood behind. Even if she could, she would have to move Niall also. And in his condition, she believed it would kill him. Besides, she could not ride a horse, and she didn't think he could as sick as he was, either.

Praying no one followed her, she strode home, walking as fast as her legs could carry her.

But then she heard footfalls behind her and Anora's skin chilled as she turned and touched her *sgian dubh*.

A girl hurried to intercept her—'twas the tavern keeper's daughter, six and ten, Anora thought, and she took a relieved breath of air. The girl was a pretty redhead with sage green eyes and a smattering of freckles across her nose. She'd hardly ever spoken to Anora, whenever she chanced to see her in the village—which was rarely. Mayhap five or so times over the last three years. She was the same height as Anora, wearing a dull brown wool dress as she worked in the tavern, serving ale to the patrons.

What did she want? For a moment, Anora thought the girl might have word about Gunnolf's whereabouts and wished to tell her in private.

"Tesslyn," Anora said in greeting. "How now?"

"I overheard Father speaking to you. Men are looking for you," Tesslyn said, as if she knew a big secret and was dying to tell someone of it.

Anora tried hard to mask her alarm as she continued to walk home, her step never slowing. What if the men who were looking for Anora began to offer silver for the information? Would the girl tell the Highlanders or the Frenchmen where Anora lived if she had the chance?

"My father said the reason Matthew will not offer for me is that he is still interested in you."

This was not good. Anora had never thought Matthew would be seeking another girl's hand in marriage. The thought disturbed her that he might be chasing after another lass, while continuing to ask for Anora's hand in marriage. If Matthew was only Anora's friend, it would be one thing. Otherwise, she felt it dishonest of him to profess only an attraction to her.

If Anora were to begin seeing another man and found some fascination with him—which instantly brought to mind Niall, but t'was not the same as he was only here for a brief time and not pursuing her—she would have told Matthew right up front.

Anora glanced at Tesslyn. "Matthew is free to choose whoever he wishes. I have told him I am not interested in marriage."

The girl's eyes rounded. "Really." She didn't say anything for a while as she kept up with Anora's long stride.

Anora hoped that would set the girl's mind at ease. But she wondered if Tesslyn only fantasized about Matthew's notice of her or had he truly pursued her and had not told Anora?

"He does not buy you the meat from his father to give to you, you know," Tessalyn said in an irksome way.

Anora stared at the girl. Of course Matthew did. Or his father gave it to her out of generosity himself.

"Laird Callahan pays for it. 'Tis all a joke at Banbh. He did not wish his people to know he buys the poor shepherdess food to put on her table. And so Matthew takes all the credit."

Anora couldn't have been more shocked to learn the truth. But then again, she knew how tight Matthew was with his money. She thought that one day he planned to have his own shop and that's why he saved his money like he did.

"'Tis very generous of Laird Callahan to do so," Anora said.

"If *he* would marry you, then…"

Anora glanced at Tesslyn when she didn't say anything further.

"Laird Callahan is not marrying me," Anora finally said, when Tesslyn did not finish her statement.

Tesslyn snorted. "If someone would take you away then, Matthew would marry me. He said he would."

Anora's heart pounded with anxiousness. The threat was implied in the girl's tone of voice and in her words—"*if someone would take you away then…*"

Anora feared then the girl would offer information to whoever was searching for her, if she had the opportunity, and she wouldn't even need to be bribed. The notion Anora would no longer be in Tesslyn's way so she could marry Matthew would be enough of an incentive.

"But Matthew has not asked my father for my hand in marriage," the girl continued.

Again, Anora wondered if the girl had dreamed up that Matthew wanted her for a wife. Why else would he not ask her since Anora would not accept his proposal?

"We have lain together several times already. I may even now have his bairn growing inside of me." The girl smiled mischievously.

Anora's heart stuttered. Was the girl lying? How could Matthew have lain with her when he professed he wished to marry Anora?

She clenched her teeth in irritation. She didn't want

Matthew for a husband, so why was she so upset over all this? Because Matthew had told her nothing of it. He had always acted as though she was the only one he was interested in. And the thought he was so dishonorable—joining with an unmarried young girl—and not asking for her hand...

Anora attempted to quash her annoyance. With the girl—who taunted her with this, and with Matthew—for being so underhanded.

"Does your father know?" Anora asked, trying to sound unconcerned.

Anora could not believe Matthew would kiss her in front of Niall when he was sleeping with Tessyln. Unless... the girl lied. Mayhap Tesslyn thought she could upset Anora into fighting with Matthew the next time he tried to see her.

"My father does not yet know. But he will soon enough." Tesslyn rubbed her belly, and Anora couldn't help looking down at her.

She saw no swelling to indicate the girl carried a bairn. "I will tell Matthew that he must do the honorable thing and ask for your father's permission to marry you." She would tell him much more than that, if she learned it was true.

"Nay," Tesslyn said, fury in her voice. "You will not speak with him further. Or... you will tell him you hate him or some such thing. For if you do not, and I learn he is still seeing you, I will let others know who the Frenchwoman is that they are seeking." Then the girl turned and ran back toward the village.

Cold chills shook Anora. She feared Tesslyn would not

wait for Anora to tell Matthew to stay away or to do what was right and marry the girl. Not before Tesslyn found the Frenchmen or Cian and his men, should they return to Banbh, and told them where Anora lived.

What if Tesslyn intended to search for the Frenchmen as soon as she reached the village?

CHAPTER 11

Charlie barked when he saw Anora. Her heart gave a little startled jump. He bounded out of the nearby woods and ran to intercept her. She gave him a quick hug, loving him, and realized if she had to abandon her croft, she hoped Niall understood she would not leave Charlie behind. She hastened inside the cottage and found Niall sound asleep, still feverish, muttering incoherently. She knew Niall had to leave. She had to as well, though she hated to think of that. She couldn't bear waking him while he slept so soundly.

Her heart heavy with concern for him, she had to find his tunic and mend it for him so he'd have another to wear on his journey. She dashed out to the byre and searched until she found his torn tunic hidden beneath the hay. Returning to the cottage, she lit a candle in the main room, though it was still light outside. With needle and thread, she sat down at the hearth and began to stitch the tears in the fabric, a million thoughts rushing through her

155

mind.

She didn't wish to leave her home behind, or her sheep. She could easily defend her home, herself, and others she cared for also. So she did not think of herself as a timid soul. But traveling across lands she didn't know, with a man she didn't know very well, to a place foreign to her— she felt overwhelming trepidation. And yet, what choice did she have? 'Twas either that, or face the Frenchmen or Cian's men, and what would they do with her? At least she felt Niall was here to protect her.

Trying to concentrate on her sewing so she could get it done as quickly as possible, and then check on Niall again, she attempted not to worry about that which she had little control over.

When she finished mending his tunic, she noticed Charlie raise his head as he stared at the main door. His ears perked straight up, and then he twitched them back and forth while he listened to the sounds only he could hear. Her heart thudding, Anora set her sewing aside, then ran to retrieve a knife from her table, though she also had her *sgian dubh* sheathed at her waist.

Charlie turned his head toward the sleeping room. Niall stood in the entryway to the small room. His dark eyes still burned with fever, his face flushed, and he was wearing John's tunic again. Niall looked ready to collapse.

"Oh, Niall," Anora said, dropping the knife on the table and rushed to wrap her arms around him. "You are still burning up. Come, you must lie down now." She helped him back to the bed and covered him with the sheepskin.

"I worried for your safety, lass," Niall said, his voice

rough and weary. He reached up to touch her face. "I woke earlier and called out, but you were no' here. I looked for you in the byre."

She kissed his hand and held onto it, his hand much too hot still. "You should have stayed in bed. I... I was enquiring about Gunnolf in the village."

Niall tried to sit up, but she placed her hand on his shoulder, keeping him down. "He is well, according to the tavern keeper, and looking for me. The tavern keeper did not know where Gunnolf was. I... I let it slip that he is your friend."

"Ah, lass, I didna want you to go enquiring about him, for your own safety. But 'tis good he is alive and well."

She was glad to see the relief in Niall's face at learning about his friend. "Aye, but I had to learn if anyone had seen him. What are we to do now? You cannot stay here."

"Tell me what was said." Niall's eyes were merely slits as if he could not keep them open any wider.

She explained about Cian and his men. She rattled on, worried that any of them might barge in at any moment. She was afraid she wasn't making sense. "Michael, the tavern keeper, said I have to leave." She bit her lip. "Oh, Niall, are you truly here to help me?"

His brows furrowed a bit. "You are the one I seek?"

"I... I believe so. Cian's men queried those in the village concerning not only you and Gunnolf but about a Frenchwoman's whereabouts."

He sighed a little. "We knew this already, aye, lass?"

She moistened her lips with her tongue, not

wanting to tell Niall the next part because she was certain the stranger in the village and those with him would soon learn where she lived. And Niall couldn't move from here— not until the fever abated.

"Lass, speak the truth." He squeezed her hand with encouragement.

She took a deep breath. "The count you spoke of is my uncle. I was... I was being delivered to my betrothed when another ship attacked ours. But I did not know about my uncle fighting in the Crusades alongside your cousin, James."

"Aye, continue," Niall said, as she took the cloth she'd used before and soaked it in the pail of water, then wiped his brow.

"Everyone was killed aboard the ship but me. The captain of the English vessel said he had a little girl my age at home, and I reminded him of her. He took me to Banbh because he was afraid the English king would learn I was on English soil and he would take me hostage." She looked away from Niall. "When he arrived in Banbh, the captain made inquiries of the laird—the current laird's father. They were Saxon and had fled when the Normans conquered England. But his wife was Norman and she would not have me living in their home. The shepherdess was selling sheep there when she overheard the lady's complaints. And when the captain thanked the laird and began to leave the walled-in castle, the shepherdess chased after him and begged the captain to allow her to raise me as she had lost her own child the year before."

"Jane and her brother."

"Aye. Old Laird Callahan died six years ago and his son took over. He has always treated me with kindness and buys my sheep when no others will."

"Because he knows who you are," Niall said. "That you are of noble blood."

"Of French nobility. Laird Callahan's father allowed Jane and her brother to raise me, and as far as I knew, the laird did not tell anyone of my birthplace. Even so, it seems the word has gotten out. I am sure I spoke a good deal of French when I was young until the shepherdess could break me of the habit."

Niall touched Anora's cheek with a sympathetic caress. "Now that we know these men are coming for you, we must take you away from here at once."

"You cannot travel. I… cannot leave my sheep behind. My cottage."

"Lass, you canna stay here. If Cian's men discover what we have done, and that you are who you are, he will slaughter your sheep, burn your cottage, and hand you over to whoever is paying him. If the French get hold of you— well, you willna be allowed to stay here any longer, either. And your uncle stated emphatically that you could be in grave danger."

She couldn't tell him about the tavern keeper's daughter. Niall was too sick to leave. "But… you cannot travel, Niall. I forbid it."

His lips quirked upward in a small smile.

"I am serious," she said, angry.

"Allow me to sleep for a short while longer. We will leave a couple of hours before sunset and then travel for another couple of hours during gloaming. If Gunnolf is alive and well, he will find us. The sun rises early so we will only have to find another place to sleep for a little over four hours before the sun begins to rise. At least we will be far away from here."

Anora was torn. She wanted Niall to sleep. The longer they stayed here, the worse the danger was that the French strangers or Cian's men would arrive. Niall was sure to be a dead man because she knew he would protect her with his life.

"I will pack food and be ready," she said. "First, let me help you off with your tunic and wash you to attempt to bring your fever down."

Again, his mouth curved up a little.

"I am *not* doing it to see you half naked, you barbarian."

He chuckled. "Aye, Anora."

He was still smirking as she helped him to remove his tunic. When she returned, she washed his skin with cool water, and he shivered.

He finally closed his eyes, and she thought he had fallen asleep when Charlie rose from the spot on the floor where he'd lain and emitted a low growl. Someone was outside her cottage. Her whole body chilled with fear.

Had the Frenchmen seen her leave the tavern and followed her home? Or Tesslyn, had she found them and told them where Anora lived? Even Cian's men could have returned when they couldn't find their own men.

She touched her *sgian dubh* sheathed at her waist, but feared the knife would not deter anyone from killing

Niall or taking her hostage.

She grabbed Niall's claymore, barely able to lift it and uncertain if she would be able to wield it. Not like she could her pitchfork. Why had she returned it to the byre?

The front door creaked open. "Niall," a man called out in a low, gruff voice.

"Gunnolf," Niall said, his voice just as low, but sounding much relieved.

"Your friend?" she asked quickly. If it was his friend, she was comforted to learn he was truly alive. And here now.

"Aye," Niall said.

"We are in here," she called out, not leaving Niall's side, ready to defend him if this Gunnolf was not alone.

The man peered through the doorway—a blond bearded man with steel blue eyes, who first considered her holding Niall's sword, and then Niall in her bed. She couldn't believe he would grin at them. The heathen. His friend was sick and could be dying and Gunnolf was grinning?

What kind of a friend did that?

"I should have known you would be in a lass's bed while I have been searching for you everywhere. Not to mention trying to locate our horses, and the lass we should be finding. Is the woman protecting you with your own sword, mon?" Gunnolf laughed.

"He was wounded and is now feverish. There is naught to jest about," Anora said harshly.

Gunnolf laughed again. "I hope you plan to wed the lass, Niall. She appears to be just the one for you. Every mon needs a woman who will fight to protect him."

"She is the woman we seek, Gunnolf," Niall said weakly. "She is a French countess. I am no' certain she would wish to marry the likes of me."

She stared at Niall open-mouthed. Marriage?

Gunnolf considered Anora from the top of her head to her shoes and said, "She truly is the one we were sent to fetch and protect?" Then he smiled again. "Here she is protecting you. But 'tis our good fortune."

"Even in his weakened condition, he fought the men who stole your horses," she said, furious with the Viking. "He has not been lying around in my bed. And you now have your horses back, thanks to him."

Gunnolf's smile only broadened. *Infuriating man.*

"Help the lass pack, will you, Gunnolf, while I rest a moment? Several will want our heads anytime now," Niall said.

"Sleep, Niall. We will wake you in a while," Anora said, patting his shoulder.

"Only as long as it takes you to ready the horses," he warned, then closed his eyes again.

"Come, lass," Gunnolf said, serious now, as if he had the right to order her about in her own cottage.

She brushed past him and he said to Niall, "Aye, Niall, you would do well to keep this spirited filly for your wife." Then he shut the door and followed Anora out of the cottage.

"You are the French countess?" Gunnolf asked Anora, his voice low for her ears only as she made her way to the cellar.

"Aye," she said, glancing up at him. "I am not sure

Niall can travel just yet."

Gunnolf helped her gather food and mead for their journey. "How badly wounded is he?"

"He took a sword wound in his side. I stitched him up and the area seems to be healing fine, but he has a fever now."

"Who was he speaking of that would descend on this place of yours?"

She explained the trouble they were in as they headed back to the cottage. There, she gathered blankets and clothes for herself, John's spare tunic, and Niall's mended one.

"We must leave right away," Gunnolf said.

"Aye," she said. "But what of my sheep? And what of Niall? He needs rest, most of all."

"'Tis too dangerous for us to remain here from everything that you have said."

She'd been fighting tears with the thought she'd have to leave her beloved home behind, the only one she'd truly had. But then a new dread consumed her. "I cannot ride a horse."

"I doubt Niall will manage the journey well, considering how sick he is. You will remain with him and ensure he stays upon his horse. He will need you. I canna ride with him as it would weary my horse too much."

"Me?" she asked, incredulous. "I cannot ride. And my dog. How will we take him with us?"

"We canna take the dog with us, lass."

"Nay. I will not leave him behind."

Gunnolf looked so annoyed with her, she scowled

163

right back at him. "You take Niall and disappear. No one wants to kill me, I do not think. Or... I could ask Laird Callahan for his protection. But you and Niall must go."

"And leave behind the lass we promised to find, collect, and return to Craigly Castle?" Gunnolf snorted.

The Viking was impossible.

"Is there anything else you need before we depart, lass?" Gunnolf asked.

She took an unsettled breath and looked over her cottage. "Nay."

"I will help Niall onto his horse, and then you will ride behind him."

She could do this. To save Niall's life, she could do this. "Then you will carry Charlie on your horse."

Gunnolf looked incredulously at her, but she wasn't backing down.

"Or I will stay."

"Niall will *have* to marry you," Gunnolf said, and smirked.

She shook her head at the Viking, then woke Niall and helped to slip his tunic over his head. "You will do this for me, or I will not go," she said to Gunnolf again, as he waited to help Niall out of the cottage.

"'Tis no use fighting with the lass," Niall said wearily. "You will lose the battle, Gunnolf. No matter what it is about."

Gunnolf shook his head, then helped Niall to stand, and with his arm around his waist, he helped him out of the cottage. "I tell you, she is the one for you."

Charlie bounced around them as Gunnolf helped

Niall onto his horse.

"I cannot leave my sheep behind," she said. "Can we… can we leave them in the pastureland near Laird Callahan's keep?"

"Nay," Gunnolf said. "'Tis in the opposite direction that we must travel."

"All right, then. We must leave them at a sheepherder's lands I know of. 'Tis a long way from here on foot, but on horseback, it should not take too long. Charlie will guide them there. I can pen them up with the man's own sheep, and…" She took a deep breath. "He will care for them."

"Aye," Niall said, "but we must be on our way, lass." He frowned at Gunnolf. "Where have you been all this time?"

Gunnolf snorted. "I was like you, nearly killed— except the mon struck me such a blow that I fell into the burn and was washed downriver several miles. I only just kept enough of my wits about me to keep from drowning. I didna have a lass to prepare meals for me, or to offer me a bed."

"Niall slept on the floor," Anora quickly said, as she hurried to open the gate to the pen and called to Charlie to bring them. She would not have Gunnolf or anyone else believing she was a wanton.

Gunnolf smiled.

"He was only in the bed this time because of his fever." She frowned up at the Viking, his blue eyes smiling back at her.

And the other time—when Niall first slipped into

her bed, and she poked him in the back with her pitchfork, but she wasn't going to mention that.

Then she reconsidered the Viking and said, "You… you are all right, are you not? If they nearly killed you with a blow to the head, and you almost drowned in the burn, you… you are all right?"

Gunnolf's teasing smile shifted to kindness. "Aye, lass," he said tenderly. "I thank you for worrying, but my head is even harder than Niall's."

She let out her breath. "Good. I could not keep you both on your horses for the duration." As much as she wasn't sure she could manage just riding with Niall. "The tavern keeper said you were looking for me in the village."

"*Ja*. Was my good fortune that I went to the tavern after you did and learned from the tavern keeper that you had inquired about me and had something of mine here. He wouldna say what, but he seemed the honorable sort, and I found the place and waited, attempting to hear what I could inside before I opened the door. I thought I heard Niall speaking to a sweet lassie." Gunnolf shook his head. "He has all the luck."

With much trepidation, Anora allowed Gunnolf to lift her onto Niall's horse and with a fierce grip, she hugged Niall practically to death, careful that she kept her arms wrapped around him high enough to avoid touching his injury. Her heart was beating so fast, she was afraid Niall would feel it thumping against his back.

Niall chuckled. "I was feeling a wee bit chilled, but no longer, lass."

She felt feverish herself then—not from sickness,

but from embarrassment. She had never held a man like this, so close, his body hot with fever, his smell so masculine and appealing. She kept telling herself she had to do this, to keep him safe, upright in the saddle, and from falling off the horse. That he wasn't thinking anything about her arms wrapped securely around his waist, and her breasts pressed against his back indecently, intimately. Most likely, Niall was too delirious to take much notice at all.

Which was good. Though she couldn't help but enjoy the feel of him in her arms. She didn't think anyone would truly believe her holding him close had all to do with her taking care of an ill man.

Even if she had wanted to loosen her hold on him, she couldn't. So she was glad she was warming him when he was feeling cold.

When Niall kneed his horse to move, Anora believed she was going to fall to her imminent demise and held on tighter.

***

Having a devil of a time staying awake in his feverish state, Niall knew the only thing that kept him from dropping off to sleep was the knowledge he, Gunnolf, and the lass were at great risk of discovery.

Though he had to admit, he was having trouble breathing as tightly as poor Anora clung to him, careful to keep her arms well above his injury, on the ride to the other sheepherder's croft. He loved feeling her arms wrapped around him, her sweet, soft body warming him while he was chilled to the bone.

He wasn't certain the dog would corral the sheep in

the direction Anora told him to take them, but Charlie was an excellent sheepdog and continued to nip at the sheep's withers, keeping them headed their way. When they finally reached a shieling cloaked in darkness, the only light shining was from the full moon glowing overhead. Gunnolf quickly dismounted and helped Anora down from Niall's horse.

Niall instantly shivered once he lost Anora's warmth and couldn't wait to have her arms around him again.

She hurried Charlie to direct the sheep to the pen. Before she successfully reached the gate, the door to the cottage creaked open. A man stepped onto the stone porch with a lantern in one hand, a knife in the other. "Who goes there?"

Niall stiffened, his hand on the hilt of his sword, ready to defend the lass no matter what.

"'Tis me, Master Torridon, Anora, the shepherdess, from the croft by the river. I must... I must leave my cottage and wish to gift you my sheep."

She sounded so sad, Niall wished to comfort her.

"Anora?" the man said, moving toward the pen, sounding unsure.

Niall couldn't blame him. Here the lass was with her sheep, her dog, and a Highland and Viking warrior with their horses and swords ready for a fight in the middle of the night.

"Aye. I have no choice. I... I..."

Niall hated that her voice was full of tears, her eyes glistening with them as well.

"I must leave," Anora said, sounding disconcerted. "And I cannot... take them with me."

"They... they are after you?" the sheepherder asked, frowning, his voice filled with tension.

"Aye."

So the sheepherder knew something of the lass's difficulty. Mayhap he had heard the news about the men searching for her in the village.

The sheepherder looked up at Niall still seated upon his horse, and Gunnolf standing on the ground, holding his horse's reins. "Who are these men?" He looked like he wished to defend her if need be, but he only had a knife. A sheepherder was no match for two armed warriors.

"These are friends of... of a relation of mine who wishes me safe passage. We must go. Will you care for my sheep?"

"Aye, lass. Be off with you then before the brigands search for you here." The man sounded kindly, fatherly.

"Aye, thank you."

She closed the pen, then allowed Gunnolf to help her onto Niall's horse again. Even for the short distance they had managed, Niall noted she walked stiffly, her body probably sore from riding. He imagined how difficult it would be for her traveling the much greater distance they still had to ride.

She turned to Gunnolf. "Wait, you must take Charlie."

Gunnolf grunted. Niall smiled, knowing the feeling. He much preferred riding with the lass. A squirming dog, no.

"I will hand him up to you," the sheepherder said, attempting to hide a smile. "A good sheepherding dog is hard to find."

But Charlie was more than that to Anora. He was her loving companion, and Niall wouldn't have had the heart to leave him behind, either. Even early this morn when Niall had left the cottage before Anora had awakened, Charlie had stuck close by him like a loyal friend.

Once Gunnolf had mounted, Master Torridon lifted the dog up to the Viking with a pained groan.

Surprised Charlie didn't seem to mind riding with Gunnolf, Niall and his friend rode off.

Anora sniffled as she hugged Niall tight again. "Are you all right, Niall?"

"Aye, lass. With your arms wrapped securely around me, I could do no better."

Gunnolf shook his head and Niall smiled. "What about you, lass?" Niall asked, worried about her state of mind.

"I am relieved to know Master Torridon will take care of my sheep, but saddened, of course. In one fell swoop, I have lost my home, my livelihood, and my way of living."

"Aye, lass, but you will be safe. And you canna put a price on that." At least he prayed they could keep her safe.

They didn't speak again for over an hour as he tried to focus on Gunnolf riding ahead of them—the dog having fallen asleep in his lap—and keeping upright in his saddle.

Much later, they reached a foaming burn where they allowed the horses to drink and rest. It was gloaming by then, the sun sinking behind the mountains, leaving a band of bright yellow, pink, and orange to highlight their craggy tops, a light smattering of clouds clinging to the pale blue sky.

"Come, lass," Niall said, spreading a blanket on the grass. "Lie with me." When he saw her wary expression, he let out an exasperated sigh. "I am frozen to the bone. Every time we separate, I lose your warmth and am chilled all over again. Whether 'tis the fever or no' I could use your warmth, lass."

Frowning, she joined him then. "John never said a man would say such things to me so that I would concede to lying with him."

Smiling, Niall wrapped her in his arms as they lay down on the blanket, trying to get comfortable. "Aye, lass, I wouldna imagine he would have thought it would come to this." Then he closed his eyes.

The sound of the stream gurgling nearby, the lass's heartbeat, and her light breath fanning his neck faded away.

"Riders," Gunnolf whispered, waking Niall and Anora from their sleep a short while later.

Anora's heartbeat accelerated as she tried to move away from Niall without waking or hurting him.

"Your dog," Gunnolf said, "hasna barked as I feared. I told him to be quiet and shushed him and he has been good."

Anora said in a hushed voice, "He can be good if you say the right words." But she realized now why Gunnolf hadn't wished to bring him. If the dog barked, he could alert the men. If they knew that Anora and her party traveled with a dog, 'twould be more trouble. Had she made a mistake in taking Charlie with them? But she could not have left him behind. He would have searched for her and if he couldn't have found her, died trying.

She petted Charlie's head and whispered, "Good dog. Quiet." To Niall, now standing, looking a bit shaky, she said, "What do we do now?"

"Wait them out. Rarely will men travel during gloaming, unless 'tis essential," Niall said. "I fear they are looking for us now. They are headed downstream, searching for a place to cross."

She reached out and squeezed Niall's hand. He didn't feel as feverish, and she quickly felt his forehead. "Thank the heavens," she whispered. "Your fever has broken." Being out in the cold night air without enough rest, he could still become feverish again.

She had never ventured in any direction other than the loch near her cottage, the village, and Laird Callahan's keep and so had never been this far northwest. She was curious as to what the landscape looked like. But she loathed sitting upon the horse for any more time. She ached in places she'd never hurt before.

"Is there any place that we can take refuge?" she asked, rubbing her arms, a cool mist cloaking them.

"Aye, we are headed in the direction of the McEwan's Castle. There, we can rest up, and I am certain the laird or the Chattan brothers, who should be there, will provide an escort for us so we can reach Craigly Castle safely. We could even stay at the Clan Chattan's holdings at Rondover Castle, if need be," Niall said. "One of my cousins has married the laird's daughter."

Her spirits lifted, she asked, "Aye, good, how long before we reach it?"

"'Tis a three-day journey to McEwan's castle, lass," Niall warned.

Disheartened, she said, "Oh."

"We will make it," Gunnolf said, his voice adamant, though she thought he spoke in such a way as to convince himself as much as he wished to convince her.

Before they could remount, Niall had to lift Charlie to Gunnolf this time.

"You are truly better?" Gunnolf asked, sounding just as worried as she'd been.

"Aye, my friend. Much better." Niall lifted Anora onto his horse next, and this time he sat behind her.

It felt so much different this way, instead of her hugging his back with a grip meant to keep Niall from falling off—and herself also—to his arm wrapped snuggly around her, keeping her back close to his chest.

It seemed more... intimate, though the other way had been just as scandalous. Considering her circumstances as they continued on their way, she thought about how her whole world had been turned upside down as soon as she had found the wounded Highlander sleeping in her bed.

And now? She was riding a horse, no small feat in and of itself, in the arms of that same Highlander—something so strange she would never have imagined such a thing—with his good friend. The Viking was just as hardy, carrying Charlie in his lap—away from a danger that had never before existed. And she was seeing lands she'd never visited before. Well, by gloaming, everything was darkening further, so she couldn't really observe much. But she could just imagine viewing all kinds of new wonders once it was light out.

If they managed to evade their pursuers.

Four more times, they stopped, watered the horses, and rested them and themselves before mounting again. Each time, she snuggled with Niall either on the ground, or in his arms as they rode forth. Whenever they paused in their journey, she would feel Niall's forehead to see if he was hot and noticed each time, Gunnolf looked worried to hear the outcome. She was glad to report Niall's fever had not returned.

Every time they mounted was getting harder than the last time, her body aching from riding the horse. She hadn't moved around much once she'd dismounted, barely able to, and she was afraid when she had to walk after riding the horse for so long, she'd have a time of it.

Gunnolf suddenly stopped his horse in a stand of birch. It had not been all that long since the last time they had stopped, so she suspected they were in some kind of danger.

No one said a word. She was dying to know the matter and wanted so to observe what Gunnolf could see ahead of them.

Fog had settled thick in the woods and surrounding glen. The day was dawning, but dark clouds threatened rain. Niall could not be out in this weather, she feared.

Then she heard men's voices in their direct path. Who were they? Was Gunnolf able to see them well enough to determine who they were?

Charlie let out a little woof, nearly giving her a heart attack. Gunnolf said, "Shhh, Charlie, quiet," in a low voice.

They sat like that forever, and she feared the horses would whinny or snort and give them away. What was Gunnolf waiting for? In the worst way, she wanted to get off Niall's horse and rest her weary bones.

Niall leaned his head down and whispered in her ear, "Gunnolf is waiting to see if the men ahead of us are dangerous or not. If they are, we will change direction. For now, he is judging their actions."

As soon as the words were out of Niall's mouth, his warm breath against her ear, Gunnolf turned his horse and walked him in a more easterly direction. She feared that meant the men they heard speaking were the enemy.

It was killing her not to ask. They had to be quiet. Still, she thought it ironic that she had lived alone for so long and didn't have anyone to speak with and here talking could mean a matter of life and death, and she was dying to ask questions.

Besides talking to Charlie, the only one she really spoke with was Matthew, though she'd always liked talking to Charlie better. *Matthew*. Oh, heavens, he would be terribly shook up to learn she had vanished. She took a deep breath. She should have left him a message.

But she couldn't have. Well, she didn't even know where she was going. Not that she would have told him where she was off to had she known, but she could have at least said she'd fallen madly in love with her distant relation and had run off with him. Or something.

Oh, aye, he would have believed that in a heartbeat.

They had walked forever it seemed before Gunnolf

kicked his horse, and they began to dash off across the glen at breakneck speed, her hair flying, her body bouncing up and down on the bony hard back of that massive beast Niall called *Spiorad*—Gaelic for spirit, he'd informed her.

And he *was* a spirited horse. If it hadn't been for Niall's arm tightening around her body, holding her hard against his own, she would have bounced right off miles ago. Worse, her arse would be permanently bruised from the experience.

Then Gunnolf eased his horse to a canter, and the rains began to pour down from the heavens. She knew the worst was yet to come.

CHAPTER 12

So far, their luck had held out, but when Gunnolf spied men ahead of them in the exact location they were going, Niall knew things could only get worse. Particularly with the rains threatening to spill. Then they came down with a vengeance. Niall tried his damnedest to wrap his plaid over Anora and himself, attempting to keep them dry. He knew Gunnolf would head again northwest for McEwan's castle in a short while, though the current route they were on was taking them out of their way. They still had a hard two days' ride ahead of them, and they weren't making progress like they needed to.

The horses were tired and so were the riders. The only one getting any rest was Charlie.

Despite all that she'd been through and not being used to riding a horse and being fearful of them, dealing with the cold, and losing everything she'd ever known, Anora was holding up well. She had remained silent when she needed to, and without complaint, had done all that they had asked of her. She'd only given her dog hell once, when she'd been alone in the woods relieving herself and Charlie had startled a squeak out of her. And then got a low harsh scolding from her. He and Gunnolf had shared smiles.

Niall wasn't used to traveling with a lass and her dog. He was proud of her for being such a good traveler despite everything.

She hadn't said a word about his comment concerning marrying her. If she was of the French nobility, she might not wish to marry him. But still, he was of the mind he would change her thoughts concerning the matter—despite that he had no title or lands to call his own. What Highlander could say that he had a wife who would fight a Highland warrior, wielding only a pitchfork, or that she would raise a Highlander's sword to fight a Viking warrior to protect him?

Her stories fascinated him, and he was thinking that if he had a bairn with her, how she would tell the child her delightful tales. And he would settle down with them to listen, too. Most of all, he loved the way she worried about his health, snuggled with him as if it was for more than warmth, and even kissed him back when he weakly attempted to kiss her earlier.

"I see a place up ahead to rest," Gunnolf called out to them in the now gale force rains and wind.

Niall was hoping for an abandoned cottage, but instead he saw a protective rock overhang. It would have to do.

When they approached, he realized—with great relief—the shelter was big enough for their horses, too.

After they rode under the rock overhang, he dismounted and helped Anora down, but she was barely able to stand. He quickly made up a blanket bed for her on the stone floor beneath the overhang. "Rest, Anora. We should be safe here for a while." He glanced at Gunnolf, who spread out a blanket of his own against the opposite wall.

Charlie stared out at the waterfall flowing over the edge of the slab of rock protecting them, the water hitting the rocks and splattering.

"I have come to believe there is nothing worse than having a dog riding in your lap," Gunnolf said, though he sounded serious, Niall noted his eyes glinted with humor. "I smell like wet dog now." He pulled off his belted plaid and shook it off.

Niall smiled, doing the same with his plaid. "I smell like a shepherdess's sweet lavender."

"Then we shall have to trade riders on the next part of our journey," Gunnolf said, winking at Anora as she reclined on the makeshift blanket bed. "Do you know the dog kicks in his sleep? I thought he would wear a hole in my leg from all the scratching he was doing."

Anora and Niall chuckled.

"So, what did you see ahead of us back there," Niall asked, "when we heard men's voices and had to stop for so long?"

"Half a dozen men wearing dark gray cloaks were speaking to a man at his shieling. He was shaking his head, indicating he hadna seen whoever they were looking for. They searched his shieling and byre and continued to talk to him. I thought we might wait them out and settle there after they left. But decided against it. 'Twould be better if no one saw us during our travels, if we can avoid it, and no one could be forced to tell them what they wished to know."

"Were they Laird Callahan's men mayhap?" Niall asked.

"Nay."

"You would have said if they had been Cian's men," Niall said, which left only one other possibility.

"They were not dressed as we are. So nay," Gunnolf said, settling down on his blanket.

"The Frenchmen I saw in the village," Anora said wearily from her blanket bed.

"*Ja*," Gunnolf said. "I suspect as much."

Niall glanced down at Anora, her eyes closed, but she was shivering. "May I rest with you, lass?"

"Are you feverish again?" She sat up at once as if she had neglected to ascertain his health first before she tried to rest.

"Nay, lass. I am well, but you appear to be shivering."

She glanced at Gunnolf, who quickly hid his grin and closed his eyes.

"Aye, you may," she said, and Niall tried not to show how eager he was to hold her close again.

Before she snuggled against his chest, she felt his forehead, just in case, and he took her hand and kissed it. "No fever, aye?"

"You are fine, thank the Lord." And then she cuddled against his chest, and he believed, despite their circumstances, he had found a bit of heaven.

Nearly drifting off to sleep, he listened to the sound of the rain pouring down off the hillside and their rock shelter like a waterfall, splashing hard on the rocks. The wind howled, the air filled with the fresh scent of a cleansing rain.

Gunnolf suddenly exclaimed, "God's..." Then he bit off the curse and said, "I didna invite you here to join me, dog. 'Tis bad enough I have to ride with you. You... are... wet. And... smelly."

Anora and Niall chuckled.

Everyone was quiet for a few minutes, then Gunnolf said, "Dog, can you breathe the other way. Your breath smells as foul as fish rotting on the shore on a hot summer's day."

Niall smiled. He was glad for the sweet smelling lassie tucked in *his* embrace.

Several hours later when the sun began to rise, the rain let up and Anora rose to pull something from one of the packs. "Bread and cheese," she said, then fetched mead for them.

"Why do you fear horses so much?" Niall asked Anora, as she sat down on the blanket next to him to eat her meal.

"Well, you see, once there was a page..."

"Not Pierre, perchance," he said frowning.

"The one and the same. He liked to play tricks on whosoever he could. But one day he made the mistake of loosening the straps on my horse's saddle..."

"You mean at the time you were unafraid of horses? You have ridden horses before?" Niall couldn't believe it.

"'Tis only a story."

"Aye, of course, continue. I learn so much from your

stories." And now he believed they were not made up in the least.

"As soon as we galloped out of the courtyard, the saddle came off, and I fell. I struck my head on the stone pavement and was knocked unconscious for two whole days. Of course, I do not remember much about that, and my memories of earlier times suffered for it, but poor Pierre..."

"Poor? I would have killed the lad. I would think he deserved whatever was coming to him," Niall growled.

"*Ja*," Gunnolf said. "I would agree."

"True, but actually he was quite smitten with me and since my horse was found to be suffering from some malady that morn—though I know not what, the stable hand had traded mine for one of the other page's horses. Pierre, thinking it was one of the other boy's horses..."

"I see. So he hadna meant to injure you. Just the same..." Niall ground his teeth.

"Aye, just the same, the fall could have killed me or anyone else who might have taken the spill. He was whipped, though things like that normally did not happen to lords. Even so 'twas not a good practice to knock the lord's daughter senseless for two days just to play a prank on someone else."

"I should say no'. Who was your father?" Niall asked.

She chewed on her bottom lip. "Julian Frederick Ponsot."

"Brother to Count Jacques Ponsot?"

"Aye. Is there naught that you are afraid of?" she asked Niall.

"A lass wielding a pitchfork, mayhap," Niall said very seriously. For a moment, in his weary and wounded state, he hadn't known who was poking him with the prongs of the fork that day. It could have been a hulking brute of a man.

She shook her head. "You were not afraid of me."

"Oh, aye, I was. Terrified. Did you no' see me trembling before you?"

She chuckled. "You were yelling a battle war cry and cursing me in Gaelic—no doubt—and then swinging your great sword."

"She used a pitchfork on you?" Gunnolf asked, sounding much intrigued and more than a little amused.

"Aye, she was a mighty foe. And even after I knocked it from her grasp, the lass went for it again instead of dashing out of her cottage like a scared rabbit. I must say I dinna believe I have ever had such an opponent."

"I tell you, she is the one for you, Niall."

"What do you plan to do with me, after we arrive at Craigly Castle?" she asked, getting serious. She hadn't thought about what it would be like living at the castle. What would it be like to live in the Highlands, among a people she didn't know?

If they learned who she was, would they be accepting?

"We have no idea how long it will take for your uncle to reach Craigly Castle," Niall said.

"But that could take weeks, could it not?" Anora said. "What would I do in the meantime? I do not take sitting idly well."

"Ah, lass, there is always much work to be done, but I

wouldna wish you to help shepherd a flock of sheep in the surrounding countryside. 'Twould be much safer for you to stay within the castle walls."

"And Charlie?" she asked, still not liking how this was going. She loved being independent, relying on herself and no one else, not being told what to do. And she was used to raising sheep.

"The dogs…"

Before Niall could tell her they lived in the kennel, she said, "He stays with me. He would howl and bark and make such a ruckus if he was forced to stay elsewhere."

"Mayhap no'. If he finds a she-dog to his liking," Niall said.

Gunnolf chuckled. Anora shook her head.

"The rain is letting up," Niall said, reluctant to leave the overhang, glad to get some much needed rest. He was feeling much better now, and he knew they could not tarry any longer now that the day was dawning at the very early morning hour.

"Aye," Gunnolf said, rising.

Niall rose to his feet, but this time when Anora stood, she looked like it was killing her to do so. "I wish I could make a hot bath for you, Anora, so that you could soothe your sore muscles."

At the suggestion, she flushed beautifully.

He smiled. But he worried about how she would take to living in the castle. And how his people would take to her. She was different—a lady of a highborn rank—yet all this time she'd been living like the common folk. Everyone in the clan worked hard, but he suspected even his aunt and his cousins would not wish the lady to work as his people did. And she was French, but more Lowland Scots in her ways. He wasn't certain how his people would view this.

He hoped she would feel comfortable with living among them. Though he knew her uncle was en route, Niall already did not wish her to return to France or leave them behind for any other location.

He'd never felt that kind of an attachment to a lass. Mayhap he was just getting so used to lying with her that it felt right. Like they were already husband and wife. Or mayhap it was because he loved her wit, her challenging him, and her sweet vulnerability.

"Did you wish a wee bit of privacy, lass, before Gunnolf and I take our leave for a minute or two?" Niall asked.

"Aye, I would," she said, suddenly looking uncomfortable with the notion, and turned to dig out something from her pack, and tried to hide it from him.

A bit of cloth, he thought. "Do not stray far," Niall warned, not wishing her to be alone for a moment.

"I will stay close," she said, and gave his hand a squeeze as if to reassure him she would be all right.

Gunnolf grinned and shook his head.

When the lass moved away from their nearly cave-like resting place, Gunnolf said in a low voice, "You are nearly as good as married to the lass, Niall."

"She is a highborn lady. Think you she would want the likes of me? Or that her uncle would wish her married to me?"

"She has been living as a shepherdess for all these many years. And you have but to see the way she treats you to know she cares for you."

"Her uncle has no doubt other plans for the lass," Niall said, hating to admit it, wishing that there could be some other way for this to end.

***

Glad the rain had stopped completely, the sky dark overhead, the pink and yellow of sunlight just beginning to appear during the early hours of dawn, Anora had not planned to move very far from their protected resting place. Just a quick jaunt into the piney woods nearby to relieve herself. She rushed through the golden-flowered whin to reach the woods. But once she had finished her business in the shelter of the trees, she thought she heard a puppy crying. There was no way that she could leave the woods until she saw to the matter.

She made her way to an alder tree-lined burn and saw a black and white sheepdog—well, puppy, old enough to be weaned, but not old enough to be out here on its own— near the water's edge. Was a shieling nearby?

She suspected her traveling companions would not be happy to see her return with a puppy, but she couldn't leave it here to fend for herself and most likely die. Wolves and wildcats would make short work of her. Anora prayed Niall and Gunnolf would not tell her she could not bring the puppy with her because they could leave her behind if that was the case, and she'd stay with the puppy and Charlie.

Charlie had remained behind with Gunnolf when he brought out some cheese for her dog to eat. So much for being her ever loyal and faithful companion. *Traitor.* Yet, despite all Gunnolf's grousing last night about the dog curling up to sleep with him, when she woke this morning, she'd smiled to see his arm wrapped around Charlie's body, her dog's head planted on Gunnolf's neck. Mayhap, Gunnolf would champion her cause, and Niall would have to agree with it.

But she could have used Charlie's help now in catching the young dog.

She coaxed the small puppy as she walked slowly toward it, making momma sounds, cooing to her. The puppy watched her with big brown eyes, her long ears, not fringed yet like Charlie's, lifting a bit as she listened to Anora. And then the vixen darted into the underbrush further away from where they'd camped.

"No." Anora said, her voice said in an annoyed but hushed way. She needed to reach her and return to camp before Niall stopped her and made her leave without the pup.

Anora scrambled after the puppy, calling to her, coaxing her to come to her. Then something moved in the woods. Anora froze. The puppy suddenly ran to her, as if whatever was in the woods was scarier than Anora. She quickly scooped her up in her arms, speaking softly to the pup, reassuring her. She turned to head back through the trees and across the glen to the hill where the men waited for her when she heard the sound of horses moving among the trees.

Niall and Gunnolf's?

She quickly crouched, barely breathing, her heart pounding—praying the puppy would not whimper.

The horses moved in her direction. Six riders all

187

dressed in charcoal gray cloaks circled around her. The riders knew she was here already.

She had nowhere to go but the icy river. She would have to leave the puppy behind, and it tore at her heart to do so. Before she could run for the river to lunge in, she was surrounded completely by the five men and a woman. The Frenchmen who had been inquiring in the village about where she lived.

"We wish you no harm," the lady said with a heavy French accent. "Do not call out or the men who stole you away from your croft will be dead."

They were too far away. They wouldn't hear her cries if she called out anyway. Anora desperately wanted to dash into the burn, but she tightened her hold on the pup. She knew the man sitting astride his horse behind her would prevent her escape.

The lady motioned to one of the men. He dismounted, then helped the woman down.

"I am Andrea Rochelle, Anora, your *soeur*, baroness of Carcassonne."

"Sister?" Anora said, her voice arching with disbelief.

"*Oui*," the woman said, then grasped Anora's shoulders in a claw-like grip and leaned over and kissed one cheek, then the other in a perfunctory manner.

"You cannot be. I have no sisters." Anora glowered at the raven-haired woman who smiled back at her. "What do you wish of me?"

"You are to come with us to Devon, my dear, where you will *joindrez la famille*."

"I will not, Lady Rochelle. I have other plans."

"We did not know until recently what had become of you. Your uncle sent me to bring you home once we *verifie* you were Asceline. You do not know how we all grieved when we feared we had lost you."

Had the woman? Anora couldn't tell. She looked over at one of the men and seeing his familiar black eyes, the one she had met in the village of Banbh, she stared at him for a moment, then faced the woman and shook her head. "I do not know you and will return to Braybrooke Castle now as I work for Laird Callahan, and he will be missing me soon."

She hoped the mention would make these strangers take heed that Laird Callahan and his force of men would be too much for them to handle.

The sound of another horse's hooves clomping closer, and Matthew whistling his nonsensical tune as he approached, had Anora's heart skittering. What was he doing out here? He'd gone to Coventry, aye. But how could he have come across them so unexpectedly when she had been traveling in the opposite direction?

One of the gray cloaked men drew his sword.

Anora quickly said in a hushed voice, "He is only a friend of mine. The butcher's son. He means no one any harm."

The lady motioned for the knight to sheath his sword.

Anora wanted to bolt for Matthew, to make him go back the way he had come, to ensure he did not get involved in this. She also was afraid he'd be shocked to see her here and ask too many questions. She feared these people would kill him.

The black-eyed man swung down from his horse and seized her arm as if he believed she would dash off. *"Vous nous accompagnerez, ma dame, comme le baroness le souhaite de vous,"* the knight said to Anora.

"I will go nowhere with you, but will return at once to Braybrooke as I have said."

Anora struggled to free herself from the man, but the baroness said, "I will have my knight kill your young friend, if you fight us, my dear."

Knights. French knights. Even Niall and Gunnolf couldn't fight these men. Not as many of them as there were. She didn't think. It wasn't the same as Niall fighting the Highlanders who had been divided, and busy with drinking or sleeping, and caught unawares.

Anora contemplated alerting Matthew to go for help, but she feared he would never be able to outride them. She quit struggling and the knight released her arm. They waited quietly for Matthew to approach.

When she saw him, her heart sank. He was riding his horse, armed with a sword and a dirk, but he was no match for any of these men. He glanced only briefly at the knights and the lady, then smiled broadly at Anora. "I am surprised to meet you here, Anora. Are these more of your relations?"

She couldn't believe he'd act so unconcerned about it. As if she abandoned her cottage on a regular basis while traveling for miles, distancing herself from her home in the company of strangers. She glanced at the woman to see how she should respond. The woman bowed her head ever so slightly.

"Aye," Anora said to Matthew, her throat dry with fear.

"Where is your... other cousin?" Matthew asked, a brow arched.

"He left. I told you he was leaving early the next morn," she quickly said, glad she had said so previously so that it did not sound like a lie.

"True. May I have a moment to speak with you alone, Anora?" Matthew asked, not dismounting, and then she thought mayhap he knew very well she was in trouble.

"I am leaving with my sister for... Devon," Anora said.

The baroness nodded in agreement.

"Devon? What is this all about? I did not think you had a sister."

Play along, Matthew, she silently entreated. He was going to get himself killed. Her heart beat frantically and her hands grew clammy, the puppy at least quiet in her arms.

"Aye, well, it turns out that I do have a sister and so you must tell Laird Callahan I will not be working for him as I had planned when you see him next, and I must cancel my engagement in Dover. He is marrying Lady Hayley."

"Who?"

"Laird Callahan. He decided to marry her quickly, then they will have a wedding at Windsor when this trouble in the region is quite over."

"*Nous devons aller*, Anora," the baroness said.

"The lady says I must go now, Matthew. Tell Laird Callahan that I am sorry to have to run out on him in this way. Tell him," Anora said, petting the puppy, worried they would not let her take her with her, "tell him I regret not having my pitchfork."

Matthew frowned at Anora. "You are not making

sense, Anora."

She wanted to slap Matthew for not going along with the conversation. And for getting a girl with bairn, if he had done so, and had pretended still to want to marry Anora.

"Mayhap you can see me in Devon, sometime, Matthew, though I am not sure I will see much of the place myself. Give your parents my love, as I must be on my way. My Danish relations will not be happy if I should delay our blessed reunion much longer."

Matthew shook his head. "If I should see Laird Callahan anytime soon."

"Laird Callahan must know," Anora said. "He will worry that I have left without word. Please tell him, Matthew. Tell him I will have fish on my platter soon enough… that I will see the deep blue seas again."

Mayhap, Laird Callahan could send men to her rescue if he understood the message, and he did not mind getting involved.

"You cannot take the dog with you," the knight said to Anora before he helped her onto the horse.

"Nay, she is my puppy. I cannot leave her behind." She tightened her hold on the pup. Anora's body was rigid with tension.

"You cannot travel with him," the knight with the black eyes said, his expression pleading with her to give the puppy up without causing any further trouble.

Another knight wrenched the puppy from her arms, and she screamed. She hadn't meant to, afraid Matthew might react, but she couldn't help herself. The knight dropped the puppy on the ground, and pulled his sword as if he was going to kill her if Anora didn't do as the baroness demanded.

"Nay! Do not kill her! I will go with you." Tears filling her eyes, Anora allowed a knight to lift her onto his horse, the whole time glowering at the other man. If he killed the pup, they would have to kill her.

She glanced back at Matthew and hoped he would get the puppy, but mayhap he was afraid. She couldn't read his blank expression, but he didn't dismount.

The brigand of a knight, who would have killed the puppy, sheathed his sword and mounted, and then they rode away from Matthew and the hills where Niall and Gunnolf were still. Anora looked back to see Matthew head toward Banbh, leaving the forlorn puppy behind. She whimpered and Anora fought to hold back the tears filling her eyes. Barely breathing, she watched as two of the French knights milled around behind them, observing Matthew. If they harmed him or the puppy, she would fight them with every ounce of strength she possessed.

When Matthew faded from sight, the knights rejoined the escort. They had to have been only ensuring he left and didn't follow them. The puppy sat down, not about to follow the big horses.

Anora took a deep breath, relieved Matthew would live another day. In a way, she was glad the puppy had not followed them, or she was certain the one knight would kill it.

Yet, her heart ached for the puppy and she prayed if Niall came looking for her, he'd find the pup and take care of her. But she knew he wouldn't. His focus would be solely on freeing her from the French.

Still, mayhap Charlie would find the puppy and take care of her, like he did her lambs.

For now, she was just as grateful Niall and Gunnolf hadn't had to fight these men, either—not without a way to battle fewer at one time—like Niall had when he fought the men separately at her croft. Then again, what if Niall didn't find her, or come to her rescue? What if she never saw him again, or her beloved Charlie?

And she couldn't stop thinking about the puppy.

She ground her teeth, angry with these men and the baroness, wishing she had her pitchfork.

She had every intention of freeing herself, first opportunity she had. And somehow, she had to go back for the puppy.

CHAPTER 13

Gunnolf had taken their horses to graze while Niall had gone to check on Anora, worried she was taking so long. But Niall hadn't wanted Gunnolf to see Anora if the lass had been bathing in the river. Niall suspected she might have been, which was why she had slipped the cloth out of her bag, attempting to hide it from him.

Once he'd heard the woman speaking to Anora in French in the woods some distance hence, and he had observed the five men with the woman, he'd hidden from everyone's view. He wanted to kill every bloody one of them, but he couldn't, not when he was one man against five. And from what he could see of the lay of their cloaks, all of them were heavily armed.

He'd stared at the puppy in her arms. Where had she gotten it? When the knight took the pup from her and Anora screamed, it was all Niall could do to stay hidden. He feared for her safety, certain she would give her life for the pup's, if the knight had attempted to kill it.

As soon as he could rejoin Gunnolf, the two of them could take the men on, but they had to ensure Anora wasn't hurt in the process.

To his astonishment, he had heard Matthew approach on horseback, headed straight for the cluster of Frenchmen. Or what had sounded like the man, as he whistled the same nonsensical tune as he had when he had visited Anora's cottage. Niall thought the bloody fool would have gotten himself killed.

But when Matthew didn't and rode off, the Frenchmen and woman took Anora away. Niall suspected the two knights they had left behind planned to kill Matthew once he was out of Anora's sight, so that she would not fight them. Niall had every intention of eliminating the men before they could murder Matthew, but he feared a sword fight would alert the others. And they would return to help their fellow knights. Then Niall would be in the same situation, alone, and facing all five knights. But he would do it if he had to in order to protect Matthew's life.

Or mayhap, the Frenchwoman was Anora's kin, as she had said—she only wished to take Anora home—and they had no plan to kill Matthew or harm the lass.

But Niall had to know that for certain. He watched the two remaining knights leave and follow the rest of them and was relieved the men had no intention of killing the butcher's son. Before Niall had a chance to dash back to Gunnolf and the horses, Matthew circled around and spied him crouched in the trees.

Surprised to see Matthew's actions, Niall straightened.

What was the man doing? Had he intended to follow Anora and her escort after all? One man alone?

Foolhardy notion if that's what Matthew had in mind.

Niall was about to signal him not to say a word, afraid he would speak and give them both away, but Matthew seemed to understand Niall was on *his* side and rode up to Niall and whispered, "Are you a friend to Anora or foe?"

Well, mayhap he wasn't all that certain.

"My friend and I were taking her to my cousin's castle in the Highlands for safekeeping," Niall said, his hope that placing his trust in Anora's friend was not a mistake.

They needed to even up the odds, though Niall wasn't certain Matthew could fight well against the knights, given that he was only a butcher's son. Niall suspected now that Matthew had not just chanced to come upon Anora in the woods, but had followed these gray-cloaked Frenchmen and woman, in an attempt to locate Anora. But what had he intended to do beyond that?

"Where is this friend of yours?" Matthew asked.

"That way." Niall motioned in the direction of the rocky brae.

"Get on, and I will take you there." Matthew held out his arm.

Before Niall could take his arm, he stalked over to where the puppy sat, her big brown eyes watching him, and then he scooped her up and slid her into his tunic, his belt around his shirt helping to make the perfect pouch for her. She settled against his chest, warm and furry and content— which he was grateful for. He could just imagine the pup clawing to get out, and he didn't want to leave her behind.

When Matthew saw that Niall intended to take the dog with him, his eyes rounded a bit, but he didn't say a word. Wisely.

He helped Niall to mount behind him, and then Niall directed him to the rock face where they had slept during the night.

"Tell me the truth about what is taking place," Matthew said, his voice dark with antagonism as he kicked his horse to a gallop.

So the man had some spine. Niall hadn't thought so when Matthew had been with Anora, mayhap trying to appear more of a gentle soul.

Niall gave him an abbreviated telling of the tale—about the trouble he and Gunnolf had run into with Cian's men and now these cloaked Frenchmen and the woman.

Matthew shook his head. "Her byre was torched, the thatched roof of her cottage and everything inside burned."

"Bloody hell," Niall said, his gut churning with fury. "Dinna tell the lass that when we free her." He never wanted Anora to learn of it.

"She had no intention of returning?" Matthew asked, sounding disappointed.

"Nay. My cousin is laird and had word from her uncle that she would be in danger. He and the French count of Carcassonne had fought alongside each other during the Crusades. I dinna know beyond that what is to become of her. Because of whatever danger she is in, she canna return to her cottage."

"What happened to her sheep?"

"She gifted them to another sheepherder."

"What about Charlie?"

"He is with my friend, Gunnolf."

"The dog will be a problem if we are to use stealth," Matthew warned. "And the pup?"

Niall shook his head. "Charlie has been fine thus far."

"And the whelp you now carry?" Matthew again brought up.

Niall said nothing. Time would only tell, but he couldn't leave the pup by itself in the woods.

Gunnolf unsheathed his sword as soon as he saw Matthew riding toward him, Niall sitting behind him.

"Where is the lass?" Gunnolf called out, troubled.

"The Frenchmen who were asking in the village concerning her whereabouts have taken her," Niall said, dismounting from Matthew's horse. "And this is her good friend, Matthew, the butcher's son of Banbh."

Charlie immediately began to jump all over Niall, not only in greeting, but wanting to see the puppy in his tunic, sniffing, trying to greet her as well. The puppy was a little shy with him, though she and Charlie touched noses, and then he licked hers.

"I am going to marry Anora," Matthew said, very seriously, as if he wanted to get that issue straight between them.

Gunnolf stared at the puppy's head poking out from Niall's shirt. Thankfully, but a small smile curving Gunnolf's mouth, he didn't react.

Niall didn't comment about Matthew's claim that he was marrying Anora. The lass would not marry the likes of the butcher's son. Not with the way she abhorred his mother and she saw Matthew only as a friend. And besides, Niall didn't believe it would be safe for her to live near Banbh any further. Too, he assumed her uncle would object.

"Matthew learned of the men asking about Anora and followed them to us," Niall told Gunnolf, as they quickly readied their horses.

"Actually," Matthew said, "I spoke with a man who rented land some distance from Anora's and hoped mayhap I would learn if she had gone that way. The French party arrived and asked if he had seen her. I was inside the cottage and heard everything. They did not pay me any mind, thinking I was the farmer's son and left. I was ready to fight them if they had thought to kill the farmer."

Niall hoped the man could fight. At least he was armed.

"Can you fight well?" Gunnolf asked, handing Charlie up to Matthew, voicing the very concern Niall had.

"As well as any Highlander," Matthew said, sounding a bit miffed that they would question him. Niall doubted the butcher's son had fought in many battles—if any. Living in the village would not have given Matthew many opportunities, Niall didn't believe.

Matthew frowned at Charlie sitting on his lap, looking up at him with his big brown eyes, his tail brushing his leg. "Cannot he run alongside the horses?" Matthew asked, as Charlie licked him on the mouth. He jerked his head aside before the dog did it again, then wiped his lips with the back of his tunic sleeve.

"He might warn Anora and the Frenchmen we are on our way," Niall said, mounting his horse, the puppy again curling up inside his tunic as if she was getting ready to sleep.

They headed in the direction of the woods where Anora had been taken. He and Gunnolf had to have their hands free to fight if necessary so Matthew's taking care of Charlie for the moment suited their purpose. Though Niall wasn't sure what to do about the pup if he got into a skirmish.

"She was trying to tell me something, but she did not make any sense," Matthew said. "Did you catch our conversation?"

"They are forcibly escorting her to a coastal town, taking her by ship somewhere, I gathered," Niall said, not intending to allow them such.

"And the pitchfork?"

"She wished she had a weapon, as if to say she wasna going of her own freewill," Niall said, not about to mention to Matthew how she'd poked him with it.

"Laird Callahan is not marrying anyone that I know of. Did you understand that?"

"Lady Hayley." Niall mulled it over. "Doesna that mean 'of the hay meadow' in English? Anora, of the hay meadow."

"But she has no intention of marrying Laird Callahan," Matthew said, sounding as though he objected greatly to the notion.

If the laird had wanted to wed her, why wouldn't he have kept her safe at his castle? Because he was interested in another lass? Mayhap he didn't believe the count would want his niece married to the Lowland Scot.

"What is the plan?" Gunnolf asked, quiet up until now.

"We will have to attack when they least expect it," Niall said, "as we are only..." He nearly said two in force, then remembered Matthew, though he didn't believe he'd help. "Three against five armed knights."

"And if they wish no harm to come to the lass? That they truly are her kin and wish to move her to some other location where she will be safe among her own people?" Gunnolf asked.

That was the part that worried Niall the most. Not knowing whether to kill the men when he knew that they would fight Niall and Gunnolf. Or let the Frenchmen live and risk their own lives and Anora's.

***

Anora hated that her escort was taking her farther away from Gunnolf and Niall and farther from the McEwan's castle where they might seek refuge. She suspected Niall and his friend would realize she was in trouble as long as it had taken her, and she had not returned. All she could do for now was attempt to learn who these people truly were and if they wished to keep her safe, or not.

"You say, my lady, that you are my sister. Are you younger or older than me?" Anora asked.

The baroness smiled. "What do you think, my dear?"

A question for a question? That didn't bode well.

"You appear to be older, but I had no sisters when I left France. I thought mayhap you meant that you were a half-sister..."

"I am older than you. Father had sent me away to marry."

"How old were you?"

"Two and ten. You were younger when they arranged your betrothal."

"And the man I was to wed?" Anora frowned.

"When we thought you were dead, he married another woman, but died several years ago."

"But Father was with me on board the ship, aye?"

"Father *sur un* voyage to *obtenir* articles from *Italie* when the *Anglais* boarded her. We did not know you survived the onslaught. Only recently had we learned you were living with the sheepherder near Banbh. Who knows what the *capitaine* had on his mind when he brought you to *Anglais* shores then took you north to live with the sheepherder."

"And yet some of our family moved here?"

"Some did. We found *plus d'advantages dans habiter dans* Devon."

Her blood chilled with worry, Anora didn't believe her. What if she was put on a ship and taken somewhere else— and not to join family?

Anora nodded, amicably, as if she agreed with them, planning to escape them the first chance she had. She turned her attention to one of the knights who watched her. The one who looked hauntingly familiar. "What is your name, Sir Knight?"

"Pierre, my lady."

Her heartbeat quickened. "Pierre?"

The knight nodded, then looked away.

Anora stared at his features—he had been a tall boy when she had known him, but he was a man now, though his eyes—they still looked at her in the same way—as if he cared for her.

"Not the Pierre I knew when I was a little girl?" The knight said nothing in response. Anora studied him further, then said, "Not Pierre Frederic Fainot, son of Jean Pierre Fainot and Catherine Julie Roux?"

The knight glanced at the baroness, who motioned at him to move along. As the knight kicked his horse, Anora said, "Wait!" He stopped and waited for Anora to catch up. "Do you remember me, Sir Pierre?"

"*Oui.*"

"Were you the one who placed a water snake in the ladies' bath then, causing several to run from the room off the kitchen in only their towels?" She studied the man's face as a faint glimmer of a smile appeared. "And the one who set the live crab on Lady Olivia's plate when everyone else's was perfectly steamed. I had never seen the lady move so fast from the table in my life. We did not even need the jester to entertain us that day, as most of us laughed through the rest of the meal."

The knight's smile broadened.

"And the lad who kissed the wrong maid at a festivity that had been given in honor of the king's birthday celebration? I will never forget the look on his face when the other girl pulled off her mask and wished for the page to give her another kiss. When he saw me watching him, his face turned absolutely crimson." Anora smiled as the knight chuckled. "You know, I had wished he had kissed me that day, but after his blunder, he was too afraid to try again."

"He has grown up, my lady," Pierre said, his voice so

much deeper now.

"Aye, well, 'tis too late now," Anora said, thinking about the way Niall had kissed her and how she wished his arms were wrapped tight around her, while he was kissing her, and loving her. She would have to escape. She had to. "Do you live in England, now, too? I cannot imagine you would be anything other than a vassal lord to the King of the Franks."

"I do not believe in many of his policies, my lady," he said, very low, but the knight she rode with could hear his words also.

Hope sprang anew that he might aid her flight.

Anora glanced over her shoulder to see the baroness following close behind as she strained to hear their conversation. "Tell me about King Philip then, Pierre."

"He is married to a...," he hesitated to say as he considered his words carefully, "a countess who will never gain the people's love for her."

"Where are you really taking me?" she asked, hoping Pierre would still care enough about her to tell her the truth. He glanced back at the baroness and she knew then he would not.

***

"Did you no' go to Coventry as you said you would?" Niall asked Matthew, as they searched for the French party's trail. "It seems to me you wouldna have had time to go there and turn around and look for Anora."

"I did not trust you had Anora's best interests in mind," Matthew said honestly. "I knew you were not her cousin, distant or otherwise. So tell me the truth. Where did they come from and who are you to Anora?" Matthew asked, his voice hard.

Niall knew he couldn't hide the truth any longer, not if Matthew had become an ally. "One of Cian's clansmen managed to get the best of me."

Matthew glanced at Niall, looking puzzled.

"I… suffered a sword wound." There, Niall said it. He wouldn't have mentioned it, if he hadn't felt he needed to explain why he had taken refuge in Anora's cottage.

Matthew's jaw dropped as his gaze shifted to look Niall over. "God's truth?"

"Aye."

Matthew remained quiet for a while, then said, "I believed you thought you were too good to aid Anora in her chores. That was why you wore John's tunic. Yours must have been ruined. And… Anora was washing it. Not because it was torn by a branch and only soiled, but a sword had sliced through it… and it was bloodied."

"Aye."

Matthew let out his breath. "Why did you not say so?"

Niall cast him a look that asked if he was touched in the head.

"Aye, you did not trust me. You thought I might even be a friend of this Highlander named Cian?" Matthew shook his head.

"You have the right of it. What would you have done in my place?" Niall asked.

"I suspect the same." Matthew looked back at the forest. "We are headed away from where you wished to take Anora, are we not?"

"Aye, that we are," Niall said. "We must go northwest again as soon as we can."

But when a drenching downpour again soaked them, they had to seek cover and once the rains let up, they could not discover any sign of the French parties' trail.

Niall was beside himself, looking for any clues for where they had gone before it was too late.

CHAPTER 14

Anora had every intention of slipping away from the woman who claimed to be her sister and her knight escort as soon as she was able.

But all she could think about was Niall, Gunnolf, and Charlie. And the puppy. She didn't know how well they could track the Frenchmen and woman, but she wanted to leave them clues that she had passed this way, if she could.

The rains had finally ceased. She was wet and cold, the day gray and stormy still. If she could scratch something in the wet earth... but could Niall or Gunnolf read? What if it rained again and washed her message away? She would make the attempt, no matter what.

Three of the men had started a fire from kindling they'd stored in waterproof packs on one of the horses. Some of the men had hunted birds and were roasting them over the fire. She shivered, glanced around, and saw Pierre watching her. She stiffened a little.

The baroness was still in the tent sleeping, Anora suspected.

If Anora could mayhap stack a few rocks and point them in the direction they were headed, or she could just set them in a particular pattern that would indicate someone had arranged them that way—that it was not a random occurrence, maybe Niall or Gunnolf would come this way and notice.

Then again, Charlie could find her with his keen sense of smell, even if she just touched a few of the rocks.

She frowned at Pierre. He smiled at her, looking his usual charming self, except he was much older than he'd been.

She looked for a special stone, then picked it up, and rubbed her hand softly over the moss.

"Put it down, my lady," Pierre said quietly, his tone a command.

"It feels so soft," she said, irritated with his highhanded manner. He had no right to tell her what to do, but she didn't have a whole lot of choice. "Have you ever felt moss under the palm of your hand?"

She hoped she left enough of her scent on the rock for Charlie to recognize it... if he came this way.

"*Non.* Put it down."

Did he think she intended to use it as a weapon? With two men still nearby, tending the fire?

"Come closer to the fire so you can warm yourself and dry your clothes a little," Pierre said.

She set the rock carefully down so that he didn't believe she intended to use it as a weapon. She could hear the river flowing just beyond the stand of trees, and she desperately wanted to make her escape that way. Not that she wanted to get any wetter or colder. But she was certain the further south they took her, the less of a chance she had of freeing herself.

"Where are you taking me?" she asked again.

He glanced at the other men. She sighed. If they could be alone, maybe he would tell her. But it wasn't going to happen soon enough for her.

She thought to say she needed to wash, but she was so wet that wouldn't work. Instead, she made the decision— right or wrong—and dashed through the woods for the river. Her heart pounded as she feared she'd never make it in time to escape their grasp. But she was desperate.

"*Non!*" Pierre shouted, and she heard him and the other knights as they took chase, stomping on the underbrush, knocking aside supple tree branches blocking their way.

She didn't believe she'd make it as twigs snagged at her hair, slowing her down as she tore at them to free herself, and she stumbled over tree roots. Then the churning river was before her. She might make it after all.

A white frothing burn, trees growing along the rocky banks, some leaning out like leafy covered fingers stretching for the water—if she could only reach it before they stopped her. She dashed across the slippery, moss-covered rocks lining the river's bank and caught herself before she fell—and kept moving.

She splashed through the shallower edge of the river and was ready to lunge into the deeper part to allow the swiftly moving currents to sweep her away when someone grabbed her arm.

That startled a shriek from her. Instinctively, she swung back and slugged the knight in the chest, surprising him. In that precious moment, he lost his grip on her. She turned and dove forward into the icy, swift-flowing water.

"Get the baroness and the horses!" Pierre shouted.

She couldn't watch their progress as she floundered in the rough water, trying to keep her head above it, allowing the current to carry her away.

She feared if she didn't get out of the water soon, she'd be too cold to be able to swim in it. She imagined the French knights were slipping all over the stony beach, trying to follow her progress, while the rest of them returned to the camp to get their horses and the baroness. But none joined her in the treacherous water. Mayhap none could swim.

Cold, freezing, Anora was free—aye, but for how long?

Not long after she took the plunge into the cold water, she saw movement on the opposite bank headed in her direction, racing along the shore—men in belted plaids— Cian's men, the same men who had visited her croft. Her heart flipped in slow motion. Did they realize who she was? That she was the same woman who lied to them about their missing men?

If they got hold of her, would they murder her, turn her over to the French, or were they working for someone else?

***

Niall didn't know what to make of it. A fire was blazing in the camp, birds skewered over the flames, but no sign of anyone. Had Anora and her French captors been the ones to make the camp?

Matthew put out the fire while Gunnolf confiscated the roasted birds, and Niall searched for signs of where the party had disappeared.

He quickly found muddy tracks in the woods and evidence they had hurried along the riverbank going in a southerly direction.

"They took off, headed down the riverbank," Niall said as he returned to camp. "The tracks the horses left indicated they were in a hurry."

"Surely, we didn't alert them," Matthew said, his brow furrowed.

"I am no' certain what made them run, but the horses were galloping when they ran along the river bank."

"You dinna believe the lass fell in the river," Gunnolf said, as they all rode in the direction the French party had taken.

"Nay. I suspect if they were no' trying to outrun someone else, Anora jumped into the river, attempting to get away—if she could swim," Niall said, not liking the scenario one wee bit. He glanced at Matthew. "Can she swim?"

"Aye, she can," Matthew said.

"And you know this because?" Niall asked, not meaning to sound so angry, but he didn't like the notion that Matthew knew she could swim.

Matthew's mouth curved up some. "The shepherdess taught her."

But what Niall wanted to know was whether Matthew

had seen Anora swimming and how had she been clothed at the time? Even if she had worn a chemise, wet, it would have looked like a second skin. He knew it was a foolish thought, considering the peril Anora was now in, but he still couldn't help being irked.

Not too much further downriver, they heard the Frenchmen shouting, but other men as well—only those were yelling in Gaelic.

A shiver stole up Niall's spine as he realized not only were the French after her, but Cian and his men. Niall and his companions pulled their horses to a stop in the woods.

Everyone was hollering about reaching the lass first. What the hell?

Then from the edge of the woods, Niall spied the Frenchmen and woman, and Cian's men across the burn, galloping along the bank.

All eyes were on the burn and that's when Niall saw her. *Anora.* God's teeth. She was bobbing up and down in the river, barely able to keep her head above the foaming water.

"They will not catch up to her. The shoreline ends there," Matthew said, pointing ahead to an area where the cliffs rose high above, creating a canyon. "I know this area well. I used to come here with others when we were lads. They will either have to join her in the burn, or go the long way around. But I doubt anyone would be foolhardy enough to jump in after her."

True to Matthew's word, the French party and the Highlanders all moved away from the river, to go the long way around, skirting the cliffs to reach the other side of the burn where they could again gain access to the river.

"'Tis two miles before they can reach the river's banks again," Matthew said.

Niall quickly handed the puppy to Gunnolf. "Take care of her for Anora." He didn't wait to hear Gunnolf's response, only saw his jaw drop for a second. Then Niall kicked his horse into the river. "Take care of my horse," he said to Gunnolf, knowing he need not have, but the words were out of his mouth before he could stop them.

Then Niall leapt off his horse and into the river, the icy water shocking his body instantly. His wound ached— bloody hell—every inch of him did as the bitter cold sliced through him. James had not said just how difficult bringing one wee lass to Craigly Castle would be. Yet, he would do everything in his power to rescue her and take her to safety.

He worried, too, how badly Anora had to be feeling, as much as the frigid water was affecting him.

"Can he swim?" Matthew asked, concerned.

"Aye, like a fish," Gunnolf said.

And then Niall couldn't hear anything more that his companions said, his body shivering as he attempted to keep afloat in the churning water as it carried him along. If he and the lass survived this... His teeth chattering, he wasn't certain what they would do. If she and he were carried down to where the Frenchmen and Cian's men could reach them, they would be in dire straits.

Not too much further, Niall reached the canyon that cloaked the river from everyone's view. Even a mountain goat could not reach the top of the cliffs.

He saw Anora then, clinging to a mossy rock in the

middle of the river and felt a guarded relief that she was safe and had not continued to flounder in the water, trying to keep from drowning. She was hidden from anyone's sight, who remained ashore, and this was good news. He swam that way until he was nearly to the rock, attempting to maneuver in its direction so that he could catch onto it. Then the force of the water slammed him into the rock only a foot away from her.

"Lass!" he yelled to her, his voice drowned out by the rushing river as he grabbed hold of the moss-covered stone. The water tugged at him with such fierceness, it was like it had a mind of its own and was intent on yanking him from his precious hold.

Anora was staring at the rock, clinging to it for dear life, seemingly unaware that he had nearly reached her.

"Anora," he called out to her when she didn't respond. He made his way over to her, his chilled fingers gripping the cracks and crevices of the water-worn, slippery rock for purchase.

She turned her head, her eyes widening in shock. "Niall," she managed to get out, her teeth chattering. She looked chilled to the bone, her skin pale, her lips blue.

"Aye, lass." He glanced at the shore behind them, but other than sheer cliffs that touched the rushing river, there was no place for them to get out of the water on that side. Glancing at the other shoreline, he could see caves about twenty feet above the narrow rocky beach. "We are going to shore now. Grab my back. I will get us to that cave."

"Aye," she said, barely able to speak, she was shivering so hard.

She reached for him and he prayed she would be strong enough to hold on. And that he would be strong enough to swim against the swift currents and not miss their chance at reaching the beach.

"Hold tight, lass." He was afraid she was so cold, she wouldn't have the strength. "Whatever you do, dinna let go."

She grabbed hold of his back and he waited a moment until he felt she had a tight enough grip. Then he let go of the rock, determined to swim to the shore at all haste.

Niall felt numb from the cold as he struggled to swim to the rocky shoreline with Anora clinging to his back. She provided the warmth and the encouragement to make it across as the river's strong pull carried him away from the cliffs. Silently cursing their predicament, Niall vowed he'd reach the bank before they lost the chance. Rocky cliffs again loomed ahead, but the stone faces were sheer sheets of granite stretching all the way to the water.

Then his feet found the rock bottom, and he reached back and pulled at Anora's arm. "Lass, try to gain your footing."

He felt her anchoring her feet against the rocks, helping him to withstand the tug of the water. As he made his way to shore, he slipped his arm around her waist, helping her against the swift currents. She stumbled, ready to collapse, but he held her up. She couldn't crumble on him now. They still had too far to go.

"Just a wee bit further, bonny lass. 'Tis just a wee bit longer, and we will have shelter."

Then they were on the shore and he helped her back

along the stony beach to reach the caves above. He would have carried her, but she needed to walk, to keep the blood flowing, to help thaw her icy body.

She clung to him, her movements stiff, her body shivering violently as much as his was. He wanted to build a fire, but he suspected they would not have the means.

"Anora, we must climb those rocks," he said, drawing her against his body. "We must." He wasn't about to ask her if she could make it. She had no choice.

But he didn't believe she could climb in her long *léine* and brat, both garments—water-repellant because of the wool's natural properties in a light rain, but swimming in them—they were soaking wet and clinging to her body.

"Your gown will cause you difficulty when we make the climb," he warned.

She nodded, shaking so hard, he wasn't certain she understood what he was saying. "I will tie them in between your legs so they will be like a man's breeches."

Her eyes widened.

"'Tis the only way, lass."

She again nodded.

Thunder boomed overhead and two flashes of lightning speared the trees in the distance. "A storm is coming." They were already wet enough. He wrung out her brat the best he could to reduce some of the weight she wore, then did the same with her *léine*. Once he finished with that, he tied her gown in between her legs so that she could climb better, her legs now exposed.

"'Tis time to climb."

"Aye," she said, her voice shaking with cold.

She reached for a handhold, carefully, but so painfully measured, he assumed every muscle was rigid with the cold as half frozen as he was also. She slipped twice, nearly making his heart stop.

"Hold on tight, lass." As if he needed to tell her. He made his way up the rock face, following her, hoping if she fell, he could catch her and still hold onto the cliff himself.

They made the climb agonizingly slow—Anora having trouble reaching hand and footholds, slipping thrice more, and nearly giving him a heart attack each and every time.

When she finally reached the lip of the cave, she peered in. He wanted to tell her to hurry before the rains and wind hit them and threatened to tear them from their tentative holds. But he suspected she was afraid of what might have taken refuge in the pitch blackness already, and he didn't want to rush her into taking a misstep at this point when they were so close to finding shelter inside.

"Dark," she said, her voice an icy stutter, and she climbed the rest of the way to the cave's entrance.

"Aye," he said, and as soon as he joined her in the cave, he took her into his arms just as the rains poured down off the top of the rocks like a waterfall. He looked around at the dark cave, and saw nothing to use to make a fire. Though even if they'd had a way, he worried they would have no way to ventilate the smoke. And if they had, those searching for Anora might see the smoke and realize where she was hiding.

This way, mayhap those chasing after her would think she had drowned. How could she have survived the rocks and the wintry water all on her own? At least, that's what he hoped they would believe.

All he could think of was thawing her frozen body when she said in her chilled voice, "Niall, are you all right? Your wound."

The sweet lassie was more at risk, to Niall's way of thinking, and yet through it all, she still was more worried about him?

"Ah, lass, 'tis your health that concerns me most. We canna start a fire, and there is but only one thing we can do to warm us."

"We must stay close to share our heat," Anora said, holding Niall tight. Neither of them could quit shivering in the chilly, damp cave, their wet clothes clinging to them and making them even colder.

"We have to get out of our wet clothes and huddle together," Niall said, concerned with how pale her face was and how hard she was shivering. Though he was shaking just as much.

She attempted to unfasten the brooch clasped to her brat while he removed his plaid, then squeezed out the water. She only managed to prick her finger and drew blood. He quickly unfastened her brooch, wrung out her brat again, and laid it on top of his plaid to make a wet bed over the stone floor of the cave.

The place was dark except for the faint light from the stormy day beyond the cave. He could still see every bit of her body, the way her *léine* clung to her curves, her ripe nipples, the curve of her full breasts, the lay of her skirt between her legs.

When he reached out to help her with her gown, he

saw the distress in her expression right away.

"Nay, I cannot remove my *léine*," she said, her voice worried, a frown appearing across her brow.

"Lass—"

"Nay, I cannot," she said, sounding desperate.

"I mean only to warm you, naught more, Anora," Niall said, attempting to reassure her, but he worried she thought he meant to ravage her. "I willna have you die on me due to the cold because we havena done everything we could to prevent it."

She held his gaze and he was certain she understood how dangerous it was for her to resist the idea.

"Lass, tell me what you fear," he said, taking her chilled hands in his and holding them tight to reheat them. Not that he didn't know. She was an unmarried lass and if she'd only considered Matthew as a friend, she had probably never had a lover before.

She shook her head again.

Niall wasn't going to argue with her. He had to remove her wet clothes, and then they'd snuggle in an attempt to thaw out. He took off his boots, and then her shoes. Hoping he wouldn't distress her too much with his nakedness, he pulled off his plaid and then he yanked off his tunic, and removed as much water from it as he could manage.

Her gaze dropped as she took in every inch of his naked body. She didn't seem shocked or afraid, more curious than anything. Which was a good thing as he didn't want to make her feel apprehensive.

"Now for you, Anora."

"Nay. I will be fine. Truly."

He reached down and untied her *léine*, allowing the hem to drop to the cave floor.

"Niall, I will be fine, really."

He didn't allow her any further argument, and lifted the *léine* up and over her head and tried to ignore the way her chemise clung to her, making it appear as though she wore nothing at all.

He quickly turned to squeeze the water from the fabric away from their makeshift bedding, and then added the gown to the rest of their clothing. Then he slipped the sopping wet chemise off next, wrung it out, and quickly tossed it on the bedding so he could close the distance between them. Having noticed her gaze focused on his body, he had to fight a smile—when he was trying his damnedest not to look every bit of her over—right before he noticed she wore the torque he had offered her. Pleased beyond compare, he pulled her into his arms and hugged her in a tight embrace.

"A man should not be with a woman close like this when she is… she is… not married to him," she said, her teeth chattering from the cold.

"Shhh, Anora. 'Tis the only way we can warm each other the best we can if we are to survive. We do this only to keep from getting sick from being so cold."

Although he kept thinking how natural they were together, how much he wished it could be.

He began to rub her back, and she did the same to him, her ice cold fingers warming against his skin, her breasts and torso and legs pressed against him, heating his front.

He worried his body wouldn't behave despite being

chilled to the bone once she was rubbing her body against his. He feared he'd scare her off. But no matter how he couldn't control his arousal, he couldn't let her back away, either. They needed this intimacy—though he kept telling himself it wasn't so much intimacy as a necessary condition. Yet, it went way beyond that for him. Ever since the wild shepherdess had poked him in the back with her pitchfork, he'd wanted her—wanted to play with her, wanted—this.

Not in a cold, damp cave, however. Her bed would have been preferable.

But he didn't want her to fear him or his intentions.

She continued to rub his back vigorously up and down just to the tip of his spine, and he wanted to tell her his arse was cold, too. He smiled as he rested his head against the top of hers, alternating from rubbing her arms to rubbing her back, and then continued lower.

She paused.

"Dinna stop, lass," he whispered against her head. The moment she quit touching him, his skin grew icy again. "'Tis like rubbing your hands together on a cold winter's day. Dinna you feel better also?"

She snorted and he chuckled.

"I suppose you wish me to... rub you lower also, aye?" she asked, a hint of a smile in her voice, though she was still shivering. Her hair was wet, the cave cold, and her skin still moist.

"Aye, lass," he said.

She moved her hands lower, tentatively, then feeling his arse was ice cold—her hands hot against his bare skin, she began to rub vigorously. "You are so icy."

"Aye. Did you think I wished your hands there for some other reason?" He tried to sound serious, but he was afraid she could hear the humor in his voice as much as he was smiling.

"I distinctly remember you telling me when we first met that if I was not careful, I could wake the dragon from its sleep."

He smiled. Oh, aye, he was well awake—her sweet body rubbing against him, guaranteeing that.

"I have nearly finished with you there. Where else do you wish me to warm you?" she asked.

He didn't think she would like to hear his answer.

"Your arms?" she asked.

"Nay. I wish to continue rubbing your skin, and keep our bodies close to share the heat at the same time," he said.

"Oh, Niall," she said, choking back a sob.

"Lass, we are all right for the moment. What troubles you?" He couldn't stand to hear her so distressed.

"A puppy...," she said, nestling her head against Niall's chest.

He smiled. "She is safe with Gunnolf."

Anora looked up at him, her teary expression full of disbelief. "You found her?"

"Aye, I witnessed them take you and saw the puppy the knight tore from your arms. I feared you would attack the man, and I would have to fight all five knights at once."

She smiled through her tears. "Oh, Niall." She wrapped her arms around his neck, her breasts pressed against his body, which quickly reacted to her in a much too interested way.

He chided himself for his body's response to hers when they only needed to reheat their chilled bodies and maintain some sense of decorum.

"Where is Gunnolf, Charlie? Your horses? The puppy?" she asked, sounding worried, but he was glad she was able to think clearly as frozen as she'd been. Her gaze was on his, and then lowered to his lips. He thought she wished to kiss him but was afraid to initiate the kiss.

"Safe, I hope. Matthew is with them," he said, hating to mention him at a time like this, but he had to let her know he had joined forces with them, helping them to find her. Did she truly care for Matthew more than as a friend?

Anora's eyes widened. "Matthew?"

"Aye. He said he was looking for you and knows I am no' your cousin. But I fear he isna a warrior."

She let out a ragged breath. "I cannot believe he is traveling with you. He found me with the French knights and the baroness—did you know about that?"

"Aye, lass. I overheard them speaking. And then Matthew intended to follow them when he spied me listening in. Then he joined us. He said he will marry you." Niall studied Anora's response, hoping that she would not like that Matthew still thought to marry her.

When she pursed her lips, her eyes narrowing, Niall smiled and hugged her closer. The Lowland Scot did not have a chance with the lass.

CHAPTER 15

The damp chill in the air was not as noticeable now as Niall's hard, hot body warmed Anora's. She had never touched a man so intimately. Or seen one as naked as Niall. She should have acted like an embarrassed maid, looking shyly away when she saw him, but she couldn't. Not when he was so beautiful.

Not just on the outside either. He was beautiful inside. After learning he had saved the puppy just because she had tried to take care of it—she loved him for it. How could she find anyone who was as protective of her and as kind as he had been to her?

Even though he had tied her up to her chair the first day they'd met. But if she'd not fought him, she assumed he would have been honorable and kept her with him on her bed, slept after having been injured so, and would not have done anything more than that.

Rubbing against him was a different story—knowing

her body was reacting to his and his was reacting to hers. She kept telling herself it was necessary so they wouldn't die from the cold. That Niall's fever could return. That she could become just as ill. Yet, telling herself these things did nothing to lessen the discomfiture. And the intrigue of it all. She wanted to feel more than his body touching hers. She wanted to feel what it would be like for a man to love a woman.

"Matthew is still saying he will marry me, even though he must know I slept with a man who is not my cousin?" Anora took a deep settling breath. Everyone would know the truth once she returned home. If she could return home. Again, she felt badly about abandoning her cottage, her garden, and her sheep. She didn't want to bring up the tavern keeper's daughter's story. What if the girl had made the whole thing up?

"Aye." Niall must have seen the question in Anora's gaze. What was to become of her? "I dinna care who you truly are, Anora. I couldna help being attracted to you from the very first—envious when I thought Matthew had stolen your heart and hopeful when I learned he had not. I still dinna know what the consequences could be if I wed you, lass, but if you would have a husband who is an orphan with nothing to his name and who is cousin to two Highland lairds, would you have him?"

Anora was trying not to feel embarrassed to the tip of her frozen toes as she rubbed against the Highland warrior not her husband in an attempt to warm them both. Yet, it felt right somehow, the way he had protected her and saved her life. The way he had come to rescue her from an unknown danger when he had not even known who she was. She loved how they could converse, and he didn't even mind her storytelling. Most of all, she loved this—the feel of his hard body against hers, the way he tried to warm her without insisting they take this further than was prudent. And now, he was offering to marry her?

And the manner in which he did so. She suspected men did not normally offer to marry a woman while both were completely naked.

Niall was warm and caring and so gallant. She had no idea what lay ahead for her in the future. How could she agree to marry him when he and his clan might have to deal with the drastic consequences of such an action?

Yet... She rested her head against his chest again, glad to hear his heart beating stronger, faster, louder—unlike it had when they had been so very cold at first. "If I were only a shepherdess..."

"Then 'tis an aye," he said, and lifted her chin to kiss her. As if she were still only a shepherdess and that had sealed the bargain.

"*If*..." she said, about to remind him of their precarious predicament, but he kissed her instead.

She was still shivering, as chilly and damp as the cave was, and her hair was still wet, though they'd finally rubbed each other's skin dry, and the stroking and the snuggling had warmed her significantly.

She realized then her lips had been cold—but no longer. Her whole body heated, as he held her tight against him, his mouth brushing hers, then pressing, his tongue licking her lips, and then seeking entrance. She didn't know a man and woman kissed like that, though she eagerly wanted to share the experience.

She tried to ignore the way he was so aroused, the way his nipples were hard as pebbles just as hers were, even the way she ached between her legs for a man's touch. How could she when they were not married?

But she ignored all the self-doubts and kissed him back, her arms wrapped around his body, her mouth pressing against his. And then he stroked her tongue with his. Startled, she glanced up at him. He was looking down at her, his eyes darkened with desire. She kissed him again, and wanted everything he was willing to offer her—whatever an orphan who was cousin to two lairds had—and if it wasn't much, they had Charlie and a new puppy, and she could be a shepherdess again.

Niall's hand was on her lower back, keeping her against him as he licked her lips, and then kissed her mouth again. His hand was sweeping up and down her back, his other holding the back of her head so she wouldn't melt on the rock floor. Then he finally broke off the kiss.

And she thought he was going to tell her they needed to stop before they went too far, when she didn't want him to stop. She hardly noticed the chill.

"I want you for my own, Anora," Niall said, looking down at her, his expression serious, full of craving.

But could she agree to this? What if she put him and his family in the gravest of danger? And yet, she wanted him and wanted this union. Was she mad? "But what if—"

"You are the one for me, lass. 'Tis all I need to know." And then he kissed her again, and she gave into the momentary madness, wanting his kisses, and his love, even if it could never come to pass. She'd been alone for so long, she hadn't realized just how lonely she had been.

For one moment in time, he was hers and she was his.

"If you agree to be my wife, Anora, 'tis all we need to do to be married," Niall said, very seriously, his hands shifting to her shoulders, rubbing, still holding her close to keep the chill out.

Her lips parted in surprise. He was that earnest?

"By the Highland ways," she said. "I have heard of such a thing."

"And?"

She smiled a little at him. "You are really, truly resolute in this, Niall?"

"I have never been more serious in my life, lass. A man doesna ask a lassie such unless he means what he says."

"But what of my French family?"

"You were lost to them many years ago. Unless you wish to return to that way of life?"

"Nay, I would not know it. I can imagine how people would treat me. I would be considered the noblewoman who served as a shepherdess all her life. I do not think the notion would be well received."

He smiled down at her then. "I could think of no one I would rather marry than a sweet lassie, who wields my own claymore against my Viking friend and a pitchfork against me, who is the loveliest shepherdess I have ever chanced to meet."

She smiled at him.

"If you wish to wait though..."

Again, she couldn't help the startled response to his suggestion. Did he... did he mean to bed her in the cave?

"We can wait, but we may be warmer if we dinna," he prompted.

She laughed. "You may be right, but I suspect only a man would think in such a way."

He smiled down at her. "Are you agreeable?"

She took a deep breath and nodded. "But what about your cousin? What if he is not agreeable to your marrying me? What if my family causes trouble for him and your clan?"

"You are a shepherdess, lass, and my wife—*since you have agreed*—and naught more." With that last comment, he pulled her brat from the rest of their damp clothes, then he took her hand and led her to their damp-garment bed.

As soon as Anora lay down on the cold, wet clothes, she shivered.

"Are you going to be all right, lass? Do the clothes pad the floor well enough for you? You could sleep on top of me, but I wished to warm you with my body and with you being on top, you would be colder."

"The bed is fine, Niall," she said, getting colder the longer he stood there talking about it. She wanted him to hurry and warm her.

"I dinna intend to sleep right way," he warned, as he covered her with his body and then pulled her damp brat over them.

She shivered, partly from the cold and partly with expectation of what making love to Niall would be like. "Aye," she said, and wrapped her arms around his neck, pulling him down to kiss her.

His mouth on hers was slow and easy at first, his tongue gently pursuing hers in a kind of sword play. Their lips met and they both smiled. She loved the way he kissed her between being sweet and passionate.

And then he moved off her a bit as if he wasn't going to make love to her, and instantly she began to feel chilled from the loss of his body heat and anxious that he wanted to wait. Until he began to stroke her between her legs, touching her in a special spot, making her arch and moan and want more, and yet wanting the sweet pain of pleasure to end.

Her body was on fire, his tongue licking her lips and then driving inside her mouth, just as he inserted his finger between her legs. She was shocked at the intimacy and more so at her response as her body pressed against his finger wanting him deeper. Wanting more.

A hot wash of pleasure rushed through her like she'd never known before. She was still trembling with excitement from the experience when he moved her legs apart with his knee and centered himself on her.

She knew it would hurt. Jane had told her so. Anora braced for the pain, but then Niall began to caress her breasts that felt so heavy and achy, and she luxuriated in the feel of his touch. He kissed her lips, making her forget all about his ready staff.

He entered her. She felt his hot flesh fill her—so big, yet he continued to caress her, kiss her, trying to take her mind off any discomfort she experienced. His tenderness touched her.

Then he began to thrust deep inside her. She forgot how cold she was, that they were in a cave making love for the very first time, and that men were trying to hunt her down, and send her far away. All she thought of now was of Niall, his pleasuring her, and how much she loved him.

Niall felt Anora tense right before he entered her and suspected John's sister had warned her what to expect when she first made love to her husband. But thankfully, Anora had relaxed enough that he could penetrate her without causing too much pain, he thought.

She began rocking against him, and he couldn't have been hotter or harder or more than eager to please her. He loved the way she was making their joining so much more memorable. Yet, he hated to take her in this manner—in a chilly, semi-dark cave, on a rock hard floor—yet, he couldn't deny that the friction between them heated him through and through. And he hoped it was doing the same for her.

Her bucking against him was unexpected and made the experience all the more pleasurable. He had envisaged she'd just lie there quietly—until she was more used to him, and they could experiment further later. He kissed her mouth, their tongues mating, their lips pressing together afterwards, hungry for more.

He felt the end coming too soon—he'd wanted this with her for far too long—and held on, wanting to stay inside her for as long as possible. Thrusting over and over again. And then he exploded inside her.

She smiled as he bathed her womb with his hot seed.

He pumped into her again and again until she had milked him thoroughly. Sated to the point of satisfaction, he lay half on top of her to keep her warm, and half off her so he wouldn't press too much of his weight against her. But like he had said, he wanted to be the one on top to keep her warmer as the chilly air surrounded them. He hugged her tight, loving the feel of her soft body in his embrace, thinking how much better this would be once they reached Craigly Castle and he snuggled with her on his down mattress.

"*Is tú mo ghrá*, Anora," Niall said, kissing her cheek. "You are my love."

"You will always have my love, Niall of the Clan MacNeill. Always," Anora said.

"And mine," Niall said, hating where he'd had to do this, but pleased she had agreed to be his wife.

Anora didn't think she could sleep since she couldn't quit thinking about the way Niall had made love to her—how wondrous he had made her feel—and wondered how long before they could do it again.

For a while, they just shivered together until their bodies warmed each other enough, the brat keeping some of the heat in, but she was still too cold to sleep. And she wanted to know more about Niall, wishing she'd taken the time to ask him more before this. Not that she thought she'd change her mind. 'Twas too late anyway.

"Tell me about your family, Niall." It wasn't an idle question either. If she had to live with Niall's family, she wished to know what she was getting herself into.

"My da died in a skirmish with a neighboring clan when I was eight. My mother died the following summer of a fever. Losing my father was difficult enough. He had been the one to teach me how to live off the land, hunt, and fight. He wasna a tender man—but a warrior through and through. But when my mother died, I was... angry. She had been so good to me, loving me, defending me when I couldna defend myself."

Anora stroked his arm and kissed his head resting on her chest. It seemed odd for him to be nestled against her breasts, but it kept her warmer than if he lay by her side. She thought about Niall's mother and father and wished that she'd had even that much time to have spent with her own when she was little.

"I was angry at the world," Niall continued, his warm breath tickling her breast. "Angry that my cousins had each other and a mother who adored them. Their father was another matter. But enough said about the dead. I didna want to live with my cousins as their brother or have my aunt replace my mother's affection. This is not to say I didn't care for her or my cousins. I did. But you see... I couldn't give up my mother just yet."

"I am so sorry, Niall. But I completely understand."

He kissed her breast and she smiled.

"They were so good to me, lass, when I was too angry to want their kindness. No' to say my cousins coddled me. James, the eldest, straightened me out many a time."

"Nay."

"Aye, but I well deserved it. I told my aunt she wasna my mother and couldna tell me what to do during one of my numerous outbursts. Shortly after my mother's death, I had attempted to push everyone away. But you see, she *could* tell me what to do because she was the lady of the keep and because she was my guardian. James and I fought in the inner bailey that time, his younger brothers watching, but not interfering. James held his punches because he was so much older than me, whereas I didna. I was too angry and would have fought the whole world if need be." Niall sighed.

"He understood, did he not?"

"Aye. He is a good leader of men. It wasna too many years after that when he was still a lad that his da, our laird, died, and James took over the leadership. He was voted in by all the clan—he is that well-loved. I have always tried to emulate him, truth be told. Though if you told him thus, I will deny it to my dying day."

She chuckled. "He sounds like he is a good laird." Which relieved her mightily.

"Aye, he is. I gave him a black eye and all he did was laugh. He allowed me a few more punches, but his laughing curbed my urge to strike him all that hard. 'Twas more that I couldna give up the fight with so many others watching. I couldna be seen as weak. And then James knocked me on my arse and told me not to get up, if I knew what was good for me. I saw then, he had to prove a point to the rest of the clan and to me. I needed to change my ways—to accept that my aunt would now be like my mother—that my cousins were now like the brothers I never had. He held out his hand, and I accepted his friendship, and later, I secretly apologized to my aunt."

Anora wiped away tears. She couldn't help it. She really loved the boy that had been so lost. She loved the man he had become. "She loved you, did she not? Just like she loved her sons?"

"Aye." Niall was silent for several heartbeats, then he said, "She actually hugged me to her breast and wept."

Anora smiled.

"I was afraid James would learn that I made her cry, and I didn't want to make her sad, so I said the only thing I could think of to make her quit crying, 'You are getting me all wet, my lady.'"

Anora chuckled. She could just imagine his aunt comforting her orphaned nephew and how his words had affected her. How, if she had been his aunt, they would have affected Anora.

"She laughed, a tearful laugh. But then she looked down at me and gave me another warm hug and said, 'I love you, Niall, as I always have, even when your dear mother was alive. I love you like one of my sons, and none of that has changed. If any give you grief and James doesna take care of the matter to your satisfaction—come to me, and I will.'"

"Did you? Have to see her?"

"Nay, 'tis no' a warrior's way. I fought my own battles and except for that one last time, James and I never came to blows again."

She shook her head. "Men."

"What about you, Anora?"

She sighed. "I never really knew my mother. She died when I was just an infant and I was raised by nannies. I barely remember my father, either. Except that he was on the ship with me. He was never around much. Some say 'twas because of the fall I had suffered that I have so few earlier memories. I remember the accident, and my uncle telling me stories afterwards, but I do not remember a whole lot before that happened. I would have loved to have had family like you have. Though, John and his sister, Jane, treated me like their own."

"Anora, you have never once called them your mother and father, though they raised you as such."

"I thought of them that way, but they warned me that I was someone important, and I could never call either of them my parents. Besides, it would have been awkward to call John my father and Jane my mother when they were brother and sister. When she first brought me home, John was angry, fearing the French would swoop down and kill him and his sister for taking me in. And likewise, the English. He took Jane into the sleeping room and shut the door and though his voice was low and angry, I heard what he said while listening with my ear to the door, when I was supposed to be asleep by the fire."

Niall shook his head. "You were willful even when you were six."

"Oh, aye. John was so angry that his sister had taken me in, that when he took the sheep to pasture and his sister planted in the garden early the next morn—while I was supposed to be raking the byre with the pitchfork that was so much bigger than me—I ran away."

"Anora," Niall said softly.

"I... I did not get away."

"'Tis a good thing that."

"Aye. I thought that John did not want me there. That he was afraid that harm would come to him and his sister.

237

But their dog, Whiskers, grandsire to Charlie, came and tried to corral me home. He acted so viciously, nipping at my heels and snapping his jaws at me whenever I tried to make a move further away from the direction of the cottage, that I could not make any headway. He kept barking and growling and scared me half to death. Yet, the night before while I slept beside the hearth, he had curled up next to me as if I was one of his puppies."

Niall kissed her skin. "He was taking care of you like you were one of his lost lambs."

"Aye, but I did not know that at the time. He grabbed hold of my *léine* and started to tug. I tugged right back. He was determined, and so was I. So, there we were, me holding onto my skirt, trying to get loose of his grip, and him tugging and shaking his head as he tried to pull me with him. I never had been around dogs like that before. My family used them for hunting, naught more. I was never allowed to play with them. Then John dashed through the woods and witnessed how far I had run away and saw Whiskers and the way he wasn't letting me go."

"Ah, Anora, you couldna have known how precious you truly were to them."

"I did not think so at the time. John looked horrified. I thought that meant the dog was going to kill me. I burst into tears, and John yelled at Whiskers to let go of me and he did, instantly. And then John lifted me in his arms, and I thought I heard him crying. But I have never heard a grown man cry. So I did not know what to think."

Niall laughed. "Ah, lass, I can see where you could make any grown man cry, given the right circumstances."

She smiled up at him. "Not you."

He kissed her throat, but didn't say either aye or nay. "So then he talked to you and said you were to stay with him and his sister."

"Nay. His sister was so shook up, she was furious with him when we arrived back at the cottage, Whiskers was bouncing around all of us. She made John sleep in the byre for three whole days. I was not sure about Whiskers, after the way he acted toward me in the woods. But when he curled up next to me beside the hearth, I realized he was just taking care of me. After that, John never said another word about me living with them or not. But Jane constantly worked with me so that I would speak only English and no more French. When she died, I grieved terribly. John and I lived together for several more years before he passed on. I truly loved them dearly."

"Sometimes all we have is a short period of time to love those who love us, and we must make the most of it while we can. 'Tis easy to forget that when we are so busy doing whatever we need to do."

"Aye, 'tis true, Niall."

"So, they told you stories?"

"Aye."

"And now you tell them." Niall snuggled closer to her. "Tell me, how did you learn to swim?"

She thought she heard a hint of concern in his voice and wondered why. "Have you ever made up a tale that made a story sound better than the truth?"

Niall laughed. "Mayhap the fish I caught was smaller than the one I bragged about, you mean? The one that got away?"

"Aye, like that. Did you truly tell a story like that?" Somehow she couldn't believe Niall would make up stories. He hadn't so far with her.

"Once or twice. So tell me how you learned to swim."

"There was a young girl, who when she was not doing her chores, which were considerable, liked to play along the edge of the loch. But John and his sister oft told her not to go near the water. Have you ever done anything your elders told you not to do?"

"Often," Niall said.

She suspected as much. What child could resist? "Do you know how tempting the water is on a hot summer's day? Ducks were paddling across the loch, white clouds drifting overheard, reflecting off the blue waters. A yellow and black winged butterfly fluttered nearby. Then Whiskers ran straight for the loch, and into it, until he was swimming, trying to chase the ducks. I watched him for some time, then figured if he could do it, I could also. I stripped off everything but my chemise, intending to stay near the water's edge, just leaning over to get wet to cool myself. But the shore dropped off, and I was suddenly over my head.

"Matthew heard me screaming and came to my aid. He stripped off his boots and tunic, and dove in. And after that, he taught me how to swim."

"For that, I am grateful," Niall said, stroking Anora's hair.

But Anora thought she heard a hint of disapproval in his voice. "Aye, or I would never have escaped my French escort," she reminded him.

She and Matthew had been young when he taught her how to swim. She had been ten, and he—two and ten. Did Niall believe she had swum with Matthew so indecently much later? She explained how old they had been, not wanting him to believe she had done so recently.

"And later?" Niall asked.

She sighed. Niall *had* thought she had swum with Matthew when they were older. She really couldn't fault him for being concerned though.

"Nay. I learned to swim—I am a quick learner—and then I went in when I knew Matthew would not be around. First, we had fun. But then John caught me swimming with Matthew and told Jane. She warned me what could happen between girls and boys, since Matthew was older than me, and that was the last I went into the water with him."

"Aye," Niall said. "Even though I am certain Matthew would have been most honorable at first, the challenge would have been there had the water play continued as you grew older. I would have liked to have swum with you on a hot summer's day."

"I bet you would."

He chuckled.

Then she wondered how it would have been if Niall had been the one to teach her how to swim. "What would you have been like?" she asked.

"If I had been there instead of Matthew?"

"Aye. You are the most honorable of men." He had been all along. She could not see Niall in any other way.

"We would have wed by the time we were old enough

to."

She laughed. She loved how he could take a serious subject and add humor to it. "I think I would have liked it if you could have been the one to teach me to swim."

"As enticing as you are to be with—I am certain I would have taught you much more."

***

The rains had stopped, though the water continued to roll off the cliffs like a light waterfall. Both of them still naked, Niall had covered Anora with most of his body, and they had slept the night away on top of their damp clothes as husband and wife. He could not have been more pleased that she had agreed to be his wife. But something in the predawn light had awakened him. Some noise that seemed to deviate from the natural rhythm of the river or the rainfall still dripping off the cliffs. Now he listened carefully as he moved off Anora, trying to clarify what had caught his ear.

She quickly rose to her feet and lifted her damp chemise off the stone floor of the cave and pulled it over her head. Then she hurried to dress in her *léine*, as Niall quickly dressed.

The river flowed down below, but something else had caught his attention. Splashing. In the water. Fish? Or man? *Bloody hell.*

If it wasn't Gunnolf or Matthew, Niall knew he'd be in for a fight.

CHAPTER 16

Niall quickly donned his clothes and helped fasten Anora's brooch to her brat. She pulled the wool over her head to form a hood, and was already trembling from the cold and dampness in the cave, their clothes still uncomfortably clammy.

A couple of rocks slid down the cliff below the cave. Someone was climbing up the granite rock face. To see if Anora was here?

Cian's men? Or the Frenchmen?

"Do you have a *sgian dubh* I can use?" she whispered to Niall, as he remained focused on the cave entrance. "They took mine from me."

He glanced back at Anora, saw her sweet face in the early morning light, looking worried but determined to aid him. He reached down to retrieve his and arm her with it but it was not there. Angry at losing it, he cursed under his breath. "I must have lost mine in the river." He'd only managed to keep his sword.

He reminded himself that those coming for her didn't want her dead. Though if she'd had a pitchfork, she could have kept at least one man at bay until Niall could protect her.

He studied the cave and wondered what his best battle tactic would be. He could fight the intruders at the mouth of the cave, having the advantage of being above those who were climbing to reach them. But if several scaled the cliff all at once, they could easily overwhelm him. And then Anora would be at risk of capture.

"Mayhap there is another way out—a tunnel through the cave," he whispered to Anora.

"I will see," she said, as he watched her, still listening to whoever was climbing up the rock face to monitor their progress.

Anora walked toward the back of the cave until the darkness engulfed her, and then he could hear her light footfalls as she carefully made her way into the blackness. She virtually disappeared, and he thought they might be able to hide there, but he didn't like that he couldn't see her. Then she headed back, materializing out of the darkness.

"There could be dangerous pots deeper in the cave. Without some light to aid us, we could fall into one," she whispered.

"Aye. We will move into the shadows and watch and wait. I could not see even a hint of you as you moved deeper into the cave." Niall edged his way back with Anora, being careful to ensure every step he took met with solid rock, while he ushered her into the darkening gloom. It appeared the cave continued for some distance, maybe even led to a tunnel, but Anora was correct. Without a source of light, it was too dark to navigate and could be much too dangerous.

Niall unsheathed his sword. He did wish he could fight whoever attempted to climb the cliff before they could reach for their weapons. With their hands gripping the rocks, they wouldn't have a chance to fight back. But if he fought and killed them, would whosoever had sent them send more? Unless, the others waiting for them thought these men had been lost to the treacherously cold river. Surely, not all of the men could swim, and Niall didn't believe all who would attempt it would manage to reach the cave before the swiftly-flowing burn swept some of the men on past.

Still, Niall didn't want to chance being overwhelmed if several came over the lip of the cave entrance at the same time. If a man studied the blackness deeper in the cave, he couldn't see Anora or Niall if they hid there and mayhap the brigand would report she was not here.

In the early morning light, a man's head crested the floor of the cave—his hair wild, wet, and red. As he made the rest of the way up, Niall identified him as one of Cian's men. The very same man who had nearly killed Niall and left him for dead, a pale scar running along his cheek and angling toward his chin. Green eyes narrowed as he studied the dark recesses, and though Niall knew the villain couldn't see them, he still felt as though he could, his skin crawling with trepidation. Not for himself—but with worrying that if he couldn't hold these men back, Anora would be vulnerable.

Anora was at Niall's back, standing close enough to him, he felt the warmth radiating from her. He wanted her to stand farther away from him in the event he had to fight.

More rocks slid down the cliff. Another man was coming, maybe even more. The man Niall had fought earlier stayed where he was, waiting for reinforcements. The brigand continued to stare at the black cave when someone down below cursed in Gaelic. Another of Cian's men. Mayhap the devil himself. Though Niall didn't believe Cian would swim in the chilly water to find the lass. Most likely, he would wait on shore for them to bring her to him.

Niall wasn't certain how anyone would accomplish it. Even Niall wasn't sure how he'd get Anora out of here and avoid the Frenchmen or Cian's men who were probably searching for her downriver.

Niall readied his sword. He would kill every last one of them before any of them could touch Anora.

Two more sopping wet men reached the cave and stared in Niall and Anora's direction. "Can you see her, Tagan?" a golden-haired man asked.

"Nay, but she could well be hiding back there." Tagan motioned to the black cave. "We didna see a body floating down the river. Unless the men found her farther down after we returned to search for her in the cave, she has to be here."

A darker-haired man snorted. "Think you the lass could have withstood the cold, made it to the shore, and then climbed all the way up into the cave? Bah."

"Come out of there, lass," Tagan said, as if he knew she was there. "No harm will come to you. You are too valuable to us."

They waited. Anora moved closer to Niall, her breasts touching his back. He wanted to tell her to get back against a wall, but he was afraid they might hear her footfalls.

"You dinna want to make us come for you," Tagan said, his voice more of a warning now.

The men's swords were still sheathed. Were there more down below, or just these three?

"We know you helped the Highlanders escape—the ones we were hunting, lass. Our clansmen, who searched your croft, had left by the time we had arrived," Tagan called out. "You told Cian that they had gone north. But later, we found our men—dead—and nearby, their horses were grazing in a pasture several miles in the opposite direction, due *south* of your croft. Most telling? Two of the horses were missing. The ones belonging to the two Highlanders that we had been searching for. Mere coincidence, lass? We think not."

So how would they explain that he and Gunnolf had stolen *their* horses when they belonged to Niall and his friend in the first place? The man had dug a hole for himself on that one. Unless he assumed the lass knew the right of it already, which was why she had protected Niall.

Anora touched Niall's back. He reached behind him, and ran his hand over her hip in silent reassurance.

The men continued to observe the darkness, listening for movement, delaying a response. Niall grew weary of this—waiting and watching—though he would do anything to keep the lass safe. And if that meant staying still to postpone fighting these men, he'd do it. But he'd so much prefer killing them and finding a way out of their predicament before others arrived en masse.

"They will send more men if we dinna return soon. Shouldna we do something?" the darkest haired man said, glancing in Tagan's direction.

Niall had been certain of it and he and Anora could not stay here forever.

"Aye. We canna take all day," Tagan said. Then he folded his arms and spoke again to Anora, as if he knew she was hiding in the black cave, "Did you know that one of your kinsmen was discovered to be one of King Philip's spies? King Henry had him hanged. Rumors abound that others who were with him—the same ones that you ran away from—are plotting with King Henry's brother, Robert Curthose, Duke of Normandy. Did you know the duke has asked for King Philip's aid, since the king of the Franks is his liege lord, to aid in Robert's fighting his brother, Henry? 'Tis no' safe for you here any longer, should the king locate you and your kinsmen."

Tagan glanced at the other men, as if seeing whether they thought he should continue. Or whether it was worth his breath if the lass wasn't even there.

They nodded to him.

"We will protect you and see you to a ship bound for your homeland, lass. The French knights will be slaughtered before they ever reach a port, and you with them—as everyone will assume you are as much a spy as them. More so, mayhap, as you have been secretly living among the people of the village of Banbh all this time. And who better to use as a spy than one who had befriended the people all these years, grown up with them, pretending she was one of them. 'Tis said you have made several excursions into England, gathering information for Robert Curthose and King Phillip."

Niall wondered if Tagan spoke any truth at all. Though it was true that Henry and his brother, Robert, were at war again. And the King of the Franks was the Norman duke's liege lord. But the part concerning Anora's kin, that's what he was concerned about. Not that she would have anything to do with any of it. She would never have abandoned her sheep to do such.

Tagan moved forward then, still not removing his sword, most likely believing if the lass were here, she had to be alone. Anora stayed close behind Niall as the other men joined Tagan, though as they approached the blackness, they slowed their steps.

"I wish we had a torch," the quieter golden-haired man said.

"Aye, spread out, wave your hands about, and see if you can find her," Tagan said.

Niall reached back and touched Anora, in a silent way telling her to move more toward the cave wall if she could. With her still at his back, together, they carefully stepped away from the men as they approached. But Niall's foot swept over a loose rock as he took another step. It moved. His heart stuttered, and he barely breathed. The sound of the rock's movement was slight, a clicking of rock against rock, and the men's footsteps were heavy, so he hoped the noise they made had covered his.

Yet they all stopped walking, and Niall was certain they had heard him.

"Did you hear that?" the dark-haired man asked.

"Aye, over there, to our left," Tagan said.

They all hurried in that direction.

Anora seized Niall's arm and pulled at him to move across the cave in a hurry. Their footsteps were virtually silent as the other men tromped in the direction Niall and Anora had been only moments before.

The men were to Niall's right still, heading for the cave wall when Niall heard footfalls behind him. He turned and peered into the blackness, but couldn't see a thing. Anora had stayed behind him, her hand touching his tunic as if to reassure herself Niall was still standing there with her, or to confirm to him that she had not made the noise. The other men were still to his right, but as soon as they heard the footfalls in the back of the cave, the men all headed that way.

"You canna escape us, lass. 'Tis only a matter of time before we find you. Make it easy on us and come out from your hiding place, or we will make you pay for the trouble you are causing," Tagan ground out.

A scuffling sound ensued as Niall tried to determine what was happening. Until one of the men screamed out in terror, sending chills up Niall's spine. The man's frightened screams grew fainter, disappearing, as if the granite had swallowed him up.

"There is a pot over there!" Tagan said, sounding just as alarmed. "Watch your step, mon," he said to his remaining companion.

The notion chilled Niall to the core, thinking Anora might have made a misstep when she had explored the black cave earlier.

"We got to get out of here. Could be us next," the man said, almost pleading.

"Nay, we heard the lass in here. We have to keep looking. Cian will have our heads if we return and say she wasna here and he doesna believe us. He would send someone else, and if he found her, it wouldna go well for us," Tagan said.

"Aye," the other man said, but sounding disconcerted.

The two men moved quietly now, attempting not to make a sound so that if Anora heard them, she could avoid them. But also, they were being extra careful not to make the same mistake as their friend had.

Again, noise came from the back of the cave. Footfalls, Niall thought. But there was no light.

"'Tis haunted," the one man whispered.

"Nay, keep searching for the girl," Tagan said, growing nearer to Niall as the other man moved away.

Tagan was too close. Niall tried to move out of his path, but his foot bumped against rock outcroppings, blocking his route. Niall reached out to touch Anora, to ensure she was not in his weapon's path. She must have realized what he had to do. She moved away from him.

His muscles tight with tension, he readied to fight the man.

Tagan kicked a rock with his foot a few inches away and the stone hit Niall's boot. He prayed he could kill the man with one blow. Niall swung hard and struck into the blackness with as much force as he could—and connected with something solid.

Tagan cried out. Good. At least Niall had wounded the brigand. Niall stood tense, waiting for another sound that would betray Tagan's current location. He couldn't tell if he'd moved away, fallen, or what else might have happened.

"What?" the other man shouted, sounding terrified.

Then Tagan began breathing hard, his head lowered as if he was bending over, clutching his injury. He wasn't unsheathing his sword. Not yet. Probably trying to handle the pain Niall had dealt him, just as Niall had attempted to control his own when the bastard had sliced him.

"What?" the other man said again, his voice hushed now. He was much farther away, nearer the location where Niall and Anora had stood in the beginning. "What is wrong?"

Tagan slowly unsheathed his sword, either afraid to get struck again and was trying to be quiet about it, or having difficulty with the task. Before he could swing his weapon at his unseen assailant, Niall struck a second blow in the direction he surmised Tagan now stood.

Tagan cried out again, only this time, he stumbled toward the entrance of the cave to get away from his hidden attacker. In the early morning light, he collapsed to his knees near the entrance, holding his chest, his sword arm bloodied.

The other man was breathing heavy now, not saying a word, probably horrified that someone stood in the blackness, armed and deadly. Just waiting for him to approach. And that someone was most likely not the lassie.

Niall focused on where the other man had spoken in the dark, though he couldn't fathom where the other footfalls were coming from. They had stopped the moment Tagan had cried out in anguish.

A tunnel at the back of the cave? A way out of here? If whosoever they were had torches, Niall would fight them for the life-saving light. If he and Anora could slip out through a tunnel, mayhap they could reunite with Gunnolf and Matthew and be on their way before anyone else was the wiser.

He was ready to battle the remaining man, but only if he drew close to Niall's location. Niall wasn't about to chase him in the pitch black cave and risk being injured and unable to protect Anora, or tangle with the pot where the other man had fallen to his death.

Niall could no longer feel Anora nearby, and he wished to make a connection with her, if nothing more than to ensure he didn't swing at her, believing she was the other man.

Then someone made a mad dash for the cave entrance, the blond-haired man, his sword out. He got behind Tagan, still on his knees, leaning hard to his left, who looked ready to fall over.

"Can you make it, mon?" the man asked Tagan, his hand on his shoulder, his other gripping his sword.

Tagan shook his head and slumped onto his side against the stone floor.

"What... what should I do?" the man asked, but Tagan

didn't respond, and Niall suspected he had died of his wounds.

The man stared at the black cave for a moment, then said, "If the lass is with you, you can have her. I willna be returning here."

Niall didn't believe him. Well, mayhap this man wouldn't be returning, but he suspected he'd tell Cian what had happened, and more men would come. Niall's best hope was to fight those in the tunnel, and leave that way before more of Cian's men could arrive.

The man sheathed his sword in a hurry, then scrambled over the side as if he was afraid Niall would rush out of the cave and kill him while he was defenseless. Niall would have, fearing this man would tell Cian what had happened and create more of a problem for Niall and the lass. But he was still worried about the footfalls he had heard at the back of the cave some distance hence. And so he stayed put and whispered, "Anora?"

"Here," she whispered back, several feet away.

"Stay where you are," he said, talking in a hushed voice. "I think men are coming this way through a tunnel."

"Aye," she said, and he swore he heard her teeth chattering.

He wanted to envelope her in his arms, warm her, take care of her, but if he had to fight...

The footfalls began again in their direction, closer. A rock slid across the cave, and the footsteps stopped abruptly. Deathly quiet prevailed inside the cave, as outside, the river rushed by in its never-ending quest to reach the sea.

Niall narrowed his gaze, sure he saw the faintest glimmer of light at the back of the cave. Or was it just a trick of his eyes? No, there. Like a candle flickering in the dark abyss, so faint, it appeared to be nearly nonexistent.

"Do you see it?" Anora whispered.

"Aye," Niall said, in just as hushed a tone. "Can you move this way, toward me, lass? I want you behind me."

Her light footsteps were careful as she made her way to him. He held out his hand and encouraged her in whispered words to guide her. When he brushed her outstretched hand with his fingers, he took hold and pulled her into his embrace, thankful to have her close again. He couldn't help himself when he should have moved her behind him, but instead, he held her tight, felt her trembling from the cold and mayhap from fright. He kissed her cheek, and she slipped her arms around his waist and hugged him close.

"If we get out of this—" she said.

"*When* we get out of this," he said against her ear.

"Aye, I will stay with you if you can live with me and Charlie and the puppy—if my being with your clan does not cause trouble for you and your kin."

Despite their dire circumstances, he couldn't help but smile at her. "Aye, lass. You and Charlie and the puppy, though I suspect both have made fast friends with Gunnolf, too. We will make it happen." He wanted to mention that they were already husband and wife and so she would have to stay with her husband, but he kissed the top of her head instead.

She nodded against Niall's chest.

For some time, he held Anora close, sharing his body heat with her, welcoming hers as she warmed him, but then the footfalls and the light drew closer. She still clung to him, as if she didn't want to give him up.

"Lass," he whispered against her ear again, "move behind me."

"So cold," she said, then reluctantly released him and moved around him, her body pressed against his back.

Anora couldn't stop shivering from the cold of the cave and her still damp clothes or the fear that whoever was approaching would fight Niall.

The cave was so dark that she hadn't witnessed what Niall had done to Tagan—only heard the deadly swish of Niall's sword—or at least she had hoped it was Niall's, and not one of the brigand's—felt the air move near her as the blade sliced through it. She had quickly taken a couple more steps backward, heard Tagan cry out, and she prayed he couldn't fight back.

When he unsheathed his sword with an ominous woosh, she feared he'd swing it and injure Niall this time. Relief washed through her when she saw the man stumble toward the cave entrance. The other man's calling out had chilled her to the marrow of her bones, reminding her the danger was still near.

Now that the two men had died and the other had scrambled out of the cave, and if he managed to survive the trip down the river, he would warn Cian of what had happened. But whoever approached from the tunnels was the new trouble they had to deal with. Two footfalls were coming, she thought, one behind the other—if her ears hadn't betrayed her. 'Twas hard to tell the way they echoed lightly off the walls in the distance.

Then the oddest noise, like something scurrying, claws against the rocks, headed in her direction. Rats instantly came to mind, her skin chilling. Goose bumps quickly covered her arms.

And then she heard a hushed voice say, "Charlie, nay."

Charlie? Gunnolf?

CHAPTER 17

Charlie's nails clicked on the rock floor in a rush. Before Anora could brace herself, he jumped against her legs in excitement, licking her hands and nipping at them. She was so happy to hug him, unable to see him, but she could envision him from memory.

"Gunnolf?" Niall quickly called out.

"*Ja!* We are coming."

Praise God.

"Take care! A pot is near the center of the cave. There may be more. We canna see." Niall moved closer to Anora, and Charlie stopped licking her and bumping against her to greet Niall.

He chuckled, and she felt Niall brush her body as he leaned down to pet Charlie. "Do you have the puppy?" She shouldn't have asked. How could the Viking have carried a puppy all the way here with him, and why would he want to?

"She is tucked in my tunic, sound asleep. I think she believes I am her mother," Gunnolf said.

Anora smiled and couldn't wait to have her in her arms again. Though she hadn't even thought of a name to call her. Then she had it. Zara. French, for little princess.

"How did you learn of the tunnel?" Niall asked, as they waited for Gunnolf and Matthew to make their appearance.

Her eyes followed the progress of the light wavering as it grew brighter the closer the men got to the mouth of the tunnel that led into the cave.

"Matthew said he and a few friends used to explore these caves in their youth," Gunnolf said.

Then the light grew closer and Gunnolf walked out of the narrow tunnel at the back of the cave, his blond bearded face awash in the dim light of the ancient rosity roots burning as a torch.

Anora wanted to wrap her arms around them both, relieved beyond measure that he and Matthew were safe and had found another way out of here for them. She had feared she'd never make it if she'd had to swim in the icy burn when she was certain the Frenchmen and the other Highlanders waited for her downriver.

Gunnolf glanced in the direction of the dead man.

"Tagan, the clansman who wounded me and left me for dead," Niall said, as Gunnolf offered them both dry brats.

"'Tis good he didna have me to deal with also. Let us leave at once," Gunnolf said, as Matthew joined them, carrying another torch.

"Anora," Matthew said, and made a step toward her as

if to hug her, stopped suddenly, and she was certain the feral look on Niall's face made him change his mind.

"Come, we must go before anyone discovers our horses," Gunnolf said. "They are well hidden in a cave at the end of a maze of tunnels, but if they make any sound, someone may discover them. 'Tis good that Matthew knew his way through here, or we would never have reached you."

"Aye, we are very glad to see you," Anora said.

"I am pleased to see you both made it here. We couldna be sure, until we saw some of Cian's men return to the mouth of the canyon and begin the swim to locate the lass. So we assumed they had not located her downriver," Gunnolf said.

"How many men does he have?" Niall asked, helping to refasten her brooch to the dry brat.

Gunnolf cleared his throat. "About a dozen that we counted."

"Two less," Niall said, "if the three who came after her were part of that number."

"Aye, they were. I saw only one dead man. The other?" Gunnolf asked.

"He fell through the pot in the cave floor," Niall said, walking behind Anora as they made their way through the cold dampness in the tunnel.

But she already felt much warmer with the dry brat around her, having removed the damp one and placed it on the outside of the other. Still, she could have used a warm shelter and a raging fire to really chase away the chill. And something hot to eat.

They were quiet for a long time as she followed behind Gunnolf. Sore from making love with Niall, she was eager to be in a safe place where she and Niall could snuggle in a warm, and much softer bed. She could envision his hungry kisses and eagerly kissing him back, the way he touched her and made her shatter into a million pieces, and then... well, Jane had said the discomfort would go away—and Anora was ready to learn if that was so—only this time on something softer.

As Matthew led the way, Charlie ran in front of Anora. They continued on their way for what seemed like miles, twisting down one tunnel opening into a cave with rocks stretching down from the roof, and others reaching up from the floor, some meeting until they formed a column. The torches' lights sparkled off the crystals in the walls, and she'd never seen such a pretty sight. She touched some of them, marveling at them, realizing at once they were the same as the one in the torque Niall had given her. Then she noted Gunnolf had paused to smile at her, and she realized she was holding them up.

She should have been more concerned about their situation, but Niall said, "They are beautiful, are they no'?"

"Oh, aye," she said. "I have never seen anything like it."

Gunnolf moved his candle closer so she could see the crystals better. She looked at them in wonder, then smiled and thanked him.

And then they were on their way again.

She was surprised that Matthew had had such an adventurous time of it in his youth. She had thought he'd always stayed close to home, doing whatever his mother wanted of him.

"Thank you for coming to our aid, Matthew," she said, though she suspected he had only done so to help her, not Niall and his friend.

"'Tis the least I could do as I intend to marry you," Matthew said, his expression serious.

She caught herself before she let her breath out in exasperation and said anything about Tesslyn's claims. Or mentioned that she and Niall were already married. She would speak to Matthew of the matter when they could have a moment of privacy.

After she had met Niall, a man who made her blood grow hot with his close proximity, she hadn't wanted anything less. With Matthew—she felt he was more like a good friend, brotherly even. But not someone she would have felt right in sharing a bed with. Still, he should know what Tesslyn had said if she was making it up, so he could be prepared to defend himself if the girl tried to spread the lie to others in the village. But if she had not lied? How could Matthew even think to marry Anora after having lain with the girl, who could very well be carrying his child?

"We have to squeeze through here, Anora," Matthew said, stopping so Gunnolf could go around him. Then Matthew reached back for her hand. When he had hold of it, he pulled her through a tunnel where they all had to crouch and then walk that way for quite a distance.

She kept tripping on her *léine* and finally said, "Wait, Matthew. I need to lift my *léine* a little so I quit catching my shoes on the hem."

Gathering her skirt, she lifted it, then continued as

before, except with her free hand, she touched the moist tunnel walls to keep her balance, hoping nothing moved underneath her fingers.

Her back and legs felt cramped as they traversed the low-ceiling tunnel for what seemed like an endless period of time. When they reached the end and could finally stand, they paused.

"How much further?" she whispered.

As dark as the cave remained, the only light from Gunnolf and Matthew's torches, she worried they still had a long way to go. She was still sore from riding the horse and from the swim in the rough burn, not to mention sleeping on a rock hard floor. She would have given almost anything to be able to sleep on a straw bed again.

Charlie stayed next to her, and she was glad for that, fearing he'd run off to explore and fall into a pot. But she still didn't see any sign of an outside source of light.

"We traveled for a good while before we reached you," Gunnolf finally said, as if appeasing her without telling the absolute truth.

And she feared from the way he didn't say anything more definitive than that, that they had a very long ways to go.

They entered a larger cave where Matthew motioned to the walls. "Stay close. The floor drops off in the center. Not sure how far it goes down. On the other side, we must climb up and then crawl through a short tunnel and climb down a cliff again."

Anora's skin chilled. She suspected she would have to tie her *léine* between her legs again to form a pair of makeshift breeches. It was bad enough that she'd had to climb that way in Niall's presence, though with having to remove their wet garments last night, she'd gone further than she'd ever thought she would with him or any other man who was not her husband, until they pledged themselves to each other.

But to lift her skirts in front of Matthew and Gunnolf? Modesty aside, she knew she had to, but it didn't make it any easier.

When they reached the other side and had to make the climb, she saw light above and hoped that meant they were nearly out of the cave. Gunnolf and Matthew waited, as if they weren't sure how to go about this.

Niall quickly took charge. "Go. We will follow."

Gunnolf said to Charlie, "Ready to take a ride again?"

Anora wondered what in the world Gunnolf was going to do with her dog. Fascinated, she watched as he created a harness and secured Charlie in it. To her surprise, her dog looked like he loved his cocoon. Gunnolf slung the harness around his back, the puppy sleeping in the front of his tunic. Despite the seriousness of their situation, she had to smile.

Matthew handed a torch to Anora. "If you need help, just ask."

Gunnolf led the way and Matthew followed him.

Once Niall tied Anora's skirts between her legs, she began the climb. Her arms were not used to this sort of thing, and she was afraid of slipping and falling and injuring Niall, who had put out the torch and was climbing close behind her.

Gunnolf and Matthew had reached the top and were

waiting for her, Gunnolf leaning down with a torch to light her way. "The last little bit," Matthew warned, "will be quite a stretch for you. I do not believe you can grasp the next handhold. I will reach down and you must grab my hand."

Matthew rested on his belly, stretching out his hand to seize hers as soon as she was within range.

"And mine," Gunnolf said, setting the torch on a rock, and then he moved lower, his arms longer.

She hated to admit she felt safer with accepting Gunnolf and Niall's help because they were much more muscular and stronger looking.

She clung to the wet and slippery jagged rock with her left hand and could see from her vantage point that Matthew spoke the truth. She could not manage this on her own as there were no hand or footholds that would accommodate her shorter stature. She stretched up to reach for Matthew's hand. He clasped her hand, but panic filled her. Hers were wet from the rocks, and his were just as clammy. Immediately, she felt herself slip and her heart with it.

"Hold on!" Matthew yelled at her, panicked.

If she fell, she could take Niall with her, and they could both injure themselves badly on the rocks below.

She couldn't hold on. Her fingers were too slick. "I..." was all she managed to get out when somehow, Niall succeeded in climbing up beside her and grabbed her by the waist.

"Hold on, Lass,'" Niall said, his words rushed and worried.

Gunnolf grabbed her free arm and pulled her toward

the top, while Niall continued climbing next to her, but then reached down and slipped his hand to her derrière and gave her a little boost.

"Oh," she cried out, shocked at his touch, before Matthew and Gunnolf pulled her up the rest of the way, and she collapsed onto her knees.

"Are you all right, lass?" Gunnolf asked, his hands on her shoulders, comforting her.

"Aye, aye," she said, her voice sounding strained. "'Tis so much better being here than where we were. All we could look forward to was waiting for more of Cian's men to come for us. Or having to swim in that very cold water again and face running into them downriver, past the mouth of the canyon."

Without some source of light, should more of Cian's men come for them in the cave, they couldn't follow Anora and her party.

Niall quickly joined them and squeezed her hand, drawing her to her feet.

"We have to go down again after a short walk," Matthew said, glancing at her bare legs.

She wanted to slug him for staring. Gunnolf had the decency not to look—at least, not when she was aware of it, anyway.

She was still trying to catch her breath after the fright of nearly falling off the cliff. Niall wrapped his arm around her waist and they moved forward again. Disappointed when she saw the torchlight was what had been giving off the light, she realized the men had left them at the two points where they had to climb.

She dreaded having to climb down this time since the climb up had been so difficult. She thought herself in excellent shape, mayhap not all muscled like Gunnolf and Niall, but she was used to walking and climbing hills with her sheep. Nothing like climbing rocky cliffs though.

"I will go first," Gunnolf said, as he moved to make the descent.

The torch at the bottom of the cliff helped light their way. The cliff face was much steeper and longer than the other. She shuddered. Niall squeezed her hand.

"Send the lass next," Gunnolf said, when he reached the bottom. Then he released Charlie from his carrier.

Niall peered over the edge. "I can go down beside you for part of the way, it looks like," he said to Anora.

She took a deep breath. "If I fall, do not let me take you with me," she said, and hoped he would listen to her.

He grunted. "You saved my life and you think I would let you fall to your death, lass?" He shook his head. "Take your time. Be sure to check your foot and handholds to ensure they are secure. I will be right beside you on the way down."

She prayed this was the roughest part of their journey, and they would soon be out in the fresh air, riding. For the first time since she'd fallen from her horse as a young girl, she was looking forward to riding Niall's horse, just a little—and leaving the cave and her pursuers behind.

She heard Gunnolf right beneath her. She was just as worried she might fall and make him tumble, wishing that he'd stayed below.

She slipped, let out a small gasp, and tried to will her

beating heart to slow down. She lost her grip again, and she slid several inches before she managed to stop, her breathing unsteady, her heart pounding hard.

"Careful, lass," Niall said, when she slipped the second time.

She couldn't look down. She was so tired. Her arms ached, her fingers burning from the cold and from scraping them on the rough rocks. She hoped she was getting closer to the bottom, hoping she'd hear Gunnolf jump onto the rock floor below them soon. But he continued to descend, and she thought they'd never reach the floor.

Then she heard his boots slamming down on the rock, and felt his hand touch her leg soon after, as Gunnolf guided her down to the floor of the cave.

"How are you doing?" Gunnolf asked, as Niall quickly climbed down the rest of the way and Matthew soon followed.

"I am fine," she said, hurrying to untie her *léine* and drop the hem to below her ankles as was proper. She was weary, but so grateful to be with Niall, Gunnolf, and Matthew. Charlie, too, of course. And the puppy.

Charlie greeted her and Niall with his usual exuberance as if they hadn't seen each other in eons. She crouched down and hugged him soundly to her chest. She had feared she'd never see him again, or if he'd managed to pursue her, she had been afraid her captors would have killed him. She wanted to hug the puppy also, but Zara was still sleeping, tucked inside Gunnolf's tunic. Anora couldn't wait to hold her in her arms again, just like she had with Charlie when he was a puppy, or some of her young lambs.

As they began to move again, she wanted to ask how much further, but then she wondered if Gunnolf and Matthew had spent the remainder of the day and the night traversing the caves to reach them while she and Niall had slept. They couldn't have. At least, she hoped they had not.

Then they walked along a narrow path following an underground river. "We will not have to swim again, will we?" She didn't want to get wet again.

"Nay," Gunnolf said, smiling at her.

Then she realized Gunnolf and Matthew, and even Charlie, had been dry when they met them. Not only that, but he couldn't have carried the puppy in the river like that and so she felt much relieved. Gunnolf led the way this time, Matthew next, with Charlie running behind him. She stopped when Gunnolf had to crawl close to the rock face. Niall rubbed her back and she took a settling breath. She loved how he was always so reassuring.

Then she saw the light at the end of the tunnel, faint, and she breathed in the subtle fragrance of piney woods and earth and horse droppings. Her heart leapt with joy to know they were nearly out of the cave.

That elation was quickly tamped down when they heard men's voices nearby in the woods. Was the cave entrance hidden well enough?

His voice low, Niall said, "Anora, you must stay here in the tunnel. The rest of us will go into the cave."

Her heart beating wildly, she didn't want to be left behind, even though she knew they meant to protect her. But what of Matthew? He didn't know how to fight, did he?

"Anora," Niall said, kissing her cheek, "stay with

269

Charlie. Keep him quiet. We will leave here as soon as 'tis safe to do so."

Gunnolf handed her the sleeping puppy.

She nodded, taking hold of Zara and holding her close, and prayed those outside the cave would not find their hiding place. She sat down on the hard rock floor, patting her lap so Charlie would stay with her and not follow the men into the cave. Charlie quickly sat next to her, watching the men leave, his head finally resting in her lap. He was not a terribly small dog, so she had not often encouraged him to sit on her lap once he was full grown, but as cold as she was, she'd make an exception. The puppy in her arms helped to warm her as well.

Charlie quickly obliged, climbing onto her lap. Half of his body rested on her legs, the rest of him hanging off her, warming and comforting her. She took a deep breath to calm her frayed nerves as the men snuffed the torchlight out and disappeared into the cave, leaving her in total blackness.

CHAPTER 18

Niall directed Matthew to speak softly to the horses to calm them as they stood near the tunnel entrance. Niall and Gunnolf unsheathed their swords and moved toward the mouth of the cave. He didn't want Matthew fighting anyone if he didn't have to; afraid the butcher's son wouldn't be able to defend himself well enough and would get himself killed.

Outside of the cave, one of the men spoke again, "The mon is a fool."

Highlanders. Cian's men. Niall bit back a curse.

"Aye, do you think he lied?"

"If he did, and we dinna find Tagan's body, he knows what will happen to him. So nay, I dinna think he lied. But he should have fought the mon and finished him off." He paused, then added, "Keep looking for a cave entrance, tunnel or something. He swore that was the way the mon, who attacked Tagan, must have reached that cave."

"And the lass?"

"For now, 'tis the mon who cut Tagan down that concerns me. Yaden said he didna think the girl was there or she would have cried out when the other mon killed Tagan. But Cian has plans for her after she lied concerning the direction our men went, as soon as we get hold of her."

Niall tightened his hold on his sword. Cian would never get his hands on Anora.

One set of footfalls drew closer to the cave entrance. "What is this?"

"What?" the other man said, moving in his direction.

"Naught. It appeared the hole in the rock led somewhere, but it doesna. Just a short distance and then stops. Just keep searching along this rock face. Peer beneath the plants."

Niall barely breathed as he was certain the men would locate the cave as carefully as they searched for it.

"Here, mon," the one said eagerly, his voice and footsteps growing nearer.

Niall and Gunnolf waited, their bodies tense with battle readiness. Niall wanted to slash out at the men as soon as they stepped into the cave and before they could arm themselves, or their eyes could adjust to the dim light. The problem was Niall had no idea how many were searching now, and if they struck at these men prematurely, anyone outside of the cave could hear the fight and go for help.

Thankfully, the horses remained quiet with Matthew at the back of the cave near where Anora waited in the tunnel.

Both of Cian's men unsheathed their swords and stepped into the darkness. Cian's men didn't see Niall and Gunnolf as they rushed forward to attack.

Neither man stood a chance as Niall and Gunnolf thrust their swords and cut them down. Afterward, Niall peered out beyond the vines and other flora hiding the cave's entrance. He heard two more men talking, mayhap a hundred feet away. He couldn't see them, only heard their voices.

"Two more," Niall said to Gunnolf, his voice hushed. "But I canna see them and they are headed away from the cave."

"They will come back this way looking for their companions before long," Gunnolf whispered, "dinna you think?"

"Aye. When they find no caves in that direction, and they realize their friends have disappeared. We either wait for them to come back this way and find the cave, or we leave, hoping that the plants will hide us well enough until we are on our way."

Gunnolf pondered that, then let out his breath and spoke low for Niall's hearing only. "I dinna want to leave here with the men roaming about out there. Surely, they could hear our horses once we begin to travel away from the cave. One whinny would be our undoing. We have the advantage of staying here and fighting more of them. If we have to, we can travel back through the tunnels. Matthew knows the way through several."

"But we would have to leave our horses behind," Niall said, his voice quiet. "We canna be without our mounts."

"Aye, true."

"Where are the others?" one of Cian's men said, headed in the cave's direction now.

Niall motioned for Gunnolf to help him move the bodies away from the cave entrance. Once they had hid both of the dead men in the darkest recesses of the cave, Niall and Gunnolf again waited for the appearance of the new men as if Niall and his friend were guardians of the cave.

"Mungen! Ghille!" one of the two men shouted.

"I dinna like this," the other man said.

"Mayhap they found the cave."

"Mayhap they found trouble in the cave. I... I think we should tell Cian."

A long pause ensued as if the other man was weighing the consequences of leaving and telling Cian, or staying and searching for the missing men.

"Aye," he finally agreed, and he and the other man moved away from the cave.

Niall didn't trust the men. He suspected they thought that if they pretended to leave, they would draw out whoever they feared was hiding in the cave.

The problem was that if Niall and Gunnolf were wrong and the men had truly left, they could very well bring the rest of Cian's men and Cian himself here. What Niall didn't expect was for Anora to quietly join him and whisper, "Let me go out there."

He shook his head. Under no circumstances was he going to allow her to leave the cave unprotected.

She frowned up at him. "If I leave and they are out there waiting, watching for anyone, they will come to grab me and take me hostage. You can… you can take care of them then. But if I do not and they are not there and have gone for more help, all of us will be at more of a risk."

Niall hated to agree, but if Gunnolf agreed and thought her plan would work, he would reluctantly go along with it. Gunnolf nodded.

"Charlie, you must stay." Then she turned to Niall. "Matthew is taking care of Zara, the puppy. But I… must have a dagger," she said, "in case they rush me. I will be able to keep them away long enough for you to rescue me."

He didn't like that idea at all.

"Aye, lass," Gunnolf said, pulling a *sgian dubh* from his boot.

"Stay near the cave entrance," Niall said. "Dinna go into the woods or all will be for naught."

"What if they tell me to come closer?"

"You dinna," Niall said, vehemently. "Or you willna leave the cave."

She smiled up at him and he was afraid that look meant she would do whatever she thought necessary to help them leave this place for good. She didn't understand battle tactics or the lengths a Highlander would go when fighting another clan.

He placed his hand on her cheek and said, "Lass, dinna get verra far from the cave or they could use you to get to us."

"Aye," she said. "I understand. 'Tis just the way you order me about that made me smile. I will stay close."

He hated that she would do this, though he knew the men would not harm her, unless they knew she had a force to protect her and thought to use her against them.

She slipped out of the cave and Niall and Gunnolf watched through the vines while Matthew quickly took Charlie in hand even though her telling the dog to stay seemed to work.

But then she looked unsure of herself. If the men watched her, they gave no indication. She suddenly placed her hand on her forehead as if she were ill, and... fainted.

Instinctively, Niall made a move toward her, but Gunnolf seized his arm and shook his head. It very nearly killed Niall not to go to her, his stomach bunching in knots. Forever, they watched the woods as she lay very still as if she were asleep near the cave entrance among the trees.

No one made a move to go to her, and Niall wondered if the men were nowhere nearby. Niall kept thinking that he and the rest of his companions should leave now before the men returned with help—though he worried that the lass truly was ill. They'd had nothing to eat since yesterday and between that and being so cold—she could very well be sick.

They waited for what seemed an eternity when he heard movement in the woods, then whispers. Niall couldn't make out what the men were saying, but he was coiled like a snake, ready to strike if the men made a move toward her.

More footfalls, the sound of boots shuffling through wet leaves, drawing closer.

Gunnolf was just as tense beside him.

And then Niall saw the two men inching through the woods, looking around the area, ensuring no one was going to attack.

"'Tis her," the one man said, his voice low, his shaggy brown hair blowing in the cool breeze.

"Aye, but where did Ghille and Mungen go?" the bearded man said.

They crouched, watching her for the longest time.

"You think 'tis a trap?"

"Mayhap, but if we leave and she is truly ill, and Cian discovers we left her here, he will kill us, dinna you think?"

"Aye, or if we leave and she disappears before we return, I wager we would meet the same end."

"Aye."

Niall thought they would approach her, but they stayed where they were. Crouched. Their hands on the hilts of their swords. Their eyes fixed on Anora.

They were so many feet from the cave, it would take Niall and Gunnolf precious seconds to reach them, giving the men time to react—draw swords and fight, or run like scared deer.

Niall and Gunnolf barely breathed as Niall weighed their options.

"But where is Ghille and Mungen? If we get ourselves killed...," the dark-bearded man said, rubbing his whiskers.

"Aye."

Bloody hell. Do something. Niall wanted to shout at them. He hoped the men who served his cousin were never this indecisive.

Anora made a moaning sound and it sounded so woeful, Niall wanted to go to her, but Gunnolf shook his head at him.

The bearded man stood, unsheathed his sword, and said, "Come on."

The other man rose to his feet, not looking as though he wished to do this, and pulled his sword from the scabbard. Then they slowly walked toward Anora, their heads looking one way and then the other, searching for any movement.

Anora must have opened her eyes when the bearded man said, "Look, she is stirring."

She hadn't moved at all that Niall could see. Then the men hurried to reach her and Niall and Gunnolf bolted from the cave to fight them.

Despite being wary that someone laid in wait to ambush Cian's men, they yelled out as if surprised. Swords slashed as Gunnolf fought the bearded man while Niall battled the less whiskered one. He hoped Anora had moved back to the safety of the cave.

But when Anora cried out, Niall's stomach dropped and he glanced back in her direction and saw a man heading for her. *Damnation.* She'd gotten to her feet and slashed at the brigand using Gunnolf's dagger. Where the bloody hell was Matthew?

"Anora!" Niall shouted. The villain he was fighting thrust at him, distracting him, and Niall jumped back to avoid getting a blade in his chest.

Niall swung with such ferocity, he struck the man's sword, swiping it away from the man's body. Before the man could pull out his *sgian dubh*, Niall thrust his blade into his chest. Cian's man sank to his knees and Niall rushed to help Anora.

The villain knocked the dagger from her hand, but before he could grab her, Niall sliced at him and the man turned to face him. Gunnolf had killed the other Highlander and rushed to pull Anora away, then also engaged the man Niall was fighting.

Between the two of them, they quickly killed him. Niall seized Anora and pulled her tight against him. "You are really not ill, are you, Anora?"

"Nay, 'twas just a ploy." She trembled in his arms, the rush of battle running through her blood just as much as it had Niall and Gunnolf's.

"Good. Let us leave at once," Niall said, leading her back into the cave, wanting to fight Matthew next for not coming to Anora's aid.

Matthew was holding onto Charlie, then released him when he saw Niall enter the cave with Anora and Gunnolf. "I was afraid Charlie would attempt to bite the men and get himself killed," he quickly explained, when he saw Niall's scowl.

Niall didn't believe it. More likely, the butcher's son had been afraid he might have been injured in the fracas. "Come. You can help me move the bodies into the cave."

Once they had pulled them into the tunnel off the main cave, Niall stalked toward Anora waiting with her dog as she cuddled the puppy. Her hair tousled around her face, she appeared so sweet and innocent when only moments earlier she had attempted to fight off a brigand using

Gunnolf's blade. Niall gave Matthew another scathing glance, furious with the man for not having come to Anora's aid. Niall would not be responsible for his actions if during the remainder of the journey, Matthew did nothing to protect the lass if she was again in peril and Niall and Gunnolf were unable to defend her.

"Let us go, now," Niall said, and helped Anora onto his horse. Then he waited for Matthew to mount before he lifted Charlie to sit on his lap. If Matthew would not fight at all, he might as well be the one to take care of the dog.

Then Niall mounted his horse and held Anora closer than he needed to, reassuring himself that she truly had not taken ill.

They left the cave and headed north again, hoping this time they would avoid any trouble. She was still tense, like he was, worrying that if they were discovered, they'd be in for more fighting.

CHAPTER 19

Relieved they had not encountered further trouble, Niall and his companions stopped to rest much later that day near a stream to water the horses. Niall took Matthew into the woods to gather kindling. Gunnolf cared for the horses and watched over Anora, while she prepared something for them to eat from the foodstuffs she'd packed for the journey.

"You could have come to Anora's aid," Niall growled at Matthew, unable to let go of the anger he felt that Anora could have been injured or taken hostage and used as a shield, all because Matthew hadn't bothered to leave the cave to help her.

"She… she was fighting as well?" Matthew sounded aghast. "Why did you not yell to me?"

"Because I was somewhat occupied," Niall said. "I assumed you would have left the cave when you heard her scream."

Matthew dropped his gaze as if he'd been scolded like a recalcitrant lad, ground his teeth, then began to kick away wet leaves covering drier twigs. "I would have had I known. Charlie would have gone to you or Gunnolf's aid, and I knew if I let him, and he got hurt, Anora would never have forgiven me." He lifted his gaze and scowled at Niall. "And I *was* taking care of the puppy, too. If she had run out of the cave, Anora would have forgotten her own safety just to rescue the dog."

To an extent, Niall knew Matthew was right. But he believed that Matthew had also been afraid to come to their aid. Niall had to remember the man was not a warrior at heart. But that didn't lessen the annoyance Niall felt— that Anora could have been seriously injured, or hauled off before either Gunnolf or he could have rescued her. She definitely was not capable of successfully fending off an armed man, despite her brave attempts.

After they built a small fire and cooked some of the beef she'd brought with them, then ate, she said to Niall under her breath, "I need some privacy for a moment."

Her face reddened when she noticed both Matthew and Gunnolf watching her. Their reaction couldn't be helped. If the lass was going to whisper words to Niall, he knew the others would wonder what was up.

He nodded. "I will guard you this time."

She gave an almost imperceptible nod. He wasn't certain if it was with reluctance, or if she knew he would after what had happened the last time and she was resigned. From now on, there wasn't any way that he'd let her out of his sight until they were safely at his family's castle.

"We will take care of the camp," Gunnolf said, and Niall knew he'd ensure that it didn't look like they'd been here if anyone should be looking for them.

After Niall walked a little ways upstream to avoid the others seeing them, Anora said, "I thank you for all your help, Niall. I know you are angry with Matthew for not coming to my defense earlier against Cian's man, but he… Matthew is not a fighter. Not like you and Gunnolf. He would have gotten himself killed. The man had no intention of harming me. He only wished to disarm me."

"Aye, and if he had grabbed you up and tore off with you?" Niall asked, his gaze steady on hers.

She snorted. "The villain would not have been able to carry me far as much as I weigh, before you and Gunnolf had managed to rescue me."

Niall shook his head. "As much as you weigh, he would have gone before we knew it." He sighed. "I will turn away to give you your privacy."

"Thank you."

He heard splashing in the water and jerked around to see she was safe. She was washing her hands. "I am done."

He led her back toward the camp where Gunnolf and Matthew waited for them to go. The puppy was running around, poking her nose in fallen leaves, chasing after one the breeze tossed in the air.

"I will take the puppy," Gunnolf said, and scooped her up in his big hands, and then tucked her in his tunic.

Anora smiled up at him, and Niall knew Gunnolf had made a friend in her.

"I am going to let Charlie run for a while," Matthew said, looking at Anora, waiting for her approval.

"Aye, he needs to stretch his legs," Anora agreed.

Then they were off. Their luck seemed to be holding out and Niall was beginning to believe they might make it safely to the McEwen's castle.

***

As the sun began to set later that day, the gold rays spreading across the sky, highlighting blue-gray clouds, Niall and his companions found a shieling near a loch. They studied their surroundings for a while, watching a man tending his cattle, clothed in his plaid, a lad and lassie chasing each other in the heather, and a woman washing clothes at the stream.

"Should I speak with them?" Matthew asked, "Given that you and others not of your clan often do not get along."

Niall hmpfed under his breath. "You think they like those of you who live in the Lowlands any better?"

"Mayhap I should speak to the woman and ask if we might stay the night in their byre?" Anora asked. "Surely, they cannot object to me asking."

"I dinna know," Niall said, feeling unsure of the situation. The family couldn't see them for the trees, but he felt something was not right. "'Tis late for them to be doing the chores such as they are, is it no'? The lass should be done with her washing earlier than this and cooking the supper. The bairns should be doing something other than chasing each other in the heather. And is it no' odd that the man would tend to his cows at this late hour?"

They all observed them for a few more minutes, then Gunnolf said, "Aye, as if someone told them to do what they are doing while watching to see if anyone arrives."

"What if they need us to rescue them?" Anora asked.

Everyone looked at her like she was mad. "Lass, if there are ten men in there, you think we can protect them? In any event, I doubt they wish them any harm. If what we think might be true is the case."

"How could any of those looking for us have caught up to us?" she said, sounding exasperated as she leaned against Niall, wrapped in his arms.

He couldn't tell her riding two to a horse was slowing them down, or that letting her dog run, or stopping more often to allow her to rest was also a problem.

"We will continue on," Niall said, hating to have to ride any further as their horses needed to rest.

"I think 'tis a mistake to go further when we could take shelter in the farmer's byre," Matthew said, his voice firm with resolve.

Was the butcher's son tired of riding also? Niall suspected he didn't travel on horseback that often either. "We canna risk it."

"But...," Matthew objected.

Niall ignored him and they pushed on, or at least Gunnolf and Niall did. Matthew stubbornly stayed put.

"He is not following us, is he?" Anora asked softly.

"Nay. Either he will, or he can return home." Niall sorely wanted to mention that Matthew's mother was probably beside herself when her son didn't arrive at his home on time. "But we willna chance that either the Frenchmen or Cian and his men are at the shieling."

A short distance later, Matthew hurried to join them. Gunnolf smiled and shook his head.

Anora relaxed and Niall knew she was glad her friend was still with them. Niall had mixed feelings on the matter.

They rode for another hour and found an abandoned stone dwelling, the place empty of anything but straw on the dirt floor and ashes on the stone hearth. Spider webs hung from the ceiling, and a hole in the thatched roof on one corner let the dimming light in.

They tethered the horses outside where they could munch on the summer grasses.

"'Tis only another hour before 'tis dark," Niall said. "Mayhap if you and Gunnolf can..."

"I stay with Anora this time," Matthew said angrily, sounding as though he was tired of Niall giving the orders.

Niall raised his brows. "All right. But I will kill you myself if you dinna protect her with your life should someone come for her."

Matthew glowered at Niall.

"Come, Gunnolf. Let us get some water at the stream and find something to burn in the hearth tonight," Niall said, and the two men left the small abode, Charlie and the puppy running to catch up to them.

Anora truly thought she could fight better than Matthew could, which wasn't saying much. She couldn't help but be annoyed with Matthew, knowing he had a temper when things didn't go his way—though everyone was tired and out of sorts.

She sighed. She could understand his irritation—to an extent. She was in sore need of rest as well. Her body ached all over from riding Niall's horse. But she was making the most of the situation. Everyone was.

She wanted to broach the subject of Tesslyn, but couldn't look Matthew in the eye, not wanting to accuse him of something if none of it was true.

She began to gather straw scattered about to create beds on the floor, wishing Matthew would lend a hand. She wondered—now that he didn't have anyone to prove anything to—if that's why he wasn't making the effort. Though she believed there was more to his actions than that—as if he was angry with her and if he hadn't been, he would have helped.

From the judgmental way he was looking at her, she was certain he'd question her about what had happened between her and Niall while they had been together, alone, overnight in the cave. She suspected he would not like it when she told him she and Niall had married in the Highland way.

"Niall said he was wounded. Did you take care of his injury?" Matthew asked, his voice terse.

She was surprised when Matthew asked about that, believing what had happened in the cave much more scandalous, and that's what she feared he'd question her about. Not that she felt she and Niall had done anything wrong, and they were married. Though the rest of the world might see it differently. Especially Matthew.

"Aye," she said, not believing Matthew would have objected to such, considering the circumstances. But he looked like he was ready to have a fight with her. They'd only fought a few times—like a brother and sister who might have disagreed on some matter. When he'd told her he'd hated her cooking, she'd told him that she was fine with that and he never had to eat at her place again. What did she care if he preferred his mother's cooking to hers?

She was just as ready to tell him off if he thought to give her any grief over any of what had happened the past few days. She opened her mouth to mention Tesslyn, when he spoke again.

"He removed his tunic for you—in front of you?" Matthew asked, as his voice rose with condemnation.

Had Matthew been stewing about this all along? She almost smiled at the absurdity of it, thinking of how much more Niall had removed and what had happened afterward as they had warmed each other's chilled bodies.

"How could I sew the laceration without having him remove his tunic?" she asked, sounding irritated.

It didn't seem to matter that she was right. He crossed his arms and glowered at her. "What else did you do for him, Anora?"

She knew what he was asking—had she lain with Niall? "You were there. I fed him, washed his shirt…" She let out her breath in a huff and continued to form a bed of straw.

"And before that?"

"He slept." She stood and folded her arms. She wanted to tell Matthew that he had no right questioning her so, but she bit her tongue, reminding herself that he *had* come to rescue her. And all of this had to be a shock, since he was of the opinion that she would marry him some day—not that she had led him to believe anything of the sort.

"Then you could have come to me for help," he said.

"Niall tied me up," she said, annoyed, remembering just how Niall had found her rope in the byre and so infuriatingly used it on her.

"To the bed?" Matthew growled, and she thought he might even be thinking of fighting Niall over it.

"To a chair and then he went to sleep. In my bed. He was exhausted from his wounds, from fighting, and seeking refuge. He was in no shape to fight or do much else," she said quickly. Except he was very much ready to do battle— at least with one lassie wielding a pitchfork.

"Even so, he could not have been too tired for the likes of you," Matthew said, sounding furious.

"For the likes of me?" What did Matthew mean by that? That she had been willing? Or what?

"I cannot believe he was not your cousin. You were there alone with a man who was naught more than a Highland barbarian."

"Nothing happened between us, Matthew." Not then. Matthew hadn't even begun questioning her about last night when they had slept together in the cave—naked! She should have told Matthew she was married to Niall by mutual agreement, but she didn't believe he would think them truly married anyway. And she could imagine he'd be angry if he realized she and Niall had actually consummated their relationship in that very same cave.

She didn't want to lie to him, mostly because she was afraid he would know it this time, but also because she wasn't going to hide the truth. She wouldn't tell him all that had happened.

"He kissed you, didn't he?"

She hadn't expected Matthew to ask her that question. "He kissed my hand."

"A little higher than that, I believe, Anora," Matthew said, scowling.

Anora turned to make another bed out of the hay strewn about. "Aye, he kissed me, if you must know."

Matthew stomped his boot on the floor. "I knew it! Then the rest follows."

"He did naught else!" Anora said, furious with him. At least not before they agreed to be married. Niall had been honorable the whole time he'd been with her, and she would not allow Matthew to say otherwise.

"I do not believe you."

"I do not care what you believe." Though she truly did. She hated that Matthew would think ill of her.

"Where did he sleep, Anora? You said he was in your bed."

She let out her breath. "Only when he tied me up to the chair. You have no right to ask these questions of me, Matthew. Treating me as though we had done anything wrong. Which we had not."

"If I am to marry you, I have every right to know the answer to my questions."

True—*if* she had intended to marry him. "I am not marrying you."

She glowered at Matthew. He folded his arms, and looked as cross as she'd ever seen him. But she didn't believe he acted as though he trusted her. How could he still think she would marry him?

"I slept on my bed. He slept on the floor by the door. He was afraid I would try to slip away to find help."

Matthew stared at Anora, scowled, and shook his head. "I cannot marry a woman who lies to me."

"I was not marrying you! And as it was, I was his hostage at the first, Matthew. He told me what to say." She went back to making the beds of straw.

"And while you were with him in the cave?"

She felt her face fill with heat, and she was glad Matthew could not see it.

Matthew growled, "I will not marry you, Anora, though it breaks my heart to say so. My mother will be furious that you slept with a Highland barbarian."

"Would... you have me lie to you and say that I did not sleep with him while Niall and I were in the cave? And if we had not, I could very well have died as cold and wet as I was?" Anora asked him, hoping she didn't have to say anything more than that to him.

Matthew eyes widened as if he hadn't believed she would do such a thing, when here he thought she'd lain with Niall in her cottage.

She turned away and closed her eyes. She shouldn't have said a word.

She'd nearly finished making the four straw beds when Matthew finally said, "Is he marrying you?"

She hesitated to answer. She was certain Matthew would be angry if she told him the truth, but before she could tell him she was married to Niall, Matthew said, "I... I am sorry for asking you what I did. Will you reconsider marrying me?"

She took in a deep breath and let it out. "Niall and I agreed to marry."

Matthew's eyes rounded, then they narrowed and his jaw tightened. "I see. Then... there is no reason for me to continue on this journey."

"But, 'twill not be safe for you traveling alone," she said, truly worried for his safety.

He gave her a small smile. "I am naught but a butcher's son. No one ever bothers me. Goodbye, Anora. I do not believe our paths will cross again."

"Tesslyn said..." How could Anora say it without sounding like she was making an accusation? And what did it matter? But then again, Anora wanted Matthew to know what the girl had said, in the event it wasn't true.

Matthew's face tightened with anger.

"She said you were marrying her."

There, Anora had not said Tesslyn had lain with Matthew.

He snorted. "She knows... everyone knows, I fully intended to marry you."

"She... she says she could be carrying your bairn."

His face turned red with anger and Anora wasn't certain if he was mad at her for saying so, or at Tesslyn. Anora still couldn't decipher whether it meant he had or had not lain with the girl.

In a dark voice, he said, "I am truly sorry."

Before she could move away from him, afraid of the way he was looking at her as if he now despised her, he rushed forward and struck her in the head with his fist so hard, she felt a sharp stab of pain in her temple, the hurt of betrayal, and in the next instant, her world turned from dusk to the darkest night.

CHAPTER 20

"You will have trouble with this Matthew," Gunnolf warned, as they headed back to the shieling, their waterskins filled with fresh water, and an armload of kindling and wood to build a fire.

Charlie was watching the puppy and making sure she kept up with Niall and Gunnolf.

Concerning Matthew, Niall had noticed. "Aye. The further we have traveled west, the moodier he has become."

"Because he sees the way you and the lass are with each other. You both show a tenderness for one another that cannot be denied," Gunnolf said. "I am used to you teasing the lasses, joking with them, but I have never seen you behave as you do with Anora."

"We agreed to be married," Niall said. "She is my wife."

Gunnolf grinned at him, gave him a brotherly slap on the back in congratulations, then shook his head. "No lassie is tying me down like that. Although I have to admit, if a lass held me at pitchfork length, or wielded my claymore against a possible enemy of mine, I would consider her worthy of being my wife."

"Just you wait, Gunnolf," Niall said, smiling at him. "Just you wait."

They'd barely reached the clearing when they noticed the horses were gone. Dropping the firewood, they bolted for the shieling. Niall feared the worse. Matthew would be dead, and the lass would be gone.

They reached the shieling and found it empty. Not only was Anora gone, but Matthew as well.

"I canna imagine they would have taken him hostage also," Niall said. "He would be too much trouble."

They took off at a run across the glen for the trees where they could follow the horses' hoof prints.

"Do you see what I see?" Gunnolf asked.

"Aye, that only our horses have gone this way. There are no other tracks." Niall glanced in Gunnolf's direction. "Matthew took Anora against her will?"

"It appears that way to me," Gunnolf growled.

Charlie bolted out of the woods and woofed at them, then wagged his tail. The puppy was not far behind, and Niall lifted her off the ground and tucked her in his tunic.

"Charlie, where is Anora?" Niall asked.

Charlie raced off through the woods.

Niall wasn't certain if the dog would help or not, but they chased after him, watching for signs the horses had gone this way. Two had soon veered off in the direction of the stream. "I will head that way," Gunnolf said, his voice hushed now.

Niall nodded and continued through the woods, following the other horse's trail, the hoof prints in the mud deeper—two riders, Niall suspected.

Matthew was headed back to the shieling where the man was tending to his cattle. It would be a good hour before he reached the place and it would be dark by then. Did Matthew know who waited there? Was he in league with whoever it was?

Niall would kill the man before he reached the shieling.

***

Anora groaned, her forehead aching where Matthew had struck her. And now she was riding on her belly across his horse's back and she thought her ribs would break from the awful bouncing she had to suffer.

She moaned again and Matthew stopped, long enough to resituate her so she was able to straddle his horse.

"Why?" she asked, meaning to question him as to where he was taking her and why, but she was unable to get the rest of the words out, her head pained her so.

"I am sorry, Anora. This was always the plan." Matthew kicked his horse to a trot.

"What?" She couldn't think. Couldn't concentrate. She didn't understand.

"I really cared for you, but my mother warned me I could never have you. She told me what your family would do to me if I ever bedded you. Believe me, I wanted to. The other boys my age chided me for loving the French girl, but they never saw you like I did."

"Saw... me."

"Aye. When we swam in the loch together. You never seemed to notice how much you affected me."

She closed her eyes against the pounding sensation in her head and the knowledge Matthew hadn't been as honorable—or brotherly—as she'd thought. How could she have been so naïve? John and his sister had been right. Though she'd fought with Jane, telling her she and John were wrong. That Matthew was only a friend.

"I was only ten, Matthew," Anora said, disgusted with him. She'd been just a young girl, for heaven's sakes.

"Aye, and I was nearly three and ten. You were pretty even then."

Three years older? She had thought him only two. But she still couldn't believe he had seen her as anything more than a friend to play with.

"Then John caught us swimming and playing together in the water. After he took you home, he threatened to kill me if I so much as touched you. And if that was not bad enough, he spoke to my mother. She was furious with me, because, you see, your family would have drawn and quartered me. She said if I could not behave when I was with you, I could no longer see you. Think you I did not watch you swim as you grew older?"

She shuddered with the idea. How could he have and never let on?

"It killed me even more to see your chemise clinging to all your curves the older you got and not be able to have you. But the will to live kept me from doing anything about it. And this Highland barbarian turns up and you give yourself over to him," Matthew growled.

"But... you said you wanted to marry me. You have always said so." He'd seemed so sincere.

"Who would not? You are pretty, though you are getting old. But still, to marry a woman of the French nobility? It has always held appeal for me."

She couldn't get used to the notion that he really hadn't wanted to marry her. Bed her, aye.

"And Tesslyn?"

He snorted. "Good for bed sport. She has always been more than willing."

Anora closed her eyes, hoping that would ease the pain in her head, but it did not. "You will not marry her?"

She couldn't help caring about the wicked girl, who might have to suffer from her consequences if she were carrying a bairn.

"As if it would be mine. She has been with several men. Think you she only serves up ale in her father's tavern? 'Twas the only reason I agreed to lay with her. No one could prove any child she had was mine."

She couldn't believe this was the lad she'd known since she was a child. "She said Laird Callahan paid for the meat you brought me."

"What else did the whore say?" he asked, suddenly sounding angered.

"To tell you I hated you so you would no longer see me."

Matthew didn't say anything.

"You have to let me go," she said, feeling panicked. "If... when Niall catches up to us, he will... will want to kill you for stealing me away."

Still, Matthew remained silent.

"We have always been friends."

"God's teeth, Anora! I have always wanted to be more than just friends with you! Do you not see?"

Tears filled her eyes. "Aye." What could she say? That she had never wanted anything more than friendship? She didn't believe he'd appreciate it.

The fight wasn't out of her, though as much as her head pained her, she wasn't sure how much she could fight. Then again, she still had Gunnolf's dagger. Not that she could use it on Matthew when she was riding in front of him on the horse.

"Where are you taking me?" she asked in a small voice.

"To Cian."

She swallowed hard. The man would want her head after she helped Niall dispose of his men's bodies and their horses. "I do not understand." How had Matthew gotten involved with that man?

"I was on my way to Conventry, as I said, when I ran into Cian's men on the road. They asked me if I knew anything about a Frenchwoman who lived in the area. I thought of you at once. If there are others, who would care anything about them? But my mother always said that someday your family would learn you still lived and would want you married off to someone of their choosing."

He paused, then started speaking again. "They said they were also looking for two Highlanders who had killed some of their men and stolen their horses. I did not think of the Highlander staying with you at first because he was alone. Until I returned home and learned you had gone into the village searching for some man named Gunnolf and that he was a friend of the one at your cottage.

"I intended to return to your place and turn you over to Cian for a goodly sum—the money I could use to start my own butcher stall and get away from my mother's constant nagging—but they had already torched your cottage and you were gone."

She stifled a sob. She knew deep in her heart, she'd never return, yet some part of her had secretly wished she could.

"There was no sign of your sheep or Charlie. I found your sheep at another sheepherder's croft and since Jacob knew you and I were friends, he told me you were with Niall and his friend. The two men Cian was seeking. Though the one is not a Highlander."

"Niall and Gunnolf only wished to keep me safe. Why would you turn me over to Cian? Just for money? We were friends." She kept mentioning their friendship, trying to remind Matthew of what they'd been to each other.

"I would never have you like I wished, Anora. Do you not see? Believe me, I desired having you for my own. And then you were with that barbarian, and I saw the way he sought having you and the way you wanted him. *He* was not worried about anyone killing him, but he should be."

Which was what she was concerned about also.

"You asked me to marry you," she said, rubbing her temple. She couldn't understand why he would have kept asking her if he hadn't wanted to really marry her. "Was it all just a lie?"

"I aspired to, but my mother would never allow it."

Anora closed her eyes against the pounding in her head. It had always been about his mother.

"Then you said you would not marry me anyway, and I would never see you again if the Highlander had his way, so I figured I would rather get something for all my trouble, and I would sell you to Cian."

"If he will truly pay you and not just kill you. What does he plan to do with me?"

"Sell you to a Norman lord who will pay handsomely for you, despite your age."

If he mentioned about her age one more time, she would slug him.

"He is still interested in you because of your family lineage, but someone else wants you to marry another lord. So he assumes this is the only way to make you his own before the other lord marries you."

"I thought you loved me," Anora said, considering how dangerous it would be for her to jump off his horse. Though the way she was feeling, falling off would be all she could manage, rather than jumping off. She hoped he had loved her, at least to an extent, and would reconsider and let her go.

"I think I did love you, until everyone kept warning me that they or others would kill me if I touched you." He raised his arm around her waist and touched her breast, then leaned down as if to kiss her cheek. "If I cannot have you, the heathen cannot."

"Do not touch me, Matthew," she growled at him. "You are no friend of mine."

Then they heard horses galloping some distance behind them, and Anora wanted to shout out to the riders, assuming they were Niall and Gunnolf. But Matthew suddenly halted his horse. Her heart beating frantically, she feared he intended to kill her.

"'Tis your lucky day." He siezed her arm and yanked her off the horse.

She fell onto the soggy earth. For a second, he glowered at her. "It is not over between us, Anora."

Then he galloped off.

***

Niall had run some distance when he heard horse's hooves pounding the ground as they made their way through the trees from the direction of the stream. He turned, and with welcome relief, saw Gunnolf riding his horse, pulling Niall's by the reins. Gunnolf tossed him his reins. "Since the lass made the beds of straw for us, I dinna think they could have been gone verra long."

Niall prayed they had not, leapt onto his horse, and then raced off after Gunnolf, who had already kicked his horse to a gallop.

Mayhap it had been a mile or so, it was hard to tell in the graying and darkening sky.

"Hold!" Gunnolf suddenly called out.

Niall stopped. It was nearly dark now, and he waited impatiently to see what the matter was, suspecting the worst if Gunnolf didn't wish him to get any closer.

Gunnolf dismounted and headed for the trees as he pulled his horse along.

"Gunnolf..."

"Just stay, Niall."

Niall ground his teeth, praying Gunnolf had found Anora alive and well. But before he knew it, Gunnolf disappeared on the other side of his horse.

What the devil was going on?

Then Gunnolf rose from where he had crouched, and Niall saw he was carrying Anora.

"God's wounds." His heart drumming, Niall was about to dismount to take her in his arms, to see how badly she was injured.

"Nay, mon. Stay. I will hand her up to you."

"Is she all right?" Niall asked, before he had her in his grasp.

"Aye."

"What of Matthew?" Niall asked, ready to kill the bastard.

"Looks like the coward dumped her and rode on. He probably realized his folly, and that he couldna outrun us—that once we reached him, we would kill him." Gunnolf handed Anora up to Niall.

Niall took her in his arms and though he wanted to crush her against his chest, he was afraid she might be injured, not to mention the puppy was still tucked safely inside his tunic. "Lass, are you injured?"

She looked up at him, her eyes misting with tears. "Nay, I am fine."

"Let us go, Gunnolf," Niall said, turning his horse around in the woods and heading northwest this time. "Are you sure you are all right, lass?"

"Aye."

"Good." Though Niall truly wouldn't believe it until he could see her in the light. She would not have gone willingly with Matthew.

"We are going to Chattan's castle, aye?" Gunnolf asked Niall.

"We are." They had been traveling in the direction of the MacEwen's castle ever since they had begun their journey. But Matthew knew of it also. He would not know of their association with the Chattan clan. "Either way 'tis another day. We should begin to see the Chattan's crofts scattered about, late tomorrow."

But he knew they had to rest the horses later tonight, though he worried Matthew might meet up with someone, and they would attempt to locate them in the dark. Which could be hard to do, particularly if they were headed in a different direction.

On the other hand, mayhap Matthew had thought to steal her away from Niall, and this business had nothing to do with turning Anora over to anyone.

Niall wanted to ask Anora what had happened, but it was safer if they remained quiet as they made their way across a stream and then cut through a glen before they reached woods again and another river. They would stay here for a few hours to rest the horses until dawn when the sun was beginnning to rise. And Niall wanted to check Anora over for injuries she might have suffered.

Gunnolf quickly dismounted. Charlie, that had disappeared someways back, suddenly appeared and greeted him, wagging his tail, panting. Gunnolf took Anora from Niall and held onto her until Niall had grabbed his blankets and made a bed on the ground. At least the sky looked clear. They would not have to suffer another rainstorm right away.

Gunnolf laid Anora on the bedding. "I will get us something to eat."

"Aye." Niall knelt on the blanket and took Anora's hand in his. "Lass, tell me what happened."

"Matthew was angry that… that we were together as we were. I told you he would be."

"Aye, but what happened?"

"He said… he said he was leaving. I worried about him traveling alone. He said he would be safe. No one ever bothered a butcher's son. He hit me. I do not remember anything after that until he cursed. I found I was riding his horse on my belly. We heard your horses. He assumed you would follow and would soon gain on us. To my shock, he grabbed my arm and threw me from his horse."

Niall ground his teeth. "Are you sure you are no' injured, Anora?"

"Nay, just where he struck me. I am certain I have more bruises than I know what to do with, but I did not break any bones or such."

He was thankful she was uninjured, but he couldn't quell the anger he felt. "I will kill him."

She took Niall's hand and kissed it. "We were friends once."

305

Niall scowled down at her, not believing she still wanted to protect the bastard.

"Oh, aye, he intended to turn me over to Cian for the money." Anora quickly brushed away tears, and Niall pulled her into his embrace, wanting to chase away her upset.

She snuggled against his chest, but inside his tunic, the puppy squirmed between them, her tiny sharp toenails scratching his skin. Niall chuckled, pulled Zara out of his tunic, and set her on the grass.

"He injured you. And if he *had* turned you over to Cian…" Niall shook his head, knowing that he would have killed the man if he'd reached him, and he'd put up any kind of a fight.

Gunnolf returned with a flask of water, bread, and cheese. "Are you well, lass?" he asked, sounding just as concerned as Niall was.

"Aye, I am fine," Anora said. "And I thank you for your concern."

They ate, giving the dogs some of the leftovers from the bread and cheese, and then Niall curled up on the blanket with Anora, pulling her gently into his embrace. He still couldn't believe she was all right, as quiet as she was. Only about four more hours to travel ahead of them. The day wouldn't dawn soon enough for him.

"The puppy," Anora said sleepily against Niall's chest.

"Got her," Gunnolf said, and Niall chuckled.

***

Slowly waking from a ragged sleep, Anora was so tired as she snuggled against Niall's warm body on the blanket, the hour—early morn, the sun just beginning to spread yellow and crimson rays in bands of color filtering through the upper half of the trees. Yet, a ground fog covered the lower half in a blanket of yellow mist. She knew they had to ride again soon, and she was glad they were getting closer to the Chattan's castle, but she ached all over after Matthew had thrown her from his horse.

Then she heard the sound of horses and she was instantly awake, her heart thudding, she scambled to stand. Her warrior husband jumped to his feet, sword unsheathed and readied. The same with Gunnolf.

In the predawn light, she saw maybe eleven men on horseback materialize from the mist—all wearing plaids. *Cian's men.*

CHAPTER 21

Anora pulled Gunnolf's dagger from the sheath where she'd worn her own *sgian dubh* until the French knight had taken it from her.

To her disappointment, she saw Matthew ride in behind the rest of Cian's men, as Charlie ran beside his horse. Had Charlie found Matthew and led them to Anora?

She'd still had her doubts Matthew could do this, but she didn't have any more now.

Feeling sick to her stomach, she readied herself for a fight every bit as much as Niall and Gunnolf did.

Niall glanced back at her. "Stay out of their reach, lass," he warned.

"Give up the lassie and you can go on your way," a man with a black beard and wild curly black hair said, his eyes a vivid blue, the man who had entered her cottage, asking where Camden and the rest of the men had gone. "'Tis no' a fight we want with you, Niall of Craigly."

"She is my wife and I will give her up to no mon, Cian," Niall said, venom in his voice.

Cian's black brows lifted. He glanced at Matthew as if surprised the man had not told him the news. Matthew appeared stony-faced, as if he had not a care for her dispostion in the least. She couldn't help but be further angered and upset at the betrayal.

"Is that so?" Cian said, turning his attention back to Niall. "No matter. I am certain the French lord who wants the lass willna put any stock in our Highland ways. Not when the lass has title and owns land. Make it easy on yourself, mon. Hand her over, and we will leave you in peace. If no'..." He shrugged. "I assume you killed my other clansmen, so we will be pleased to avenge their deaths."

"Fight, you whoreson! You are no' taking the lass with you," Niall said.

"My sword will meet your challenge," Cian said and charged Niall.

Anora's heart leapt into her throat. Niall would be no match for a Highlander on horseback. She jumped back away from the horse and warrior. Niall jerked the blanket off the ground, twirled it around and around until it formed a long rope-like weapon, and hit the horse hard in the chest. The horse reared up on its hind legs, whinnying in distress.

The blanket hadn't hurt the horse, just scared it. Niall's quick action and the horse's startled reaction caught Cian off-guard. He yelled out with a slew of Gaelic words as he fell from his mount and hit his back hard on the earth.

Two of his men rode forth to attack Niall while another couple of his men engaged Gunnolf. One of the remaining men went to Cian's aid. He tried to get up, but he... couldn't. Anora was glad to see he had been injured enough that it appeared he couldn't fight. She and her party were still outnumbered. Not that she could really count herself in that number.

The last man rode toward Anora, but she managed to grasp hold of Cian's horse's reins and pulled the animal around, using him as a shield between her and the villain. She prayed he wouldn't hurt the horse in an effort to reach her. But Cian would probably kill him if the man injured his horse.

Charlie grabbed the pup by the scruff of the neck and hurried her into the woods and out of harm's way. She loved Charlie.

Gunnolf was busy fighting two more brigands. She assumed Matthew was just watching to see who was victorious. If Cian was, he'd get his money. If Niall was... Matthew had better flee for his life.

"Anora!" Matthew shouted in warning, as the man who had been trying to help Cian, came after her and approached her from the rear.

What was Matthew about now?

A swordfight began at her back and she swore if she hadn't known him better, she would have thought Matthew was a practiced fighter. And that he would fight Cian's man? She thought Matthew was with Cian's men on this venture.

Her skin clammy with concern, she blocked the other man's attempt to reach her as she continued to move Cian's horse around between them.

The man swore, then leapt from his horse and came around behind it to reach her on foot.

Heart thumping hard, she let go of the horse's reins and took a defensive stance, facing the tall, bull of a man, his red beard making his face look rounder, his green eyes narrowed in irritation. She might only be a shepherdess and she might not have the strength or skill that the Highlanders had, but she wasn't giving up, either.

"Come, lassie," the man coaxed, baring yellow teeth as he drew closer, his sword raised—he was no fool—and approached her cautiously. "Put the *sgian dubh* down and I will be gentle with you."

"Do not come any closer," she warned, but movement to the east caught her eye. A man in a gray cloak. "Nay," she groaned. If she, Niall, and Gunnolf managed to defend themselves against Cian's men, next they'd have to fight one of the French knights?

A man fell to the ground behind her, and she feared it was Matthew. She turned to look, not a good battle tactic on her part, and the man approaching from her front slammed into her. She fell over the body—not Matthew's— and she felt relief that he had not been killed, despite what he had done.

The brigand on top of her tried to wrest her dagger from her hand, but she wasn't giving it up to any of these men.

More horses arrived. The rest of the Frenchmen and the baroness. She bit back a curse. Did they not have enough to deal with?

Niall jerked the man off Anora and with one thrust, stabbed him in the chest, then shoved the man aside. Niall turned to face the French knights, offering his hand to Anora to help her stand.

"Anora is my wife, now of Craigly Castle. You have no claim to her," Niall said to the French party.

Anora looked for Matthew and Gunnolf. Gunnolf had taken a stance that indicated he was ready to fight the French next. She was glad to see he had not been injured in the fight. Matthew was lying on the ground on his back, his face ashen, his hand holding his chest, blood spilling onto the soil. Her heart stuttered.

"Matthew," she said, and went to him. He *had* been a friend and he had come to her aid at the last, despite that he had helped Cian's men find her.

"I... I am sorry," Matthew said, his eyes losing their luster as he tried to remain focused on her face. "You... should have... been... mine."

She thought he looked as though he truly had meant he'd wanted her for his wife all along. Those were the last words she'd ever hear him speak.

Her eyes filled with tears and she quickly looked away. She couldn't deal with this now, not when the French knights were sure to attempt to kill Niall and Gunnolf next.

"She does not belong with the likes of you," the baroness said, her tone haughty. "Come, Anora. 'Tis time for you to be a countess again. You should be pleased you have so many marriage prospects."

Anora moved in close to Niall. "I could not have found a better marriage prospect than I have in Niall. I will not go with you. Asceline, the countess you seek, was lost to the sea many years ago."

"We have had word your *oncle* is at the Chattan's castle. Will you ride with us there?" the baroness asked.

Rondover Castle? Anora took hold of Niall's free hand, suddenly chilled. She had not seen her uncle in so many years. What if he insisted she return with him? What if Laird Chattan agreed with him because she was a Frenchwoman of noble blood?

"We will ride with you," Niall said to the baroness, and sheathed his sword.

"But…," Anora said to Niall, not entirely trusting the French party. Then again, they were only two men against the five knights.

Niall pulled her close and kissed her lips. "We will sleep on a soft bed tonight. You and I. As husband and wife."

"My knights will help you bury these men," the baroness said, interrupting the moment.

Anora glanced at Cian, thinking he must have broken his leg or something from the fall, but he didn't appear to be breathing.

One of the knights checked on him. "His head hit a rock and he cracked his skull. He is dead."

Anora stared at Cian, remembering so long ago, the fall she had taken from her horse when she was a little girl. And the one where the squire had died from his fall.

"Are you still afraid of horses?" Pierre asked, as he took hold of one of the bodies near her with the help of another knight.

"Nay," she said, quite honestly. Not after all the riding she'd done over the last few days. She glanced at the Murray horses, all nibbling on grass nearby. She would ride Cian's horse to Chattan's Castle to prove she told the truth.

"I have never forgiven myself for what I did to your saddle," Pierre said.

"Aye, but I have, Pierre. Rest easy."

He nodded.

She walked over to Matthew and took his hand, then said a silent prayer for him.

Niall and Gunnolf approached. "We need to bury him and get on our way, lass," Niall said quietly.

She nodded. And fought shedding anymore tears. Then she called for Charlie and he came running, greeting her in his usual enthusiastic way, Zara running to catch up.

When the gruesome business of taking care of the dead men was done, they headed toward Rondover Castle. Anora wanted to go to the McEwan's instead to avoid seeing her uncle. She took a deep breath and let it out.

She would tell her uncle just what she had done—married Niall—but she couldn't quash the nervousness she felt as she rode Cian's horse through the glen. Though she was quite certain some of the apprehension making her feel so unsettled was due to riding the great gray beast all on her own.

***

Niall wanted to get this situation resolved with Anora's French family with all haste, and he was glad he hadn't had to fight any, just in case they could decide this matter diplomatically. In other words, her uncle would agree to Niall and Anora's marriage and be gone.

Otherwise, Niall was ready for a fight. He just hoped Laird Chattan wouldn't be angry with him for not consulting him first in the matter and putting his own people at risk. What if Chattan backed the French count's plans instead?

Niall had no intention of losing Anora.

Niall glanced at her. Her chin held high, she looked proud of herself to be riding a horse on her very own. She was gripping the reins as if she was afraid she'd fall off the horse at any moment, but otherwise, she appeared to be doing well. He thought her real anxiousness was due to having to meet her uncle. He couldn't blame her, either. Hopefully, Chattan would permit Niall to be present during the exchange while the French knights were excluded from the meeting.

Much later that day, they reached the first of the crofters' lands who worked for the Chattan, and Niall was much relieved.

The man had a pitchfork in hand, reminding Niall at once of Anora, and he couldn't help but smile. "We have come to see Laird Chattan. We are kin to the Chattan by marriage and are now visiting his lairdship," Niall said.

The farmer eyed Anora and the baroness, then—as if Niall and Gunnolf, and their French companions, could not be too much of a threat since they traveled with a couple of women—he nodded. "They have been hunting. Tell the gate guard what you have told me, and he should allow you in."

"Good. Thanks, mon." Niall then rode with the others toward the castle in the distance, the way clear of trees for a quarter of a mile and saw the lake to the north where he and his cousins had swum a time or two.

As they approached the castle, he studied the fortifications. The gray stone walls rose to the gray sky, the keep towering above it in the center, built high on a hill of granite, deep ravines cut around it, ensuring an enemy would have difficulty laying siege to the keep.

A gate guard and two others greeted them—stopping them—but one of them smiled broadly. "Niall and Gunnolf of the Clan MacNeill. Angus and Edana will be pleased to see you. As will his lairdship." Then he eyed the others with a hint of suspicion.

"My wife," Niall said, introducing Anora, "her sister, Baroness Andrea Rochelle, and their escort."

The guard frowned. "Is... is the lass you have married the Count of Carcassonne's niece?"

"Aye," Niall said, already feeling apprehensive about how this would all play out. He would not let the man take her away, but he hoped Anora would not be too upset by what might happen.

The guard nodded. "I dinna believe he thinks she is married." Then he grinned. "'Tis good she has a husband in you. Welcome. Come. The stablehands will take your horses."

They dismounted, Niall assisting Anora, though he noted she winced as if the travel had been too much for her. Not to mention the bruises she must have suffered when Matthew had thrown her from his horse.

The sound of horses galloping toward the castle had them all turning their heads to see who had arrived now.

Tibold Chattan, laird of his clan, and Angus MacNeill, Niall's cousin, led the pack. Angus's dark hair was windswept, making him look as wild as Niall had ever remembered it, his dark-eyed gaze taking in all of the newcomers with a quick survey.

"You found the lass?" Angus asked, hurrying to dismount and gave Niall a brotherly slap on the back, his grin spreading across his face. "One of the crofters said you had arrived. No doubt you have heard her uncle waits just inside."

Tibold approached, his dark brown hair looking to be sporting a few more gray hairs, and his eyes a vivid blue, focused on Anora. "The man will be delighted to hear she is well."

"She is my wife," Niall quickly said. "This is Anora."

Tibold and Angus's jaws dropped.

Angus quickly looked at Gunnolf as if he would say Niall was jesting, or should have ensured Niall had not done thus, or something.

Gunnolf raised his hands in defeat. "He got away from me. What can I say? The lass was right for Niall. She belongs with no other mon."

Angus shook his head, then smiled at Anora. "Welcome to the family, lass. My wife, Edana, will see to your needs and to the other lass's as well."

Niall quickly made further introductions. Tibold still hadn't said a word. What was he thinking? Would he back Niall, or stand by Anora's uncle's wishes?

"'Tis time for a feast," Tibold announced, as if food in their bellies would solve all their problems.

***

Edana hurried to greet Niall and Gunnolf, welcoming them to her father's home. But as soon as Niall explained who Anora was, his arm wrapped securely around her waist as if she needed his support, Edana smiled. Anora was glad she didn't drop her jaw with shock like Edana's father and Niall's cousin, Angus, had done.

Edana's blue eyes were as bright as her father's, but her hair was a glorious red. Angus's hair was as dark as Niall's, and his eyes just as dark a brown. He was a little taller, and when he smiled at her, Anora could see the family resemblance. After everyone had gotten over the initial shock that Anora was married to Angus's cousin, he had welcomed her with open arms as if she was part of the family now. She felt a little overwhelmed, truth be told. But she wouldn't have wished this any other way.

Before Edana could take her and the baroness to a room to wash, a dark-haired man with greying temples stalked toward Anora, his build slight as if he were a diplomat and not a fighter. Then he glanced at Niall, who wouldn't release her waist as if he was afraid someone would snatch her away. She was used to fighting her own battles, but in this, Niall was her pillar of strength.

"Who might you be?" the Frenchman asked Niall, his expression and tone of voice stern, before Laird Chattan could make introductions.

"Niall of the MacNeill of Craigly. And this is Gunnolf, who is as much a MacNeill as my own blood," Niall explained, not letting go of Anora.

Recognition shone in the man's eyes. "Your cousin, Angus, told me James had sent the two of you to locate my niece. And this, I take it, is my niece." Then the count turned to Tibold. "May I have a word alone with my niece?" he asked Chattan, as if Niall had no say in the matter.

Anora was afraid to speak with her uncle alone, even though she thought he couldn't steal her away. But still, after all she'd been through, she didn't truly trust anyone who was French.

"Nay," Niall said shortly, which brought a smile to Anora's lips.

Tibold cleared his throat. "Mayhap, Niall and I could stay with the lass while you speak with her. She has been through quite a lot, and I am certain she feels... more reassured with Niall at her side."

His brow pinched, her uncle looked annoyed, but then reluctantly nodded.

Niall's grip on Anora eased.

"Do you remember me?" the count asked Anora as they settled on benches before a nice warm fire in a small room while Niall stood by the hearth, arms folded as he leaned against the stone wall.

"Nay, not well," she said, vaguely remembering her uncle, his voice a little rougher with age, his hair grayer, his skin more wrinkled.

"'Tis understandable. You were very young when your father took you on the ship. I gave you the horse for your birthday when you were six."

Her horse had been white as snow and sweet, but after her fall, Anora had not ridden her again.

She glanced at Niall, who was looking fiercely protective of her. She loved him for it.

"You were not much older than that when your father took you by ship and the English confiscated it. I only learned you had survived while I was fighting during the Crusades and could not return for you. I asked James MacNeill, whom I had befriended, if he would take you under his protection should it become necessary."

"Aye, and Niall and Gunnolf have done so at his request," she said.

"Aye." The count took a deep breath and let it out. "Our lineage is connected directly with the royal family and once several learned you were still alive and unmarried..."

Her uncle *couldn't* force her to leave with him when she was wed—according to the Highlanders' laws—to Niall.

Her uncle frowned at her as if reading her mind. "You are not married, are you?"

"Aye," she quickly said, even if her uncle would not agree to the conditions.

"By our laws, aye," Niall added just as quickly, and the way he was standing now, tense, ready to fight for what was his made Anora stiffen a little. She did not want Niall fighting her uncle. He was her family.

"I have heard of these notions of yours," her uncle said to Niall. "As long as both parties are agreeable, the marriage is valid. But not by our standards. And the lady is of the nobility. She could not marry a..." He stopped what he was about to say, and then he changed the subject. "As I was saying, the word has spread that you are available for marriage, though you are a little old. But because of your lineage, the noblemen are willing to make do."

Niall snorted. Everyone glanced at him. He gave her uncle a disgruntled look and a shake of the head.

She arched a brow at her uncle. Niall had not seemed to mind that she was nearly an old spinster. And she was grateful for that.

"Two French counts and a viscount, in particular, want your hand in marriage," her uncle said.

"Nay," she said vehemently.

He looked disapprovingly at her, but ignored her outburst. "The one, I cannot abide. He is dangerous, and I believe because of his outspoken ways, he will end up getting himself killed before long. I would not wish you to be in such a situation. Not only that, but I fear his only interest in you as a marriage prospect is your lands and title. But he has oft had disagreements with King Phillip. If he should be executed, then you would be forced to marry some other lord—"

"Not of my choosing. I have agreed to wed Niall and the deed is done. And since I am not French and I am only a shepherdess, not someone of nobility, that should suffice," she said, determined to make her uncle see her point. She was a storyteller, after all. Why should she not make her own up to aid her in this matter? Her uncle had no way of knowing who she truly was.

Her uncle frowned at her.

She frowned right back at him.

Niall smiled.

Then Charlie and the puppy ran inside the room and greeted her. Glad for the interruption and the calming effect he always had on her, she leaned down to give him a heartfelt hug, and then lifted the puppy onto her lap. Charlie curled up at her feet, watching Niall, wagging his tail as if waiting for Niall to call him over to greet him also.

"You are my niece and you have no choice in this," her uncle said gruffly. "Another lord is—I feel—too old for you. I do not believe he has the temperament to deal with a young woman who has lived the life you have. The solution to the marriage problem is for you to marry Pierre. He has always cared for you, and now that he has his father's title, he is just as suitable to marry you."

"Pierre? He said naught of this to me when he and his companions took me hostage. Why did he fail to mention it?" Not that she had any intention of marrying him. She didn't believe Niall would ever have loosened a horse's saddle as a jest to play on another lordling when they were lads.

"For propriety sake, Anora. I am the one to tell you whom you are to marry. It is not Pierre's place to do so," her uncle said, annoyed.

Pierre had nearly killed her when she was a little girl. Oh, aye, she'd had feelings for him when she was young, loved how he'd tried to kiss her and kissed the wrong girl. But those days were long since gone and for many years she had lived a much different life. She couldn't even imagine trying to learn all about a courtier's ways. How would they treat her? She'd served as a shepherdess all that time, and she didn't believe the French nobility would see her in a good light. Especially when she'd been with Niall as husband and wife.

She was no longer a countess and hadn't been one since she was very little. She wished to be with Niall, orphaned—aye—just as she had been. She wasn't certain how all his family would treat her, but she thought his aunt, who had cried so on his tunic when he was a lad, could be like the mother she had lost. Like Jane,who had helped to raise her.

Anora rose from the bench and joined Niall and took his hand. He quickly slipped his arm around her shoulders— showing more—possessiveness, protectiveness. She loved how he was always that way with her.

"Niall and I chose each other because he works for his cousin, the laird, and I will do what I know best—take care of my sheep." Though she would have to get some more. "I am sorry that you have not found your niece, but I am afraid she died long ago on the ship that the English commandeered. Everyone aboard the ship was lost."

Her uncle considered her for an extended moment, then Niall. Her uncle finally let out his breath. "I see." Then he cast Niall a long-suffering look as if he knew just who had stolen Anora's heart without her uncle's permission. "I believe you are right, Anora. The little girl I knew was spoiled and pampered, naught like the woman I see before me."

Anora smiled a hint at the memory. Niall squeezed her shoulders, and she suspected he'd question her about that later.

Her uncle continued. "The little girl I knew could never have survived the ordeals that you have been through. I will leave you in the Highlander's care."

"How am I related to Andrea Rochelle?"

"She is my daughter, your cousin, though she has always referred to you as her little sister. She was overjoyed when she learned you were safe. She had already been sent away to marry a man when you were very young and she was widowed a few years ago. She was not happy Count Gastone wished your hand in marriage when she had hoped he would be the one for her. He is the older gentleman and is much more suited to her."

"Then mayhap he will reconsider her when he learns the younger sister is gone."

"Mayhap." Her uncle looked weary as he stood to take his leave. "Take care of her, Niall of the MacNeill. Fulfill your cousin's promise to me to keep her safe for me."

"Aye, my lord. You have my word," Niall said.

Anora truly didn't remember her uncle all that well—for the short time she had known him—but she felt she owed him much heartfelt gratitude for allowing her to stay behind and remain with Niall. She pulled away from Niall and joined her uncle, giving him a hug. He appeared startled as he looked down at her in surprise, his dark brown eyes wide. Then he wrapped his arms around her and gave her a warm embrace.

"If I had an uncle, he would be just like you," she whispered.

"And you would be the niece I cherished that had grown into such a beautiful young woman." He kissed her cheeks and thanked Chattan for his hospitality, and then he walked toward the doorway, looking a little forlorn, his shoulders stooped.

Anora wiped tears from her cheeks, but before Niall could reach her, she ran after her uncle and took his hand. "You will stay for the feast the laird is having his people prepare, will you not?"

He looked again startled and stared down at her with kindly eyes.

"I would have you as my friend," she added.

He gave her a reassuring smile. "I will visit you and see how you fare, Anora. I will be honored to be your friend."

"Pierre knows I am that little girl."

"We all know the truth, Asceline. You have your mother's looks. The same colored eyes and hair, the same mutinous look when you wish to have your way. I will make up a suitable story—mayhap that I told James I wished his cousin to marry her and prevent her from marrying a man she did not love."

"Please call me Anora, uncle. I have been known by that name for so much longer. You... you were the one who told me stories when I was little," Anora said.

"*Oui,* Anora. I did."

She smiled at him then. "I make up stories like you did."

"Then we have something in common. Would you... sit beside me at the meal?"

"Aye," she said, without hesitation. And then she kissed him on the cheeks and gave him a warm hug—just like she had done when she had been a little girl.

***

After feasting and much merrymaking to celebrate that Anora and Niall were married in the kirk—a condition her uncle had insisted upon—Niall and Anora retired to a private chamber.

Niall smiled at her as they bathed in a tub together, glad the festivities belowstairs, the meal, and an impromptu wedding in the Chattan's kirk—had all turned out so well.

"The first time I thought of you in a tub was when I spied it in your byre while I was getting the rope to tie you up," Niall said, looking at the sweet vixen sitting next to him in the tub, her skin wet and glistening, her breasts swollen from his kisses already, her smile fixed. "It was wet, and I could envision you bathing there."

She threw the soapy rag at him and it hit him in the chest.

He laughed and pulled her onto his lap and nuzzled her cheek, her neck, her soft skin. He cupped a breast in his hand and then began to caress it again, feeling her nipple poke into the palm of his hand, stirring his blood.

"And then again, when you suggested I take a bath. The only way I would have done so—to ensure you didna slip away to warn someone of my presence—was if *you* had joined me in the tub. Believe me, I couldna get the thought out of my mind after that," he said.

"You are so scandolously wicked, Niall," she said, smiling.

He grinned at her. "Aye. Dinna tell me you didna think of me sitting naked in the tub when you offered for me to use it."

Her cheeks blushed a brilliant red.

"Just as I had suspected, wee bonny lass." Her thoughts had been just as wicked as his had been. He touched the torque he had given her as it rested between her breasts. "You still wear it."

"Aye, I will always. I cherish your gift to me."

He loved her. Then he leaned down to kiss her lips.

Despite not ever believing she would be sitting on her husband's lap in a wooden tub built for two—in a Highland castle, of all places—Anora loved Niall with all her heart. She met his kisses, just as eager as he was to enjoy the intimacy between them once again. And not in a freezing cold cave, but with a fire on the hearth, and a curtained bed just waiting for them.

Earlier, she could not believe how the baroness, her older cousin—though she loved how the woman wanted to be her sister and Anora would think of her fondly in that way always—had hugged and kissed her and wanted to be her friend and visit with her in the future. Or when Edana and her sweet maid, Una, had helped prepare her for her wedding night when she'd already had one in that cold, damp cave.

She had no worries about Charlie or Zara, as Tibold had given permission for them to sleep with Gunnolf in the keep until they left. She smiled at the thought. Others might have chided him for the matter, and she thought Angus was about to, but Gunnolf had given him one of his charming Viking warrior looks that said Angus had better not. The teasing light in Angus's eyes told her he'd say something about it later, though.

She kissed Niall again, but then she stood in the tub. "In a soft bed," she said. "This time."

Niall was all for it. He was out of the tub, drying her so quickly, she was surprised and amused. Until she witnessed how aroused he was. She had only felt his hard staff against her when they were clothed, or barely was able to observe him in the dark cave. And even while they had sat in the tub, she could feel him, but not see him as well as she would like.

Now, with candles all aglow, and the fire lighting the room with a soft yellow light, she could see all of him—muscled, his wound healing, some battle scars evident from fights he must have had before she'd met him, and his staff ready—he was glorious—all dripping wet, and hers.

"You keep looking at me like that, lass, and I swear I willna have time to make it to the bed to ravish you there." His voice was husky with longing, his eyes darkened with desire.

She smiled, her whole body feeling as though it was on fire. She dried him off as he wiped her down, and then without waiting, he lifted her into his arms and carried her across the rushes to the bed.

Sinking against the soft down mattress, she was in heaven, and pulled at Niall's arm to join her.

He kissed her long and hard on the mouth, his lips scalding, showing just how eager he was to have her. She probed his mouth with her tongue, knowing just how much he loved it and she did, too. His hands caressed her body, her arms, her breasts... every touch leaving a trail of heat in its wake.

He paused to suckle a breast, and she had never experienced such intense pleasure as...

Barely breathing, she quit thinking as his warm, wet tongue caressed a nipple, and her whole body tightened with need. Enraptured by his tongue on her skin, his teeth grazing her breast, she could barely think of anything else but the way he was making her feel—loved, desirable, and needed.

And she was certain she made him feel the same way as eager as he was to please her.

His fingers tangled in her hair for a moment, as he renewed kissing her mouth, his leg wedged between hers, the rampant heat of their bodies making her burn as hot as the peat fire at the hearth. His staff rubbed against her thigh, and she was ready for him to claim her as she had claimed him for her own. His hand slid down her hip in a tender caress before he made his way to the center of her being, stroking her, bringing her to that fiery point of pleasure. The burst of fulfillment washed over her in a rush of heat, before he plunged his staff deep inside her all the way to the hilt, thrusting, his need as great as hers.

She ran her hands over every delectable inch of him that she could, his eyes glittering with conquest and desire. "Always," he managed to get out, as he pounded into her, making her feel the swell of exquisite need rising up in her as he rubbed against her.

He came inside her, his seed hot and welcome, before his breathing slowed, and he kissed her softly on the mouth. "This is the way I want you, lass. Like this... loving you, always."

She smiled up at him as he rolled onto his back, and pulled her into his arms.

"No more caves?" she asked.

He chuckled. "No' if I can help it."

"Or... the tub?"

He stroked her arm for a while and kissed her head. "Mayhap there."

"And what if we happened to be in a hayloft..."

He chuckled. "Point well taken, lass. Anywhere with you will work for me."

She smiled. "I thought so. Though I would not suggest it. But if we happened to be in such a predicament..."

"Aye, lass, though I will do my best to ensure we have a bed to sleep in."

"Niall," Anora murmured, still bothered by what Matthew had said to her about watching her while she had swum in the loch, and she had not known it.

"Hmm, lass," Niall said against the top of her head, planting a kiss there, sounding half asleep as he tightened his arms around her.

"Matthew said he watched me while I swam—even when I was older—after John told him to stay away from me."

Niall didn't say anything and she thought he might have fallen asleep, but she couldn't quit thinking about it. "He was not an honorable man."

"Nay, lass."

"Well, you would not have done something so vile, would you have?"

"Nay, lass."

Pleased with the way things had turned out between them, she stroked his belly with her fingertips as he ran his hand over her hair. She loved him.

"I would have joined you," Niall finally said, a smile in his voice.

She chuckled and kissed his chest. She could see him doing it, too. "And then John would have chased you off."

"You think so?" Niall's voice was dark and... interested.

She shook her head. "You would have married me."

"Aye, lass. Though I would have missed having you prod me with your pitchfork."

She looked up at him, his dark eyes and his mouth smiling at her. "You will not tell our children about that, will you?"

"I leave that tale to you to tell. But better they hear it from their mother than from everyone else in the clan when *they* learn of it."

She sighed deeply. "Then I will have to tell it in my own way."

Niall chuckled. "I knew you were the lass for me. Have I mentioned the nearby loch where I swam with my cousins and Gunnolf on a hot summer's day? Or even when it isna so hot?"

"You are still thinking about swimming with me?"

"Aye, and much, much more."

"There is... a loch here, as well. I saw it from the distance when we rode in."

Niall didn't say anything, just kept combing his fingers through her hair.

"I cannot sleep." She looked up at him.

He was grinning down at her. "You want to swim in the gloaming hour of dusk?"

Wickedly amused, Anora was just too precious, Niall thought as he hurried to dress, then helped her to dress also. This was one fish tale he would never tell—about the shepherdess he would catch in the loch.

ACKNOWLEDGMENT

Thanks to my critique partners—Judith Gilbert, Vonda Sinclair, and Gwyn Brodie, and my beta readers—Loretta Melvin, Donna Fournier, Dottie Jones, and Bonnie Gill, for helping make the story the best it can be!

ABOUT THE AUTHOR

Bestselling and award-winning author **Terry Spear** has written over fifty paranormal romance novels and four medieval Highland historical romances. Her first werewolf romance, *Heart of the Wolf,* was named a 2008 *Publishers Weekly*'s Best Book of the Year, and her subsequent titles have garnered high praise and hit the *USA Today* bestseller list. A retired officer of the U.S. Army Reserves, Terry lives in Crawford, Texas, where she is working on her next werewolf romance and continuing her new series about shapeshifting jaguars. For more information, please visit www.terryspear.com, or follow her on Twitter, @TerrySpear. She is also on Facebook at http://www.facebook.com/terry.spear. And on Wordpress at:
Terry Spear's Shifters: http://terryspear.wordpress.com/

CPSIA information can be obtained
at www.ICGtesting.com
Printed in the USA
LVHW04s1059290718
585280LV00001B/90/P